Where there'

"Subject has entered [...]
in his earpiece.

He remained at his position in the stairwell. A bogus maid trundling a cart now appeared from one of the rooms. Freaky heard two clicks in his ear indicating that the Aussie had entered his hotel room. Still he did nothing.

The Aussie was paranoid. He entered the room with his hand on his gun, whipping it from his belt as soon as the door was shut.

Holding his door open a crack, Freaky saw the maid remove the large smoke canister from inside the cart and pull the arming pin. Dense white smoke immediately began filling the corridor.

The maid began to scream in Arabic.

"Fire!" she shouted. "The place is on fire!"

Freaky placed the thermal-imaging goggles on his head and powered them on. By now the corridor was densely filled with billowing smoke.

The Aussie cursed and opened the door a crack, his hand on the grip of the pistol in his belt. One or two other guests were in the hallway, running toward the elevators.

At that moment Freaky stepped toward the Aussie with a silenced .22-caliber Walther and pointed it at his head.

Titles by David Alexander

SHADOW DOWN
SPECIAL OPS

MARINE FORCE ONE
MARINE FORCE ONE: STRIKE VECTOR
MARINE FORCE ONE: RECON BY FIRE

MARINE FORCE ONE

ONE

RECON BY FIRE

David Alexander

BERKLEY BOOKS, NEW YORK

This is a work of fiction. Names, characters, places, and incidents either are the product of the author's imagination or are used fictitiously, and any resemblance to actual persons, living or dead, business establishments, events, or locales is entirely coincidental.

MARINE FORCE ONE: RECON BY FIRE

A Berkley Book / published by arrangement with the author

PRINTING HISTORY
Berkley edition / January 2003

Visit our website at
www.penguinputnam.com

ISBN: 0-425-18504-4

BERKLEY®
Berkley Books are published by The Berkley Publishing Group, a division of Penguin Putnam Inc., 375 Hudson Street, New York, New York 10014. BERKLEY and the "B" design are trademarks belonging to Penguin Putnam Inc.

PRINTED IN THE UNITED STATES OF AMERICA

10 9 8 7 6 5 4 3 2 1

An evil man seeketh only rebellion: therefore a cruel messenger shall be sent against him.

—PROVERBS 17:11

book one

The Wild Beast Shall Tear Them

I will meet them as a bear that is bereaved of her whelps, and will rend the caul of their heart, and there will I devour them like a lion: the wild beast shall tear them.

—HOSEA 13:8

chapter *one*

It was windy there, high above Jabal al-Harim, outside the shepherd's cave overlooking the Straits of Hormuz in which they had passed the night. Below them lay the sea, and in the near distance, beyond the rust-colored headlands of the southern Iranian coastline, an assortment of arid, sandy islets sparkled in the just-risen sun.

Their journey had been a long one and fraught with many dangers. But God had been with them and his mighty hand had preserved them from all harm. When they emerged from the cave and saw the hawk circling overhead, his talons clutching the snake that was his prey, both knew that their mission would prove successful.

They had spent the better part of an hour carefully picking their way along a narrow, winding path to the surface of the windy promontory. Their two horses were laden with gear and often lost their footing. Yet that power that had preserved them from detection across great obstacles and distances protected them still and they reached the precipice without mishap.

The two were brothers. Not siblings but brothers in arms, brothers in mission, brothers in devotion to their holy cause. Their skills complemented one another's, yet their personal histories were as different as fire and ice. In the night before the mission they had talked, permitting themselves just this once to reflect on things they had not spoken of before.

The one who had taken the name Mabrouk, the Blessed One, stared into the cooking fire and saw images from his past life rise up in the flames. First the suburbs of Indianapolis, then the drugs and the flirtation with the skinheads at

the Aryan Nations camp at Hayden Lake, Idaho, where he
had marched and shouted himself hoarse and saluted the
leader with the rest. Then the disillusionment and the angry
leave-taking. After that the drugs again and the attempts at
suicide, until he had finally found the light of God.

With this light had come renewed purpose. The skills
learned in Idaho had given him an edge over many of the
other recruits, and besides, he was a fast learner. There was
also the connection between the neo-Nazi movement and his
new life. Those days with the Nations had not been entirely
in vain. There the leader had introduced him to Wolfram
Krieger, a man who was to be the bridge between two
worlds, and a reconciler of both. In the end Krieger had
helped Mabrouk to realize that the martyrdom operation
would be the culmination of his entire life.

The second one, who called himself Thawra, Revolution,
now also going through the procedures he had trained to
carry out until he knew them in his sleep, had come from a
very different background. The slums of Cairo had nurtured
his hatred for the satanic enemy. He had pledged to fight this
enemy, to destroy it, even if it meant sacrificing his own life
to accomplish his ends.

He had trained with Mabrouk, and though Mabrouk had
come from the enemy's homeland, Thawra had embraced
him as a brother. Still, Mabrouk could never truly be a friend.
His blue eyes, his blond hair, his pale skin, all of these
marked him as *kufr*, one of the infidel pit creatures, those
who were *al-haram,* the unclean. Still, this American had
proven himself through many trials; Thawra admitted grudg-
ingly that he could be trusted. But only up to a point. Beyond
that, never.

Now Mabrouk unshipped the olive-drab military transport
canister from his saddle and dragged it across the dusty surface of the plateau. When he reached the edge of the promontory he squatted down, unsecured its latches, and removed
what was packed inside it.

Thawra was also at work. He set up the parabolic antenna
on a tripod base, pushing the sharp spikes into the firm sub-

soil beneath the weathered sand crust to stabilize it. He then snapped open a rectangular milspec case. Inside was nestled a battlefield computer.

Thawra pulled out the keyboard, coupled the parabolic antenna cable to one of the unit's interface connectors, then powered on and booted the unit. It required another few minutes to input commands using the keyboard and integrated mouse. With the ground-based unit now tracking the satellite, Thawra looked toward his comrade and signaled.

Mabrouk nodded and returned to his task. He too was almost finished with the assembly procedure. The firing tube now squatted on its mounting platform and he was behind the unit, sighting through the target-designator scope.

Their preliminary tasks now completed, the two men watered their horses, unpacked and heated rations, then fed themselves. Then they unrolled prayer mats and pointed themselves westward, toward Mecca, engaging in the afternoon devotions. Their hunger satisfied, their peace made with heaven, they rolled the prayer mats back up and stowed them in the saddlebags. Then they returned to their stations.

The sun was now beginning to sink. Soon it would be dusk. They knew that their expected target would approach the killing zone just before sunset, but they did not know precisely when it would be within optimum range of the weapon. The task of pinpointing this moment was entrusted to Thawra, who operated the computer.

Their chance was not long in coming. Mabrouk, squatting behind the weapon, soon heard Thawra warn that the target was approaching. Soon Mabrouk could see it with his unaided eye, a small, toylike speck glinting in the reflected golden rays of the sun as it slanted over the coast of the Arabian Peninsula directly behind them.

Mabrouk now gave all his attention to the weapon and his appointed task. With his eyes pressed into the rubber cups of the spotter scope, he now saw a magnified image of the ship. He pressed the initiator switch and began tracking the target.

Forward and to the right of the launcher, a laser emitter

fired invisible pulses of coherent light at the near side of the
vessel's hull. An auto-ranging processor in the launcher analyzed the laser pulses as they were reflected back from the
ship. Soon the launcher indicated that the target was acquired.

Mabrouk pressed the trigger and launched the round.

The projectile arced out over the windswept abyss expel-
ling a contrail of billowing white smoke. Seconds later the
booster stage flamed out and its main solid-fuel engine executed a burn that rapidly propelled the projectile upward to
its tracking altitude of six hundred feet. Once it was there, a
parachute popped from its rear. Gravity pointed the round
downward.

Slowed by drag, the round began to fall into the Gulf.

Behind the Plexiglas dome set in the center of its nose, an
infrared tracking head mounted on gimbals began to swivel,
and behind this assembly, a guidance-control module began
to interpret the data that the sensor was now acquiring. This
module, a small rectangular printed circuit board, was not
the original supplied by the manufacturer, Bofors of Sweden.

The Stryx system had been designed as a tank-killer, not
a ship-killer. The original module contained a library, in
ROM, of known MBT, APC, and other mechanized armor
signatures against which it would match data input from the
IR nose sensor. The new module had been prepared in an
underground laboratory in the city of Thumrait, one of the
many burgeoning suburbs of Baghdad, by technical staff attached to the Iraqi *mukhabarat*, or intelligence service, SUS.

The techs, many of whom had received their training in
military electronics in one of the sprawling valleys of California, had replaced some of the original ICs with chips programmed with an entirely new library of target signatures.
They had made other modifications as well, but the new and
differently programmed ICs was the main one.

The new terminal-guidance modules contained signatures
of commercial ships: freighters, oil tankers, and naval vessels
of several nations. In effect the modification turned the re-
vamped Stryx into a top-attack ship-killer. While such a

weapon would be of limited use against most oceangoing military vessels, which are defended by Phalanx deck guns and similar antimissile systems, it would prove devastating against virtually all unprotected commercial vessels, especially fully loaded oil tankers. Such a ship was now the target, and it was precisely such a target that the weapon had been re-engineered to search out and destroy.

Mabrouk, as he watched the trajectory of the fire-and-forget round while quickly breaking down the launcher apparatus, knew nothing of these matters. All he knew was what concerned his training and indoctrination. But what Mabrouk knew was not important.

It was what the reconfigured Stryx round knew that was important. And the Stryx round knew that below it was an oil tanker matching the parameters in its target library. Armed with this knowledge, Stryx began its terminal-guidance routine. The round executed a terminal burn. The round then sped downward into the main chimney just above the boiler room of the vessel below.

The explosion that followed ignited approximately one million cubic pounds of crude oil. The secondary explosion that followed upon this primary blast was so great that it could be heard and seen as far away as Riyadh, in the middle of the Saudi Arabian desert.

As the hulk broke up, leaving behind no survivors, and spraying a miniature lake of flaming oil across the mouth of the Persian Gulf, the brothers in arms prepared to complete their mission. The horses were sent on their way, into the darkness. At first they did not go, but the martyrs-to-be drove them off with their whips and curses.

When the beasts had departed, Thawra and Mabrouk turned toward one another. Their faces were grave and each thought of something fitting to say; in the end no suitable words came to mind, and both merely nodded and did what they had come prepared to do next.

From within their loose-fitting *shalwar qameez*, each produced a hand grenade consisting of a cylindrical fragmentation sleeve shrouding a core of plastic explosive. The two martyrs stood to face the sea. Each looked out into the night that was now filled with the sound of low-flying planes and the questing searchlights of military helicopters. Al-Dhafra air base, in which the satanic enemy had many men and aircraft, was quite near, and U.S. forces would soon be sweeping the area. There was no time left to waste.

Clasping the grenades to their chests, they pulled the pins and quickly joined the ranks of the *shudadah*, Allah's holy martyrs, in paradise, although the acrid stench of high explosive fumes that accompanied their deaths befitted another locale entirely.

The room in the refurbished Pentagon basement bore no number or other identifying marking. Not that it needed one. The armed Marine standing guard outside it, big as a Texas outhouse, was a landmark that couldn't easily be missed.

Before a visitor even crossed the jarhead sentinel's path, he had to present ID at a checkpoint set up near the elevator. This requirement applied even to those whom the guards manning the checkpoint recognized on sight, or even to those who outranked them.

Dressed in mufti, Lieutenant Colonel David Saxon returned the sergeant major's salute and pinned the photo-ID tag he'd been handed to the left breast pocket of his leather jacket, then turned the latch on the unmarked door and entered the room beyond.

Already inside were key members of Marine Force One's operations staff including Saxon's exec, Lieutenant Frank Williamson, Master Sergeant Berlin Hirsh, and other wizards, dragons, and gnomes of MF-1's inner circle. Like Saxon, they were all in casual dress. It was early Sunday morning and the normal dress code that prevailed at the Building was significantly relaxed.

Marine Force One's new operational command center at the Pentagon was state-of-the-art, modeled after the larger war room on the fourth floor used by the chiefs during global crises, and linked to it by local intranet.

Banks of flat-panel display screens on the walls provided real- and near-real-time imaging from intelligence satellites. Workstations at modular centers across the length of the large room could be used as networked mission-planning centers, or to access the same satellite data as the large displays. Doors set in the walls opened into other rooms that included a well-stocked galley, sleeping facilities, and an armory.

Saxon took his place amid his seated staff, and let them fill him in on what they had learned during his flight up from MF-1's training compound at Camp Lejeune. Then the audiovisuals started.

The images were stark, but this was to be expected. A pathetic husk of what had been a U.S. serviceman like themselves twisted and turned slowly on a length of rope. In the grainy long shot the figure was only a blur, but as the camera zoomed in, the bruises and blood oozing from the bandages that covered his eyes, and the torn, bloodstained uniform, could not be missed. The camera lingered over the end product of weeks of torture and interrogation, mercilessly playing across every bruise and every patch of blood-spattered cloth.

A placard had been set up behind the figure. The narration, which had been overdubbed onto the original footage by CIA interpreters, stated that the Arabic characters read: "Islamic People's Jihad Center. Death to the Crusader Infidels! Death to Satanic America!"

After the AV briefing the lieutenant from the JCS Advisory Committee who had come with the DVD took over the show. He recited facts, figures, statistics, dates, and times. The prisoner was Captain Craig Michaels, USAF, formerly pilot of a B-1B Lancer strategic bomber. The captain had been taken prisoner shortly after the plane had gone down after a midair refueling accident.

"At 1735 hours, almost three weeks to the day," began the lieutenant, "a B-1B had rotated off the runway of Diego Garcia Island en route to its initial ordnance release point near Baghdad, Iraq. Awaiting the Lancer at thirty-three thousand feet some fifteen minutes out from Diego was a KC-135 tanker aircraft. It was night. The weather was clear. Visibility was good. The crews of both aircraft were professionals and maintenance records revealed no flaws in servicing prior to the mishap."

Nevertheless, a mishap did occur. The Lancer RV'd with the KC fuelbird. The boom man aboard the KC-135 flew the hose-and-drogue refueling boom down toward the receptacle located just behind the cockpit roof. He was experienced and wind conditions were good. Yet the boom missed its target. Instead of docking with the fuel receptacle, it went smashing into the roof of the cockpit.

The damage ruptured hydraulics on the B-1B. The pilot began to lose control. As he fought to stabilize the aircraft, the bomber pitched wildly and collided with the aft section of the KC-135, inside which was a bladder farm containing some twenty metric tons of high-octane aviation gasoline. Miraculously, the resultant fireball did not incinerate the Lancer.

Although severely damaged and with some of its crew seriously injured, the plane remained intact. Engines on fire, control systems almost useless, communications down, but intact—just barely. The pilot attempted to land the plane. His intention had been to put it down in Saudi Arabia. In the end the B-1B never touched down anywhere.

The huge airframe broke up over southern Iraq. Captain Michaels, his navigator, and WSO/copilot succeeded in ejecting via their survival capsules. All three crewmen were later recovered, injured but still alive, by Iraqi ground forces, who also recovered at least one, and possibly another, of the nuclear-capable cruise missiles on board the plane.

Somehow Michaels had been spirited out of Iraq to some undisclosed location in Southwest Asia or the Middle East. That much could be determined from CIA analysis of the footage, which was largely propaganda. Michaels had been interrogated chemically. The beatings were for the visual impact only, pure window dressing for the American Satan. Enough had been extracted in this way to compromise many intelligence and military operations in the region.

"Gentlemen," the lieutenant said, "what you've seen and heard is classified, and eyes only."

"We figured as much."

"I would have hoped that you would."

The lieutenant was completely serious when he said this. His audience decided to let him slide and not get on his case. He was just a greenhorn from JCS HQ and the briefing was too important.

The lieutenant next showed Marine Force One's operational and planning cell another prepared video. This one was different. It showed another kidnapped official. Though Marine two-star Kenneth Baker had obviously been through the wringer, he was not in as bad shape as the Air Force captain they'd just seen.

But the capture was only a few days old. The general's captors were bragging about their coup. The snatch had not yet made the media. DOD would suppress the news for as long as possible, plugging every media leak. Baker had been kidnapped in Athens. The general had been on the NATO planning staff, the liaison officer from JCS continued.

As best as could be determined, he and his driver had driven into a moving ambush in an isolated section of Athens. They had been forced off the road and found themselves in a district of narrow streets.

What had stopped the car was a Prague chopper. It was a trap first used against Soviet tanks in the Prague Spring of 1968. A two-ton steel I-beam had been suspended between two buildings.

As the black limousine flying the U.S. diplomatic flag passed between the buildings, the I-beam swung down, decapitating the driver and peeling away most of the cab like the skin of an orange.

Riding in the rear compartment, the general was badly shaken. However, not even the security features of the limo, which included bullet-proof glass and an armored carriage, could withstand the crushing force of the trap.

The car was surrounded, the general pulled out at gunpoint by masked assailants. It was assumed he was driven to a safe house in the vicinity and spirited by fast boat from the coast of Piraeus that night. From there many sea lanes led to Middle Eastern locations. It was assumed that he too was being interrogated.

The images of the aftermath of the snatch dissolved, and a real-time secure video teleconference (SVTC) transmission from the situation room beneath the White House replaced them. Members of the National Security Council's Deputies Committee and their counterparts from Defense and State's second-tier hierarchy were seated there.

As was usual in such situations, mid-level civilian policymakers were tasked with briefing the military. The honchos rarely interfaced with the implementers of their policy, which was just as well in certain ways, since it was frequently the deputies and junior staffers who were in closest touch with the real world, while their bosses were largely glad-handers, political hacks, and time-serving appointees of the current Administration.

The nature of the mission was fairly obvious to Saxon before it was even given to him. *The Mean One was to find the captive U.S. servicemen and either rescue or kill them before they spilled more of their guts to their captors. At the same time MF-1 would be ordered to secure and return or destroy the stolen cruise missiles from the downed B-1 bomber.* Nobody told them that the bomber crew and general were both considered expendable. Nobody had to spell it out. One's orders would certainly include a provision to eliminate them all if they were not rescuable.

The large central screen that had displayed the SVTC transmission went blank, and neither Saxon nor the other members of MF-1's inner circle saw the men in the stuffy underground chamber of the White House turn to one another.

One of them lit a cigarette. Drew smoke. His name was Congdon. He was a spook who sometimes oversaw One's missions.

"You realize we've probably sent them all to their deaths," the other man said.

"That's what they're paid for, Charlie," Congdon answered, getting up and popping an antacid tablet into his mouth. His work had given him ulcers. It was all the stress, the CIA doctor had told him.

chapter *two*

The West Virginia countryside spooled past the car. The dream spooled past his eyes. Both seemed oddly unreal, but he too felt oddly unreal, and with good reason, and besides, it was all connected and his memory was a bridge between the two.

For a moment the verdant jungle southeast of Tay Ninh and the multicolored fall foliage in the rolling hill country west of the Washington suburb of Falls Church merged into a single mass of fiery, violent green, and he heard explosions in the distance and saw, in his mind's eye, the gunships come sweeping in over yet another hot LZ.

He popped another go-pill to fight off the numbing fatigue, which was by now causing him to hallucinate. He knew that the pharmacopoeia of pills, which included Haldane for sleep and Dexedrine to keep him up, was feeding an hallucinatory cycle in much the same way that oxygen nourished a blaze, and he also knew that he had caught himself more than once recently confusing imaginings with reality, facts with fiction, past with future, and himself with somebody else who was once alive but was now not even a memory.

The fire-support mission into Viet Cong bandit country in November of '69 kept coming back to him now as he drove.

He had been the door gunner of helo two on that mission. Tuttle, the pilot, had bought it on the way in. A twenty-mike-mike tracer round had come right up through the deck plates and skewered him from coccyx to skullcap, through which it spewed a fountain of pulverized viscera and shattered bone on its way out. He remembered the white phosphorous flare and how it had gone off in his face when more twenty-mike-mike from one of Charlie's revetmented antiaircraft guns down there had tagged the Huey, and then everything spinning in a yellow spiral that became a black void, and later waking up in a delirium, thinking at first he was back in a Saigon hospital, but then realizing that the language was not English, or even Vietnamese, but something else, more guttural, plainly Slavic.

Sweat beaded his brows. He lit another cigarette and forced his concentration back to the two-lane blacktop that snaked its way through bleak stretches of wintry suburban countryside.

Between the Fourteenth Street Bridge that crossed the lower Potomac and the suburban enclaves of Arlington and Fairfax beyond, stark clusters of low-income municipal housing stood off the highway interchanges. The driver headed for one of those a few blocks from a seedy-looking strip mall and a Mobil station. Checking his rearview mirror to make certain no one had followed, he parked near the front walkway and left the car.

At a leisurely pace, he sauntered toward the complex of multistory brown brick buildings, their facades covered with graffiti. He had been seen here before, and had been confused with a welfare case worker or others from the Washington public-assistance establishment who paid occasional visits to the apartments in the complex.

Nobody paid him undue attention, and he continued into the ground-floor level of the nearest building in the complex.

The housing projects were enormous, virtually self-contained villages, and were only haphazardly patrolled. Security was a joke. The housing police had been bad when the city had staffed them, but they were even worse now that the department was a private contractor based in another state and owned by a multinational conglomerate.

Not only was security poor, but it was also invisible. The driver had been here many times in the last year, but had so far seen nothing resembling a security guard. But of course that's why his handlers had chosen this place for dead drops.

Continuing on past a small playground, he saw the first chalk mark, a red curlicue on the frame of a brown wood jungle gym. This indicated the destination of the drop, and he knew he was to turn left and proceed down a roofed-over concrete alleyway to a steel door in the center of the under-pass wall. Reaching it and noting no other presence besides a stray gray tabby cat that loped past with a single look of scrutiny, he dug into the pocket of his black camel-hair coat, producing a steel-plated key that he inserted into the lock.

A moment later he was inside a heated cinder-block pas-sageway leading to the central hallway of one of the build-ings of the complex. He heard voices faintly echoing from beyond the passageway, but the passageway itself was de-serted. A few more paces brought him to the entrance to one of the building's four laundry rooms, directly to his right.

He entered the deserted alcove, paused to listen for voices or footsteps or the trundling of the door of a service elevator at the head of the passageway as he scanned the rows of coin-op washing machines to his right and the bank of taller dryers to his left.

He found the second chalk mark on the right-hand wall. It was diagonal and colored orange. The two codes indicated the placement of the message in the dead drop by his han-dler's cutouts.

The driver went to the third washing machine from the right-hand wall on which the mark had been made, and felt behind the large appliance.

The plastic capsule, magnetized to adhere to the metal back of the machine, was just where he'd expected to find it. He removed the slip of paper from inside the capsule and slipped it into his coat pocket. He would quickly decode it in the car using a one-time code pad, and burn it later, when he returned to his split-level home in Falls Church, some twenty minutes from the drop point.

When he looked up again, he saw the child.

The little girl had wandered in from somewhere. He had not seen or heard her enter. The driver froze for a moment, fighting back a jolt of sudden, free-floating panic. He should have paid more attention to his surroundings, he chided him-self belatedly. He'd been sloppy, and sloppiness in this game was an ultimate death sentence. Then he smiled, and his cold blue eyes crinkled at the corners.

"Hello," said the child, recognizing him from before.

"Hello, Betty. Your name is Betty, right?"

His face broke into a smile. She nodded.

"See, I remembered," he replied, stroking her hair. "Anyone with you, darling?" he asked.

"Nobody."

"Not your mommy or anybody?"

"Nope."

"Where's Mommy at, honey?"

"She upstairs with Jamal."

"Who's he?"

"Mommy's boyfriend."

"You sure?"

"Uh-huh."

He checked the hall to make sure, but like before, she was alone. His pulse quickened. There would be enough time. He could chance it—again. Not here, of course; too risky. But in that storage room in the basement the girl had shown him last time, there it would be safe. Twenty minutes later, he was zipping his pants' fly back up. The little girl had said nothing as she had watched, which was all he ever wanted them to do. Watch him, that's all. Sometimes raise up their tops and show him. Nothing more. He had never harmed anyone. If it was a crime, then he could rest assured it was a victimless one.

"Now, we're not telling anybody about this, right?" he asked, pressing a ten-dollar bill into her small hand.

She shook her head.

"Good girl," he said, and stroked her hair again. "I have to go now. Maybe I'll see you next time?"

Expecting no answer, not even wanting one, he turned, left the building, and quickly returned to his vehicle. As he gripped the steering wheel his hands were shaking.

Wolfram Krieger lit a cigarette and turned his attention back to the Germanic-looking blond twins seated at a nearby table. The wet bar of the Dubai Marriot was doing booming business, as it did whenever the vest-pocket Arab oil state at the gateway to the Persian Gulf hosted a global arms exhibition.

Dubai competed with Abu Dhabi—another of the small former kingdoms of what had until 1971 been called the British Trucial Coast, and which now made up the seven main national divisions of the United Arab Emirates—for the revenue from international development projects and expositions.

These attracted a lucrative clientele of wealthy American and European business interests as well as their counterparts from other Middle Eastern kingdoms. In Dubai, unlike in Riyadh just five hundred miles due south of the small kingdom, Western travelers could indulge themselves in their favorite vices to their hearts' content.

As long as they were reasonably discreet, the restrictions on and prohibitions against those things did not apply here. There was no Mutawwa, or religious police, as in Riyadh or Jiddah in Saudi Arabia, and even if the phones were tapped and the hotel rooms bugged, it was also true that those who did the tapping and the bugging cared little about what was said and done as long as it posed no threat to the emir, who ran Dubai like a more massive version of Bloomingdale's department store.

The vest-pocket emirates made up most of a crescent of oil-rich states embracing sunbaked island archipelagos and oil platforms in the southwestern Gulf, with little Qatar forming the crescent's northernmost horn. The emirs and sheiks and their royal families, which controlled those states, were descended from forebears who were originally faithful clients of the British and then the Americans, and whose definition of Islam was far more amenable to the incursions of foreigners than the strict Wahabi Islam practiced—and officially recognized—by the House of Saud.

Krieger sipped at his drink and continued to study the twin blondes. He had heard from one of his contacts about their extraordinary gifts for bisexual fornication and girl-on-girl cunnilingus. According to his information, the duo had already performed feats for a united nations of satisfied customers so capably that their prowess had become a part of the local lore, rivaling tales of the Prophet. There was even talk of an interesting scene they had played with a friendly camel in the sand dunes beyond the city limits, although Krieger had doubted the legitimacy of that particular bit of Gulf mythology.

Krieger saw a waiter approaching and glanced at his wristwatch. Its digital face was set to Lima time, but Zulu time was also available in a small LCD window on the crystal. A third window gave time in the D.C. area where Krieger lived, or at least where he kept his main residence, a Victorian house in a wooded stretch off a spur of the Beltway.

Judging that there would be enough time, he flagged down a passing waiter and explained to him that he wanted as many free rounds of drinks delivered to the table of the legendary Swedish girls as desired. Krieger also produced a gold Cross pen and wrote a brief message on a sheet of notepaper from a small pad taken from his jacket pocket.

I want you both tonight. Room 314. 11:15. This is a down payment.

He pulled six hundred-dollar bills from a gold money clip and handed one of them to the waiter. The rest he instructed his Arabian Cyrano to give to the girls with his compliments.

A few minutes later the beautiful twins were lifting martini glasses toward Krieger in acknowledgment of a deal struck. Krieger returned the salute and signaled the bartender with a writing gesture with the forefinger of his right hand against the palm of his left. When the house bar tab voucher was brought and signed, Krieger left without a second look at the girls. He planned, after all, to see plenty of them later that night.

The evening air was cool, bordering on cold, and would soon turn frigid, but he had anticipated this and there was a warm coat waiting for him when he needed it along with the rest of the kit in the Range Rover. The hotel was right on the corniche above the beach, and the night air was scented with the salt tang of the nearby Arabian Sea, to the south beyond the Shumailiya mountain range that began just behind the littoral and extended down the peninsula to the headlands of the Gulf.

Krieger had built a nice buzz from the beers, but was rested and full of energy. The day had gone well, with several potential buyers tendering bids for his Maryland-based company's weapons systems and private security services. Two of these bidders represented Iran and Iraq, although they'd said nothing to identify themselves as such. It didn't matter. Krieger made exceptions. Business was business, and nobody's skirts were clean.

Krieger found the dark blue Toyota Range Rover parked in the hotel's underground garage, remote-keyed the left door, and slid behind the wheel. The smell of new leather assailed his nostrils. He had always wondered about that. Did rental companies spray the upholstery with something to make their cars smell perpetually showroom fresh? He had always meant to inquire but never had. Anyway, he assumed that they did.

He did not need to check the cargo compartment for what he needed to bring with him on the night's meet, because if it was not there the individuals responsible for fucking him up knew that they would pay with their lives. This fact, and the generous wages of sin they earned by working for him, kept them reasonably reliable.

Krieger produced the PDA from his pocket and keyed on the GPS function, receiving indication that seven of the twelve-satellite array were linked to it and that the unit was fully operational, then punched in the preplanned script. The small color screen of the handheld unit flashed a series of way-points along a road that stretched into the peninsula's central cordillera, which began only a few miles beyond the corniche.

Once he was safely beyond the garish supermodern city and in the eerily dark, primeval world that engulfed the largely deserted regions beyond the lights of its streets and buildings, he attached the PDA to the dash by its Velcro mount and keyed on the GPS audible indicator.

A series of beeps now accompanied the car icon that slowly crawled along the route toward the glowing blue rectangle representing his first way-point. Just under an hour later, Krieger had penetrated deep into the mountains, navigating the four-wheel-drive vehicle through a maze of gullies, draws, and the seasonally dry riverbeds, lake beds, and washes known locally as wadis.

His headlights were now extinguished—he had killed them barely ten minutes out of Dubai and then donned the monocular night-vision goggles that were part of the kit that had been stashed in the Rover's cargo bay by his trustworthy smurfs.

Krieger preferred monocular NVGs for missions that called for driving because they made it easier to scan the interior of the vehicle's passenger compartment simultaneously with the road and surrounding terrain. Binocular NODs always produced night blindness for seconds or minutes after their removal, an interval that could well prove fatal under the wrong circumstances. Always keep one eye open and drive sober was Krieger's motto.

Before long the car icon on the GPS unit's screen approached the final way-point on his bumpy journey into the primordial night. As the trip-completion tone sounded, Krieger stopped the truck, killed the ignition, and reached for the lightweight Spectre submachine gun that he had removed from his gear and laid on the seat beside him. He shouldn't need the weapon, but it was always a good insurance policy to have one handy, especially one fitted with a Sionics-type silencer.

He had known Mitch Werbell, who had designed the Sionics, in the old days, when both were whores for the Company in Thailand and other places in Southeast Asia. Mitch had always been a character. He had gotten funding for the silencer by convincing some peacenik with money that it was intended to cut down the noise of lawnmowers. Well, the good died young, Krieger thought, as he twisted the black steel cylinder into the whorls of rifling inside the muzzle of the weapon and exited the Rover.

The infrared strobe he had been expecting flashed in the prearranged signal no more visible to the unaided eye than the beams of a TV remote. Indeed, Krieger used the remote from the TV in his hotel room to signal back. It was one of his little private jokes; instead of switching channels you lit up a merc.

The exchange of recognition signals completed, Krieger warily stepped clear of the vehicle, brandishing the Spectre. The two men who approached were wearing traditional Gulf Arab costumes; however, there were the distinct guttural vocalizations of Saudi Arabic as one of the two addressed him with the agreed-on code words.

The other Krieger was not sure about, but he was darker-complected than the speaker. Like Krieger, both men who had materialized from the darkness wore NVGs strapped to their heads.

Krieger ran through his mental file of potential associates of the Saudi and decided he was either Iraqi or Egyptian, probably the former. Krieger was not an Arabic linguist, but he'd heard enough of the local dialects to recognize the special drawl, almost a kind of brogue, that marks Iraqi Arabic.

Krieger got the padded plastic case from the truck and handed it to the Saudi, who removed his NVGs and inspected its contents by the light of a flashlight held by his associate. As he lifted one of the small, foam-cushioned cylindrical objects, his attention and eyes revealed that he was much more than a simple messenger. Of course. Hamza was earning millions in speaking fees talking about the bad old days as Saddam's chief nuclear physicist, but there were others who had not sought asylum and still worked diligently in Baghdad's ongoing weapons programs.

The Saudi exchanged a few more words with his companion and nodded to Krieger. The component disappeared back into its foam swaddling; the case was snapped shut and the transaction was complete. It had been profitable, and would no doubt pay dividends of various kinds. Although Krieger only had a vague idea of the relation of the goods to the coming operation—he was sure they would not play a role in the American end, though—he was a professional and he had a suspicion of what they might ultimately be used for. If he was correct, so much the better. If not, it was really none of his business anyway.

One hour later, the Range Rover was making soft ticking

sounds in the Dubai Marriot's basement car park as its owner
rode the lift up to the penthouse suite. No one was in the
corridor, but Krieger had no doubts. There was the soft scent
of perfume—French, and expensive, he decided—wafting
from his room. Krieger smiled. The two girls were indeed
waiting for him, both well-costumed in leather and lace for
an evening's bedroom calisthenics.

After a shower and a few drinks, the hired talent got down
to business. The twins girls spoke English with heavy Swedish accents, and these were authentic. The twins were native
Swedes, but most of their background, had anyone decided
to check, was completely phony. They were graduates of
what insiders usually called the Institute but outsiders generally called the Mossad. Technically speaking they were *bat
leveyha*, female operatives, in this case recruited for sexual
espionage.

While the twins occupied their client, other members of
the team in the hotel's garage were looking over the vehicle
and its interior. One held up his fingers to the other and
rubbed them together. His mouth twitched into something—a
smile or a grimace, it was hard to tell—as he faced his companion.

Grains of sand sparkled beneath the fingernails.

Five hundred kilometers to the north, there are coves and
inlets that dot the ragged coastline above the Saudi Arabian port city of Al-Jubail. Scattered among the sea-scoured
massifs and unearthly rock formations of the headlands are
the mouths of serpentine caverns that twist into the moun-
tainside and form wormhole warrens in the bowels of the
earth.

The sea Arabs had known these places since prehistory.
The Al-Bu Shamil, the Naim and Beni Kaab, the Balush of
Mazam, the Wahibah, Janoba, the Al-Bu Falah, and the Har-
asi of the Learish region of Hugf, and still others, all had
known this wild and desolate coast.

But most of the tribal villages scattered along this coast
were long ago displaced by the omnipresent infrastructure of

international oil. The headlands lie in a wedge between the southeastern half of the Tapline—Trans-Arabian Pipeline—Road, built by the Americans in the 1950s to service the oil pipelines that begin at Dhahran on the Persian Gulf and end on the Red Sea coasts of Syria, Lebanon, and Saudi Arabia itself.

No longer do the pearling dhows set off from the villages strewn along this rocky headland. Instead, the littoral of the northern half of the Gulf is dotted with the black superstructures of oil platforms, plied by leviathan supertankers and patrolled by Western naval fleets.

The two gulfs and two seas that wrap around the Arabian Peninsula are arguably the most vital sea arteries of the world. The fossil-fuel energy resources that these waters contain, and over which the great ships full of crude sail to distant ports in North America, Europe, and Asia, are arguably the lifeline of an increasingly energy-hungry world. Were this lifeline to be severed, the power of the West and NATO would be drained like that of a strong man stabbed in the heart.

It was precisely this metaphor with which the men who now prepared their open boats for a short journey had been indoctrinated. The air was chill and the surf cast sprays of frigid salt water over them as they worked in the dark. It was treacherous going. One slip and a man could easily fall and crack open his skull.

The ordnance cases of weapons, ammunition, and high explosive that had been secreted in the recesses of the cavern were heavy, slippery, and hard to handle. Each block of Semtex, each rifle magazine, each wedge of mortar primer, each bullet, each grenade was precious and could not be spared.

They had been brought a great distance, and had taken months of painstaking work to move from caches and clandestine drop zones in the Rub al Khali Desert hundreds of miles inland, by ancient smuggling routes, to their present location.

The men groaned and cursed as they labored to load the boats and set up the weaponry and other equipment for the impending dawn raid. But they knew they would not fail, and as they imagined their objectives out in the Gulf, the satanic forces for which these stood as potent symbols rekindled the flame of hatred in their souls, and they redoubled their efforts to finish on time.

When their blow had been struck, one more underpinning of the West's power would be removed from the foundation, one more prop of false hegemony would be blasted away, one less pillar of this great evil would stand between the ultimate downfall of the sinister enemy and the darkness in which it had cloaked the world for far too long.

Before dawn, the men were finished with their grueling tasks. Some prayed, others checked their weapons, still others slept wherever they could, on the boats or on the hard, cold, wet surface of the sea cavern floor, oblivious to the salt spray misting their slumbering faces.

Tomorrow, before first light, they would depart this place, and commence the bloody work of those who have dedicated their lives to Allah, emir, and jihad.

chapter *three*

Yemen. It lay to the south of Saudi Arabia on the Arabian Sea littoral. To the east and taking up roughly half of the southern tier of the Arabian Peninsula lay neighboring Oman. To the west, just across the narrow straits that formed the dividing line between the narrow Red Sea, pointing at the Arabian Sea like a hypodermic needle into the arm of a junkie, lay Ethiopia on the horn of Africa.

The cities of Yemen were clustered on the Hadramaut, a low-lying coastal band fanned by Arabian Sea breezes but baked by the sun throughout much of the year. Unlike the other Gulf states, which included its next-door neighbor, Oman, and Kuwait at the headwaters of the Gulf, Yemen possessed little oil, its total reserves residing in two small fields inland from the coast. Being oil-poor, Yemen was rich in strife, and had always been a hotbed of local discord and international intrigue.

The coastal city of Sa'ana was one of the centers of political unrest. It was also a seat of pious learning and religious devotion, a city of mud huts and ancient skyscrapers. To say the least, Sa'ana was a place of contrasts.

The hotels along the fashionable corniche glittered like jewels, but in back streets and twisting alleys the timeless poverty of the Arab lower classes went on like a bad third act of a second-rate play. In the rundown quarter by the sea, night fell on stucco buildings jumbled together over painfully narrow streets.

Inside most of those buildings, the working poor of Sa'ana slept, ate, chewed the stimulant called *qat*, or went about producing more members of the Arab lower classes. Inside other buildings, other inhabitants of the quarter carried Kalashnikovs and patrolled courtyards and terraces late into the moonless night, waiting for something to happen.

Jump Team Welder sat shoulder-to-shoulder on opposite sides of the aircraft centerline. The C-130H-30, a stretched version of the Hercules military transport plane, cruised at thirty thousand feet above the black waters of the Arabian Sea.

The twenty-four-man rescue and recovery cell comprised the brigade's newly commissioned paraforce company, officially formed following the unit's air-land strike on an Iraqi presidential palace doubling as a weapons manufacturing plant some months back.

As Force One evolved into a go-anywhere, do-anything fighting outfit, its leader, Lieutenant Colonel David Saxon, saw the need for greater specialization in some operational sectors.

The hastily assembled and trained paratroops had done well on the mission. Saxon nevertheless wanted trained cadres with specialized skills, and with One's paratroop company he now had that capability. Although this jump showed every indication of being a cakewalk compared to Iraq, it was comforting to have sky troopers ready to go on a moment's notice.

The time to go would be soon. Because of the debarkation point's close proximity to the target, Sergeant Kelso, the jumpmaster, was already walking down the red-lit aisle giving the team a fifteen-minute warning, an unlit cigar clenched between his teeth.

The company now had to completely suit and gear up, checking belts, weapons, and everything else necessary to make the jump. Packs, ordnance, guns, ammo—whatever gear had been dumped on the deck for the ride to the drop zone was now hefted up and strapped into place on backs, fronts, heads, arms, legs, and even several other ingenious places devised by 1-Patchers to shoehorn as much hardware as possible into their bags of tricks.

Saxon was first in line. As in Iraq on One's previous mission, he would accompany and lead the strike team. Apart from being a commanding officer who led from the front rather than the rear, Saxon reasoned that the Yemen mission had more room for trouble than the Indian Ocean mission, which was being run nearly simultaneously by a second team.

There were hostages and terrorists inside the hillside villa outside the coastal city of Sa'ana, an unstable mix that called for instant judgment calls.

If there were mistakes to be paid for later, Saxon preferred them to be his own. A long time ago, Charlie Beckwith had told him that the one thing he didn't regret about the debacle at the Rice Bowl landing site in the Iranian desert was being on the ground with his men when the string of mishaps began to happen. The colonel's judgment call was a tough one to make, but years later he was still confident it was the right one and the only one.

As the men griped and kidded to ease the pre-jump tension, Kelso was already showing signs that the go was imminent. Leaning precariously out into the whipping wind and the black of night beyond the dimly red-lit confines of the airlifter's cargo compartment, the veteran jumpmaster eyeballed the terrain below.

Kelso strong-armed himself back inside the cabin and resecured the forward of the plane's two hatches. Talking around his dead cigar, he told the team to get their asses in gear because they would jump in five minutes.

As Team Welder neared its DZ, Team Bricklayer was preparing to undertake its own mission insertion.

The U.S. attack submarine *Pasadena* was a Seawolf-class nuclear boat. Its skipper, Commander Gannon Lamb, had received orders to take on a contingent of special warfare operators before his crew put out to sea from the sub pens at Norfolk, Virginia, where the *Pasadena* was undergoing refitting and repairs.

The twelve-man team that had come aboard wore black uniforms with no insignia of rank other than that pinned on epaulettes. They were sequestered from the rest of the crew in a special deep-freeze or isolation area.

No big deal. The skipper and crew had seen it all before. And with good reason. Among other things, the *Pasadena* was a dedicated special-operations-forces delivery platform, specially equipped to support undersea, surface, and littoral commando ops.

The sub had taken on passengers and provisions four days ago. In the interim, while the *Pasadena* set a course for the Indian Ocean, Bricklayer personnel worked the remaining kinks out of their plan to hit the freighter believed to be carrying the nuclear weapons captured from the downed Lancer in Iraq, refining the plan they'd developed at One's Camp Lejeune compound using scale models and computer simulations.

Many ideas, including a heliborne assault, had been rejected as unworkable. In the end, the stealth option of submarine delivery was judged most effective—any other approach would have given the crew of the freighter time to do any number of troublesome things, including radio confederates, destroy the cruise missiles that were the target of the hunt, or scuttle the ship, among other scenarios.

The decision favoring stealth narrowed the field of possibilities considerably, and meant an assault on the ship while at sea by small commando teams armed with light automatic weapons.

The teams, three in all, would use inflatable attack boats, raiding craft similar to those used by SEALs and the British SBS, to get in close to the freighter. After that, a three-man assault element would scale the hull to deck level using specialized climbing gear.

Any security found on deck would be killed with silenced automatic weapons. When the deck was secure, the remaining team members would take the elevator up, using motorized winches deployed by the first team to fast-rope up the side of the hull. The complete assault force would then fan out, commandeer the vessel, and find the missiles.

Simple in conception, but as Bricklayer's members all knew, potentially difficult in execution.

* * *

Aboard the C-130H-30, Master Sergeant Kelso watched gear-laden men do Frankenstein walks out the aircraft's two doors and disappear into cold, black, empty space, helping them on their way with shouts and shoves where these were deemed necessary.

None of these boys ever needed the full treatment—they were professionals, not greenhorns—who sometimes required literally prying a para loose from a seat and throwing him bodily out the door. Still, in Kelso's opinion, no good, clean jump could ever be accomplished without a little shouting and shoving. As a seasoned jumpmaster, Kelso knew the boys expected it of him, and he was ever glad to oblige.

On the paratroop end of things, each man experienced a familiar set of physical sensations on exiting the Hercules; not all of them pleasant. First there was the gut-wrenching, bone-jarring tug of the wind whipping the jumper away from the cabin he'd just left, a cross between being swallowed by an invisible giant and swatted like a fly.

After that, when the chute deployed, a similar sensation, only in an upward, rather than a sideward, direction, jerking the body like a marionette being pulled off the stage by a hidden puppetmaster, while above, and to left and right, were the sounds of other chutes deploying and bellying out with wind as the engine exhaust smells and drone of the C-130's turboprop engines faded eerily into silence.

Then came the fun part, for a while anyway. Drifting earthward (and on a HALO jump, such as One's para-assault element was now engaged in, a trooper might ride the wind for miles to a distant target), controlling the descent by the use of handgrips, watching lights and terrain features slide by below, gliding downward like a vengeful spirit to dispense whispering death.

The chutes used by One to make the high-altitude, low-opening drop were airfoil chutes of a type favored by special forces personnel. The crescent-shaped black parachutes were far more controllable than conventional ram-air chutes, and could be piloted much like hang gliders by those that had mastered the intricacies of the art.

If everything went as anticipated, the assault company would drop silently and all but invisibly onto their target zone in a well-choreographed series of individual landings, each at a preselected sector of the sprawling villa compound situated on one of the rocky hills overlooking the Arabian Sea.

If necessary, the assault force was prepared to take out sentries or other combatants with silenced automatic weapons as the team landed, dropping the hostiles before shedding their rigs and quickly moving in to secure the target.

Saxon hoped it would work.

He would be the first man down.

The freighter *Star of Ankara* was identified by the maritime radar of an E3-B Sentry AWACS aircraft loitering some distance from the operations zone. Its radio transmissions were also being monitored by an RC-135(X) Cobra Eye ferret plane, which would use electronic countermeasures to jam those same transmissions once the assault commenced.

The freighter was cruising at approximately sixteen knots on high, rolling seas. No other shipping traffic, commercial or military, was in the immediate vicinity. Few if any vessels were expected in the area during operations. The mission timetable called for ambushing the *Star of Ankara* at a transit point vulnerable to armed assault.

The MF-1 assault crew on board the *Pasadena* also had access to dedicated photo-imaging from an Improved Crystal satellite parked in geosynchronous low-earth orbit. The orbital spy platform provided high-resolution digital photographic data in real time, so the Marine strike force could run a last-minute mud check on the freighter.

The overhead imaging showed four sentries walking their perimeters on the freighter's deck. Sergeant Bart "Doc" Jeckyll, One's chief technical, who was part of the op, zoomed in on these and captured a few stills, which he highlighted in separate windows on the computer display screen and enhanced with some rapid-fire mouse clicks.

At higher magnification and low-light enhancement, the sentries were seen to be packing AK-class weapons—AK-74's from their telltale Y-shaped tubular stocks—and equipped with mobile communicators clipped to belts and harness webbing.

In addition to the four deck security personnel, the satellite imagery also revealed a fifth merc hunkered in shadow atop the control island above the main deck, and another unfriendly secreted in darkness at the ship's prow. The fact that there was a heavy guard posted indicated that there was more than met the eye about this beat-up tramp of the seven seas. It tended to confirm intelligence assessments that the ship might well be the clandestine carrier of the cruise missiles lost in the B-1B crash.

Doc Jeckyll changed perspective and now focused on the hull. Its steel plates appeared reasonably dry, especially rising toward the deck of the ship, but he knew that even a very fine misting of sea spray could pose hazardous climbing conditions for himself and his men.

Still, the mission appeared as doable as it was ever likely to get. Lieutenant Balls, the unit commander, was satisfied. Balls turned to his XO, Master Sergeant Death, and told him they were going in and to suit up.

"Hoo-ah!" Death hollered, glad the op was on.

Several minutes later, the assault team had suited up into scuba gear and entered the submarine's escape trunk, a pressurized compartment enabling swimmers to leave the submarine from its forward escape hatch. When the divers were free of the sub, powered inflatable boats and other equipment, including weapons, radios, and explosives, were retrieved from stowage lockers built into the deck of the submarine.

When the boats were fully inflated and on the surface, the rest of the gear (which was marked by inflatable buoys made fast to hawser lines) was collected and taken aboard. Working silently, communicating by hand signals only, the team checked over its weapons and assault kit, and donned night-vision headgear.

As they fired up the low-noise hydraulic engines that would shuttle them silently and swiftly to their objective, the attack submarine had already slipped away from the operations zone, into the dark recesses of the night sea.

Saxon's airborne assault team dropped stealthily onto the grounds of the fortified hillside estate, taking out opposition sentries during the final stages of the descent with silenced bursts of automatic fire from the compact M-11 submachine guns favored by One for close-in killing.

Even equipped with sound-suppressors, the M-11's had a small footprint and pointed naturally in the hand. The 9mm short rounds the downsized Ingrams fired were far easier to silence than the standard parabellums that most other sub-guns accepted. The only noise heard as whispering death was dispensed were the rapid clicks of the weapons' bolt actions and the inhuman grunts and bleats of the victims their bullets cut down without preamble or warning.

One by one, Saxon's paratroops dropped into their pre-planned landing positions, shucked their chutes, and moved on the objectives that they had trained to assault for the last several weeks at MF-1's Camp Lejeune headquarters, and later on Masiriyah Island off the Omani coast.

Thanks to the training, which had included computerized war-gaming scenarios, the troops felt like they were reliving an already successful mission. Saxon's hard-chargers speedily and stealthily deployed into the main building and outlying structures of the estate, taking prisoners and shooting any defender who resisted as their shock assault progressed.

Within minutes, Saxon's main team element had entered the main building, where it met sporadic resistance. Firefights erupted throughout the compound as other team elements encountered terrorists armed with small arms, some of them sentries walking their posts, other personnel awakened by the clamor of the attack and hastily grabbing up weapons to launch an ill-prepared defense.

This defense was haphazard and short-lived, though, and Welder had secured the estate well within its fifteen-minute assault timetable. One by one, elements of the Marine Force One strike package reported over the team's radio net that their objectives had been taken and perimeters were now secured.

With minimal friendly casualties, and prisoners now being searched before being herded into a portion of the main building set aside as a temporary containment area, Welder set about searching for the hostages throughout the premises.

Numerous crates containing weapons, ammunition, and military matériel of many kinds were discovered during the search, but the lost cruise missiles seemed nowhere in sight. Neither did interrogation of the captured unfriendlies indicate that the main objects of the operation were in fact present on the estate.

Faced with no choice but to extract within the timetable's outside limits, Saxon ordered his men to hustle to their extraction positions for pickup by a V-22 Osprey convertiplane. The aircraft had an ETA of under ten minutes. Saxon made yet another spur-of-the-moment command decision, which was to take the honchos of the terrorist force captured alive on the raid back to base along with the extracting Marines.

It was just possible that under further interrogation they might provide useful information. After videotaping everything of interest, including the faces of those prisoners left behind, One took its blindfolded, gagged, and Chinese-thumb-cuffed prisoners on a one-way ride, courtesy of Uncle Sam. Minus their turbans and beards, with shorn heads and wearing the latest in bright orange overalls, the terrorists were destined to trade the villa for a comfortable holding compound at Gitmo for a long time to come.

Bricklayer rapidly took control of the freighter, but found none of the lost cruise missiles on board. The commando assault team had no way of knowing that the freighter had been part of a carefully stage-managed diversion to point U.S. weapon-retrieval teams in the wrong directions.

Actually, the weapons had gone elsewhere, by another and more clandestine route. As the returning 1-Patchers were being debriefed by secure video teleconferencing, the consignment of missiles was already arriving by convoy along the sprawling Bonn-Karachi truck route at their true destination, a country across the Red Sea on the edge of north Africa: Libya.

Here, in the capital city of Benghazi, a contingent of Libyan border guards was already waiting at the debarkation point with orders to transship the precious weapons cargo to a secure underground research facility, located many miles away.

They had to work fast in order to complete the task before the regular overflight of American spy satellites, but they had practiced the drill many times and were confident of success.

Soon, the stolen weapons were hidden from sight in the underground confines of a facility in the remote desert reaches of Cyrenaica. There, teams of Libyan technical specialists began the arduous job of reverse-engineering critical systems in order to construct a military hybrid based on the captured American weapons. Though the final product would not be a cruise missile, it would be something very much like it.

Something destined to reshape the world.

chapter *four*

With the muzzle of a 9mm Sig pressed into the hole in his right ear, the skipper became cooperative.

He no longer needed the cup of hot black coffee he had been handed by the first mate five minutes out of Ras al-Qulayah in southern Kuwait. He was now wide awake and no longer felt the early morning chill of the northern Persian Gulf in winter. He was a frightened man, and was now in the unaccustomed role of taking orders instead of giving them.

Ismail, his first mate, was now giving the orders. The gun in his hand afforded him that right. The skipper listened to Ismail and did as he was told.

"Now. Kill the engines. We stop."

The weapon pressed painfully into the opening of his ear.

"Yes. OK."

The skipper cut power, and the steady throb of the twin diesels that powered the tug instantly died away. Except for the creaking of the vessel as it was lifted by swells, and the tense breathing of the two men, silence filled the cabin. Beyond the windows of the wheelhouse, the faint blue-black glimmer on the eastern horizon line marked the beginning of the hour before dawn.

"Do nothing. We wait."

The skipper made no answer. Inwardly he cursed himself for the hundredth time for having taken on the Palestinian. They were no good, these Palestinians. They had shown this before, during the Iraqi occupation, and they had been ejected from the kingdom for it. But some had remained, and still others had filtered back in to fill the menial jobs few other nationalities would undertake and no Kuwaiti would even consider.

Besides, the skipper had needed a man on short notice, one with some experience, and no one else was available. Ismail had done the work, showed up every morning on time, and had given the skipper no reason to regret having hired him on.

Until this morning.

This morning Ismail had pulled the weapon on him ten minutes out of Ras al-Qulayah and had made it clear that to disobey was to die.

"You will kill me anyway," the skipper had rebutted. "It is *khalas*."

"No, it is not *khalas*," Ismail had answered. "You will live if you follow instructions. We have no quarrel with you."

The skipper had not believed that it would not be *khalas*, though he had wanted to believe it. In any case he had no choice but to follow instructions. Perhaps it would be *khalas*, perhaps not. In any case he had no choice, this much was clear.

The minutes ticked by. The tug continued to rise and fall, heaving in the swells. Ismail was growing nervous now. The skipper felt the gun move as Ismail looked around, straining to see in the gloaming, straining to hear in the stillness.

Suddenly, there was a thud from near the stern and the tug lurched and juddered. By these signs, both men knew another craft had drawn alongside. Moments later they heard the cadences of footsteps on the metal stairs leading from the tug's deck to the elevated wheelhouse.

"Why does this one live?"

The man who had spoken was older and tougher than the Palestinian first mate. There were two others with him. They too were tougher. The skipper knew now that surely it was *khalas*.

"I thought—"

"Step away."

The Palestinian muttered something. He stared at the skipper as if to communicate that it was not his fault that he was about to die, but the fleeting contact was soon broken as he spun aside. The skipper heard his right ear ring and felt a new ache. The gun muzzle was no longer pressed against it. He wanted to rub his ear, but thought better of it.

He did not move.

The leader of the boarding party wasted no time in making the execution. The gun in his hand spoke once. The first bullet burrowed into the Palestinian's midsection. A second and third round to the sternum and stomach followed, ripping his belly open, gutting him like a fish.

Shaking his head, straining to say something, Ismail collapsed onto the deck, preceded by the clattering of his weapon.

"You are Kuwaiti?"

"Yes."

The skipper had glanced at the bleeding corpse of the first mate on the deck and found the courage to speak. The shooter followed his eyes and smiled as he glanced at the cadaver.

"I too," he said.

"There is a motor launch outside," the shooter went on. "We have no use for it. Go back and tell them. Tell them that Al Qadr has done God's work today."

"What work?"

The skipper was surprised at his own boldness, but the words were already out.

"You will see." The shooter gestured with the gun. "Go, *ya sheikh*. Now. Before I change my mind."

So it was not to be *khalas* after all, not for the skipper anyway. For the first mate, yes, it had been *khalas*, and *khalas* this Palestinian's *khalas* and may his *khalas* rot in *khalas* and *khalas* on his *khalas*, the stinking bloody son of a *khalas*, may camels piss on his fucking *khalas* in hell, and *khalas* his *khalas* forever and ever, *khalas*.

As the skipper lowered himself into the motor launch, he heard men curse as they carried something heavy and slid it over the tug's starboard gunwale. Then the tug's diesels coughed and whined to life, and the supply boat chugged slowly in the direction of the increasingly brightening horizon line.

As the skipper struggled to restart the outboard motor, he saw Ismail's corpse float past the boat. There was no point in wasted effort on this son of a *khalas*, for his stinking relatives would soon take care of the corpse, the skipper knew.

Minutes later, while he was still tinkering with the outboard motor that he now realized had been fixed so it would not start at all, Ismail's family members came for the corpse, their gaping mouths and gnashing jaws biting off his limbs and head and sawing off huge chunks of his body.

There were many sharks in this portion of the Gulf, and they were big ones too, the ones with gray backs and white bellies that were always hungry, always mean, always prowling for something to swallow. The skipper wasted no time in using the set of oars that lay at the bottom of the launch and paddling toward the coast of Kuwait as the sharks consumed the last of their bloody breakfast.

A few minutes later the supply tug was in visual distance of its destination, an Aramco oil-drilling platform that lay to the west of the Qatari coastline in the Persian Gulf.

The black bowl of the sky had by this time turned a deep indigo blue. Soon the early morning twilight would fade to powder blue as the sun rose above the line of the horizon, but this was still at least half an hour away. Enough time to accomplish their mission.

Ahead, the Aramco platform continued to grow larger as the tug approached, the *Omrikanee* flag that flew from the top of its derrick visible against the lightening sky, the blue circle of its helipad lights, the blinking red of its warning lights, the pale white lights shining through windows, all still turned on against the faltering night.

In the wheelhouse of the bobbing tug, the radio crackled. The caller's voice spoke college-textbook Arabic with a nasal American accent. He was making a request for identification. The leader of the *fidayeen* took the ship-to-shore radio's microphone in his hand and keyed the squelch. He informed the questioner that it was the supply tug out of Ras al Qulayah arriving on its scheduled provisioning run.

After the brief radio exchange, the leader nodded at the pilot, who steered the tug, then issued orders to his men. The triggering mechanism for the explosive device was activated and checked out. The leader of the *fidayeen* studied his Casio digital wristwatch. Backlighting its digital face, he saw that only a few minutes remained.

By now the *fidayeen* heard the distant drone that marked the approach of their fellow martyrs-to-be from the south. The drone grew louder as the tug approached within a few hundred yards of the oil platform, which by now had grown to fill their field of view. Just before the tug passed beneath the lower deck of the multilevel structure and reached the central point between its four gargantuan steel supports, the *fidayeen* saw the twin-engine Cessna hurtle toward the upper decks.

At the controls sat an Al Qadr *mujaheed*, around his waist an olive-drab web belt festooned with ammo pouches stuffed with sticks of TNT, each stick wired to an electrical detonator whose single-pull switch was clenched between the *mujaheed*'s *qat*-stained teeth.

The *mujaheed* aimed the plane at the center of the oil rig and pulled back on the throttle, simultaneously biting down on the detonator button. The light aircraft slammed into the rig, exploding into a tremendous fireball. The pilot was incinerated instantly, before the name of Allah formed on his lips, the euphoria brought on by the hashish he had smoked before the mission as close as he would ever get to Islamic— or any other—paradise.

With the first boom of the explosions above the oil rig, the *fidayeen* leader on board the tug gave the order to detonate the explosive charge on the boat. The two hundred pounds of TNT detonated as the three men raised their arms and shouted themselves hoarse chanting *"Allahu Akhbar!"* They were incinerated in a fervor of religious worship, becoming in that instant *shaheed,* martyrs assured of paradise. The simultaneous blasts completely destroyed the Aramco drilling platform, killing the hundred-odd members of its crew in the process.

The rig was blown off its supports and the entire super-structure was smashed to flinders. The cranes at either side of the platform broke in two and toppled into the sea. Millions of gallons of crude from ruptured storage tanks now began to pour into the Persian Gulf.

The flames of the conflagration gushed up into the air and were visible for hundreds of miles. Soon, nothing remained save for a flaming oil slick spreading out for miles on the surface of the waters beneath the newly risen sun. The *shaheed* had done their work all too well.

The Marine commandant had checked it out with the JAG. The snatch was legal, since the prisoner, Sahir Al-Gebrowny, was wanted by an international tribunal. So was keeping him incommunicado for interrogation.

Saxon did not approve of the methodology of interrogation, but it was out of his hands now and in the hands of the spooks. The Geneva Convention didn't apply here. Neither did the Constitution or Bill of Rights. The spooks called the shots and they had opted for chemicals.

In white clinical jacket, the CIA doctor sat before the captured terrorist. About fifteen feet of empty floor separated him from the small viewing area made up of three rows of collapsible metal chairs. These were occupied by a handful of persons holding need-to-know security clearances for the operation.

Saxon was among the onlookers. Like the rest, which included representatives from the president's small group of advisors and the DOD and NSC deputies' groups, as well as lawyers from the JAG and the Marine Corps Office of Special Operations, Saxon had submitted a list of questions that were to be put to the terrorist while under the effects of the medication.

Seated in a chair in front of the subject of the interrogation, the doctor consulted the vital-signs monitors and instructed his assistant in modifications to the drip rates of the four IV's stacks with tubes running into the subject's arms. Flow rates from the stacks were controlled by one of the remote PCs on a trestle table with other monitoring equipment, including the recorder for the video cameras trained on the subject.

Satisfied that the subject was in the maximum state of receptivity to questions, the doctor proceeded with the interrogation. The mixture of hallucinogens, neurochemical inhibitors, and other mind-altering substances produced their intended result.

When the hour-long session was complete, Saxon knew that the next phase of the mission would take Marine Force One back to the Arabian coastal state of Yemen, for it was in Yemen that the captives had been hidden and were now being held.

For the first time in his life, Timothy Lomax was scared to go to work. Sure, the bravado was there when his buddies were around at the depot and after work at the bar, but now, when he was all alone behind the wheel and rolling down a dark stretch of the Pennsylvania Turnpike toward Youngstown, Ohio, in the dead of night, it wasn't that easy to laugh at the danger.

Lomax was only a boy in the mid-1970s, but he remembered how his father had to wake up extra early to get gas at the pumps. He remembered driving through ice-cold mornings, passing one gas station after another until they found one with a line that wasn't too long. Then there was the long wait until their car reached the pump. They had to worry about gas-siphoners too.

Lomax had also heard the stories about how oil trucks were being hijacked by armed heist artists who sold their illegal loads on the black market. Had he not remembered it from his boyhood, the media would have recalled it all for him. TV and Webcasts were full of reports about the oil shock of the seventies, discussing the similarities and differences between it and today's version.

One of those differences was that today's looming oil crisis was being created by terrorists who had been deliberately attacking the world's petroleum infrastructure. Al Qadr, The

Glory, wanted to again use the "oil weapon" to bring Western society to its knees.

During the earlier oil crisis, it had been the big international oil conglomerates acting in concert with OPEC oil sheikhs that had been responsible for upping the price of crude. They hadn't wanted to bring the West to its knees, as did today's weilders of the "sword of oil," only bleed it dry of money.

While these historical distinctions were interesting, they didn't touch the crux of the matter as far as Lomax was concerned, because today Mullens's job was to drive an oil tanker over a lot of dark, lonely highway, and this is what the new oil crisis boiled down to for him.

Lomax was nervous, and had gotten to carrying a .38 revolver, which he kept on the floor of the passenger side of the cab. The gun gave him some measure of comfort, but he wasn't sure he would be able to pull the trigger if it ever came down to that.

What he and the guys had been talking about was armed security personnel riding shotgun on individual tankers, even the adoption of the protected convoy system to get the oil to the tank farms and the gasoline to the pumps out there in America. Management had met with the union and discussed it, but so far there wasn't much happening.

The bosses claimed that the terrorist strikes didn't amount to much yet, and didn't pose a threat domestically. The work force shouldn't get exercised over a single widely publicized incident and jump to the wrong conclusions.

So a Mobil oil tanker had been hijacked off a lonely stretch of highway between Tulsa, Oklahoma, and Lawrence, Kansas. So the driver had turned up dead in a wooded stretch midway between the two cities and the load of crude oil had never been recovered.

It didn't mean that the drivers should panic, or that it had anything to do with the terrorists blowing stuff up out there in the Middle East. Let's not jump to conclusions, management had said, and the union bosses had done nothing about it.

But that meant nothing to Timothy Lomax, all alone in

the darkened cab of a semi pulling twenty cubic tons of crude oil through highway that twisted between the Allegheny mountain passes that girded western Pennsylvania.

Not much at all.

In Benghazi, the preliminary assessment by a team of Libyan missile technicians—many of whom had begun their careers as exchange students at American universities—of the shipment was that it was of high quality.

The other materials, those received from the contact in Dubai, were also now in the facility, and were judged to be of a type that would work well with the other weapons-grade components that had recently arrived.

Having filed their early report, the technicians went back to work while the intelligence staff began to make its own study. After some discussion with *Al-Qaids*, the Brother Colonel, it was decided to activate the agent known as Hammon, named for the ram-horned deity who was to the ancient Libyans the god of the evening sun.

Soon a new chalk mark was placed at the appropriate location along the Washington Beltway, directing the intelligence asset in place to the housing project where new orders were to be retrieved.

chapter *five*

The control tower overlooked a full-scale mock-up of an urban center. Its windows were tinted a semi-opaque grayish brown and appeared reflective to any person in the open-air facility three stories below. The identities of the faceless manipulators inside the control tower could not be discerned by covert field assets deployed on the ground-level module.

"This is most impressive," said Libyan General Othmar Kayyali. "It's almost as good as the one at Benghazi designed by the Russians."

The man standing next to Kayyali, to whom he had addressed his comment, remained impassive. Wolfram Krieger's face stayed masklike, his eyes not blinking.

"It is even superior to the training facility at Fort Bragg," Krieger calmly returned. "I have personally seen aerial surveillance photo-intelligence of that installation. We have here an improvement in certain key sectors."

Krieger spoke a few words of Mandarin to the other man in the room, Lionel Soon, the Singaporean head of Imexco Corporation, which had designed and built the facility with the intention of surpassing any similar installation in the world.

"Permit me to explain," Soon told the Libyan intelligence chieftain. "The close-quarter battle range and live-fire training facility has been built to simulate every conceivable type of urban combat situation. The panel in front of you, for example, controls weapons and antipersonnel devices of all extant configurations."

The Singaporean gestured to the console fronting the tower's opaque windows. A complicated array of switches, push buttons, glowing LED readout panels, and mouse-controlled computer screens conveyed a sense of superhuman power that could be projected by an individual seated at the console.

"This particular bank of buttons," the Singaporean went on, "commands over a dozen different types of small-arms weapons which have been placed strategically on the building rooftops, in windows, and on the streets below."

Identification labels next to each button, printed in English and Arabic, gave Kayyali an idea of the capabilities that the panel controlled.

A moment's glance told him that M-16 automatic rifles, M60A3 machine guns, smoke and fragmentation grenades, Claymore antipersonnel mines, and even 80mm mortar tubes could all be remotely controlled from the tower.

"These innovations provide the capability to simulate sniper fire, ambushes of field personnel or vehicles, explosive booby traps and mined areas, house-storming, hostage abductions, and a broad spectrum of related tactical situations," Soon continued.

"It's impressive," Kayyali agreed, "there's no question about it."

"Please direct your attention to the street below, which is a replica of a sector in the proposed area of operations in the United States homeland," the Singaporean went on. "These windows are impervious to both bullets and shrapnel fragmentation and the entire structure is armor-plated."

"Has this been cleared for overhead surveillance?" asked Kayyali.

"We have timed the exhibition to coincide with a blind spot in coverage by the KH-12 photo-reconnaissance satellite currently scheduled to pass over this sector, nor are other surveillance overflies expected," Krieger said with a nod, his voice betraying a tinge of annoyance. "You may rest assured on that count."

He then nodded to the technician seated at the console, who began to manipulate the various control mechanisms in front of him.

All at once, a group of heavily armed commandos hustled

down a ruler-straight avenue from around the bend of a stop-light intersection. They were dressed in woodland-pattern BDU pants and wore matching jackets. Their faces were concealed behind black tactical face masks.

The paramilitary assault unit carried a variety of automatic field weapons. The Libyan recognized the ubiquitous Heckler & Koch MP5 SMGs that were justly famous throughout the world for reliability, accuracy, and ease of handling.

Deploying, the commandos quickly and efficiently began setting up an L-shaped ambush straight out of special forces field manuals. The point men of the unit deployed around the bend in a street, concealing themselves in vestibules and doorways.

Kayyali glanced away for a moment and looked at the men in the room, searching for reactions as he habitually did.

The American's face was impassive, but his eyes were bright in anticipation of the bloodshed to come. The Singaporean wore what looked like a half smile on his face and his nostrils flared, accentuating the hawklike quality of his features.

Suddenly, the Libyan intelligence officer's attention was gripped by the unmistakable bolt clatter from below, a sound made only by automatic weapons discharging their rounds. A lifetime of military service enabled Kayyali to instantly distinguish between live fire and even the finest recordings. This was live.

Two passenger cars of a type their intended targets would drive had suddenly come speeding around the intersection bend and driven straight into the L-shaped ambush. The first vehicle swerved hard as it was raked by automatic fire, and struck a wall as its windshield was shattered by a hail of parabellum bullets, instantly killing those in the front seat. The stricken vehicle burst into flames a few moments later as its fuel lines caught fire and began to burn, giving off dense clouds of billowing black smoke.

There was no doubt to Kayyali that the vehicle's occupants were dead: There was no way they could have stage-managed that kind of assault. For a moment, he flashed on something he had read long ago concerning gladiatorial combats in the Colosseum of ancient Rome. Most fighters had been condemned men. Where had these latter-day gladiators come from?

By chance, Kayyali caught Krieger's glance. There was a half smile on the face of the American mercenary leader as he nodded to the Libyan, as if to say, "We are not afraid to go the maximum distance in pursuit of mission objectives." Kayyali returned his attention to the action still unfolding below.

"The families of the dead will be well-compensated," Krieger said out loud as if sensing the Libyan's thoughts.

Weapons in hand, passengers from the second car had now come dashing out of the other stricken vehicle after it too had been hit by repeating small-arms fire. A pitched firefight erupted as they shot back at the ambushers with chattering automatic rifles and submachine guns.

One of the attackers was hit as a burst of SMG rounds struck him across the upper torso. A ragged, zigzagging tear of exposed red meat immediately opened up under the barrage of multiple bullet strikes. The commando shooter flopped to the blood-drenched sidewalk and lay in a death posture with arms and legs haphazardly outflung.

But the two men who had charged from the car did not survive long either. As both raced in different directions, snapping off bursts on the fly, they were promptly cut down by massed automatic fire from the surviving members of the ambush crew.

Moments later, the last echoes of battle had died away. Except for the crackling of the flames licking up from the charred wrecks of the burning crash vehicles, silence reigned in the killing ground below the observation and control tower.

The entire spasm of violence was over as quickly as it had commenced, having taken just under ten minutes from start to finish since the initial car had first sped into view. In its aftermath five people lay dead on the smoke-choked streets of the training installation.

Their weapons safed and slung across their shoulders, the tactical-masked survivors of the ambush turned from the carnage and walked toward the base of the tower.

Kayyali surmised that these concluding gestures had obviously been orchestrated along with the initial show of murderous brutality as part of the violent exhibition of the merc force's skills. All the commando shooters now removed the tactical face masks that had concealed their features and saluted those they could not see behind the tower's concealing windows. Again he thought of Roman gladiators.

The Singaporean and the American turned to the Libyan intelligence officer.

"What did you think?" asked Krieger.

"Impressive," Kayyali declared, meaning his remark this time. "You must have gone to considerable trouble to duplicate even the vehicles likely to be encountered, to say nothing of the street and building facades."

"We did," Kreiger admitted, smiling his lupine smile.

It was indeed impressive, Kayyali thought. What's more, he had just had an idea of how the skills of the ruthless assassins below could be put to use to deal with a nettlesome issue that had recently arisen. It concerned certain data that had come into possession of agents of his government monitoring the secret intelligence establishment in the Pentagon and Washington, D.C. The capture of Al Qadr operatives in a strike in Yemen had resulted in a Marines special forces contingent ordered to a fresh search for U.S. hostages.

"You said they had no idea of who actually controls them?" Kayyali asked.

"None whatsoever," the Krieger replied. "Recruitment, vetting, and training procedures are operationally compartmentalized," he went on. "Those below are separated from us by an extensive line of cutouts."

"Good," Kayyali told the both of them. "You'll be hearing from me soon regarding inserting some of your assets into the field. This would be separate from the forthcoming major operation in America." He checked his wristwatch. "However, right now I have a plane to catch. I'll be back to you as soon as things develop."

The Libyan motioned for his aide to get the door. The

others in the tactical nerve center, following suit, agreed that they all had important duties to attend to.

One by one, they began to file from the control tower overlooking the high-technology killing ground that was a preview of the real thing to come.

Somehow, the CJCS knew it would be bad news even before he answered the phone. Not that all calls early in the morning were bad news, but most of them, in his experience, had been.

Besides, he'd had a portentous feeling about letting the spooks handle the job. He'd lobbied, hell, had fought tooth and nail against it, but the SecDef had overruled him. The SecDef was the CJCS's boss and spoke for the president. You didn't argue with Zeus's messenger, you just saluted and said, "Can do."

Sure enough, the report was that the mission to take down Krieger had been botched. Too little too late. He had warned the CIA about cutting deals with an all-but-confirmed neo-Nazi, but his warnings had been ignored. And now, disaster.

Krieger had been isolated in his hotel room. Set up by the two girls used as a *bat leveyha* team by the Mossad's wet-jobs unit. But he had pulled a pistol out of nowhere and begun blasting away. No surprise there. You could practically hide a .25 up your ass, if your ass was big enough, and some, he guessed, were. Kreiger had escaped down the hall and somehow managed to reach his Land Cruiser. Later they'd found the truck but not Krieger.

The CJCS had been told the Israelis never failed. They'd told him that once before about the French too, but an SDECE hit a decade before on an important Libyan target had allowed a terrorist chieftain to escape unharmed and to cause a lot of trouble afterward. That had taught Stark-weather never to accept never when it came to guarantees of success. In this business, there were no guarantees, ever.

The CJCS hung up the phone and checked his bedside clock. He would soon be expected at the Yellow Oval Room, which faced the South Lawn of the White House, for a meeting of the president's Executive Action Group. The group had been formed from various cabinet members to keep the president informed through the growing international crisis caused by Al Qadr attacks on the global oil infrastructure.

The meeting was only five hours from now, and the general's regular wake-up time of four A.M. would come in twenty minutes. He climbed out of bed and proceeded to get his used and abused system working again.

The White House West Wing was the CJCS's destination. He went from there to the Yellow Oval Room, where he was the first to arrive. His assistant then set up various audiovisual aids.

The president soon entered. It would be an abbreviated meeting, attended only by himself, National Security Advisor Ross Conejo, Chief of Staff Marvin Lacy, and the deputy secretary of Defense, Fred Chin. Coffee and pastries were served and the meeting quickly came to order.

As usual, the president seated himself in a comfortable chair facing his advisors. Also as usual, he was first to speak.

He said he'd just read the morning intel digest and was dismayed. Troubling events had been taking place and something had to be done soon; otherwise, events would spin out of control.

"Buck," the president said to the CJCS. "You first."

The president folded his arms and listened.

Krieger sipped his Madeira and consulted his laptop computer. It had involved time and money for him to piece together the events that had driven him into hiding, but he had gradually formed a coherent picture.

His private intelligence network had lines of communication with members of the U.S. military and intelligence communities and with the staffs of both houses of Congress, to say nothing of journalists. All it had taken was a little extra money to grease the gears, and he had been able to obtain all the data he needed.

Apparently, the hit had been sanctioned as a payback for that little episode in Afghanistan that had been carried out at the instruction of the Pentagon's office of the chairman of the JCS.

Krieger's mercenary network had landed a secret contract through the same joint CIA-DOD antiterrorist initiative that was recruiting a motley assortment of operatives to destroy the remnants of the Al Qaeda terrorist cells worldwide, especially the radical splinter group, Al Qadr.

Literally meaning "the Glory," it was a name that to fanatical Muslims bespoke a Koranic passage of revelation, and therefore also was synonymous with martyrdom, jihad, and the rewards of the eternal paradise that awaited those *mujahideen* slain in holy battle.

Krieger had led his team into Kabul to retrieve a crypto module salvaged from the wreckage of a shot-down spy plane a few months before, but had neglected to return the actual module. He had reported it destroyed, but telltale signatures of the crypto algorithm that could have only come from the central processor of the captured module had later been discovered amid intercepted foreign communications traffic. Agents had been compromised, supposedly secure transmissions intercepted and decoded—things like that. That had made a number of people high up in the U.S. intelligence infrastructure, especially at the No Such Agency, very angry at him.

The luscious Swedish twins had apparently been involved in the hit, keeping him busy and distracted while the Sayaret Matkal *kidon* team, farmed out by Israeli Mossad to the Cookie Factory and the office of the CJCS's special ops details from the Building, had moved in to take him out. Fortunately, Krieger was too lucky and too paranoid to go that easily.

Krieger considered the good points and the bad points. For the moment, the bad points seemed to be in the majority, unfortunately. Krieger had been forced to make a hasty departure from Dubai, leaving his firm's pavilion in the hands of his subordinates—a not-too-trustworthy lot—and that might result in a significant loss of annual revenue in the short run.

On the other hand, he was still alive and hiding out under a false identity on a sun-drenched and balmy little island off the southern coast of Spain in a cozy villa with all the amenities, including another pair of twins, these apparently Greek or Moroccan, he hadn't figured out precisely which yet.

Krieger's next step would be to put out feelers and try to cut a deal with his former employers. They were angry today, but tomorrow they might have a change of heart, providing he managed to find a way back into their good graces. This might take some doing, but in the meantime he felt reasonably safe here on this little island—what was it called, ah, yes, Azahar—and later on, if the heat was still on, there was always Benghazi.

The Brother Colonel was still playing his cards close to the vest, but his appetite for power politics remained as healthy as ever. Krieger's next stop would probably be Benghazi or perhaps Tripoli. It had been a while since he'd spent some pleasant days in the Al Shatti hotel district of that North African city. He'd heard that Al Shatti had been completely redone to accommodate the tourist crowd that Libya was hoping to attract. It might be just the right place to lay low while things cooled off. One thing was for sure: There weren't likely to be very many tourists around to get in his way.

The vacation package included hotel accommodations, meals, and transportation to the airport. The many high-rise hotels strung out along the Hadramaut coastal region of southern Arabia were internationally renowned and catered to those involved in the oil business, high technology, and other international commercial interests.

Among the reasons for their popularity was the relaxation—for foreigners—of the strict Wahabi Muslim injunctions against alcohol that held sway in the three quarters of the peninsula to the north.

The Defense Intelligence Agency's covers directorate had

been handed a tough job in preparing false identities and
documentation for Marine Force One operatives, but had
been helped by the sizable tourist trade and the thousands of
nomadic international businessmen that amounted to a de
facto transient population of foreigners shuffling through the
Hadramaut week in and week out.

Saxon was traveling as Wallace Bradshaw, business agent
for the Lockheed-Martin Aircraft Corporation of Cupertino,
California. Saxon was told a field asset of the CIA's special
actions directorate would liaise with him in Sa'ana. Saxon
was to make contact with him in a prearranged manner.

Saxon was surprised to discover that the contact was none
other than Congdon's field spook, Lyndon Rempt, miraculously returned from the dead. Saxon had last seen Rempt
during One's operations in the cross-border regions that lay
between Turkey, Iraq, Iran, and the Southern Caucasus region of the new Soviet Union.

The most surprising thing of all about Rempt's reappear-
ance was that when Saxon had last laid eyes on Rempt, he'd
been a partially charred corpse, the victim of a helicopter
missile strike. It was interesting, to say the least, to see the
late Rempt alive and kicking instead of a stinking, smoldering mass of broiled black carbon lying on the dirt floor of a
bombed-out native hut.

Rempt explained that he had been forced to make a hasty
exit ahead of Marine Force One. He couldn't explain the
body in his hut overlooking the *peshmerga* encampment that
One had been based at, but such were the fortunes of war.
Probably, Saxon had confused Rempt's supposed corpse with
some other unfortunate's remains.

Saxon was sure he hadn't. In fact, he was also sure Rempt
had set One up for termination in the helo assault that had
ostensibly killed Rempt.

To say the least, Saxon didn't like working with Rempt
again. Apart from the fact that Rempt had almost certainly
double-crossed Saxon and his crew, and had almost certainly
been in on the clandestine helo assault on the mountain compound, there was something unspeakably evil about the man.

Rempt's dead but ever-gleaming blue eyes, his equine face

and strange way of smiling at you when he spoke to you, as
if he were party to a thousand sneaky ways of cutting off
your balls, and the curious thin red scar that began just beneath his right ear and trailed upward along his jawline, until
it disappeared into the scalp beneath his sand-colored hair,
all bespoke a malignant deceit that had been imprinted by
fate upon his flesh.

Yet there was no other choice. Like MF-1's other spook
connection, Congdon, who sometimes was in on the planning
of One's missions, working with Rempt was a necessary evil.
In any case, Rempt was basically functioning as a bird dog
on this op. His role was as a liaison only. He wouldn't be
in on the operational end.

Rempt informed Saxon that his assets in the region were
working on getting the 1-Patchers the intelligence the team
needed to conduct antiterrorist operations in Yemen. Right
now, those same assets were conducting a thorough sweep
of all likely hiding places and Al Qadr command posts, and
would soon have a detailed report.

In the meantime, Saxon was to lie low. A day, maybe two,
and there would be something positive to work on, Rempt
promised.

As Saxon returned to his hotel through narrow twisting
streets, he passed a small cafe. A Westerner seated at a curb-
side table idly glanced over the top of his *International
Times,* returned to the newspaper, then abruptly looked up
again. He thought he had recognized Saxon, and he was not
one to forget a face. Sometimes, that ability spelled the difference between staying alive and getting dead in a hurry.

The muscular man with the close-cropped gray hair and
scar-gashed forehead finished his Turkish coffee *saadeh*—
sugarless. He rose, paid his bill, and followed Saxon through
winding streets, using his tradecraft to remain invisible to the
subject.

When he determined that Saxon was actually registered at
the hotel and had probably not picked up the tail, the ground
asset contacted the Mr. Soon from Singapore whom he had
last worked for in a private demonstration some weeks
back—not as one of the Dixie cups in the killing ground,

but as part of the invisible security backup that Soon had watching everybody, including the VIPs up there in the booth with him. Mr. Soon, he knew, had certain connections that might be interested in learning about the man he had just spotted.

As it turned out, Mr. Soon was very interested indeed, and instructed the muscular man, whose code name was Hammer, to set up a surveillance team. Hammer already had two men in Yemen he could trust—fellow Brits and ex-NCOs to a man, of course—and more could be made available with a few phone calls to cells stationed in Marseilles, Malta, and Crete that he sometimes used. One was an ex-sergeant major in Her Majesty's Royal Marines, just like himself.

For the moment, his instructions were to watch, wait, and do nothing else.

Fine with Hammer.

As long as he got paid, he would bloody well do whatever his paymasters wanted, and do the job spot-on. But this here Yank was a special case. He'd heard a tale or two about this Saxon. Couple of blokes in the merc business he knew had been burned by the yob a few years back. They wouldn't mind seeing him mauled. Hammer hoped he'd get a chance to work him over a bit before Soon's mystery merc force got its mitts on him.

Yeah, that would be a treat, it would, Hammer thought as he reached into his jacket pocket and fondled the brass knuckles nestled inside. A real bleedin' treat.

chapter six

The simoom that had blown in that morning had dumped an inch of rain over Sa'ana, and a low ground fog, smelling of the Arabian Sea, had rolled in to cover the tops of the city's minarets, spires, and domes. Pools of water filled the hollows and broken places in the cobbled streets of the old quarter, and veiled, caftan-clad women returning from market were careful to remain on the narrow strips of pavement that ran unevenly along the rutted thoroughfares.

Twilight fell an hour early due to the weather, and the evening ululations of muezzins in distant minarets were strangely distorted in the moist, chill air. Bare bulbs projecting on horizontal poles from the upper stories of buildings fronting the streets came on. They cast a spotty illumination over the twisting alleys below. With full darkness, the simoom returned for another bout, drenching the city anew. Only those with good reason were out on this night.

Hamid Namjoori and his two companions were among those few. The Islamic prayer group of which they were members met on alternate evenings, and tonight was one of the meeting nights.

Foul weather was not among the reasons to stop the devout from attending to their duties. The three men, cheeks puffed out with *qat,* kept close to the sides of the buildings lining the narrow lane as they approached the entrance to the three-story building on the second floor of which the group met in the traditional *mafraj,* an apartment converted into a meeting place, in this case a mosque.

From the entrance—an ogive-shaped cutout in the wall of one of the buildings—a short tunnel ran the length of the building into a pocket courtyard at the rear. Midway along the tunnel, a locked door gave access to a flight of stairs to the second story. Namjoori had the key.

As the three backs disappeared one by one into the mouth of the tunnel, they showed up as green and black images on a small LCD screen on the end of a telescope. The telescope was clamp-mounted to the sill of a window on the uppermost story of a building diagonally across the street.

"They're in," said Doc Jeckyll as he turned from the black rubber binocular eyepieces of the telescopic nightscope to face the others in the observation post. The group included Rempt, who had set up the safe house; Saxon; several members of Rempt's local espionage cell; and Saxon's mission XO, Lieutenant Freaky.

Rempt nodded and turned to his technicals, a man and a woman in Western dress who were seated at two low trestle tables on which computer and electronic monitoring equipment had been set up. In front of each operative was a large flat-panel display screen. Virtual windows occupied the viewing areas of both displays, and the two technicals used mice and keyboards to change zoom angles and shrink or enlarge the windows.

"Here we go," Rempt said to Saxon. "The feed on the right is from Namjoori's eyeballs. The left is from the camera-mike combo in the ceiling of the mosque, and the central feed is from the eyeballs of the *sayyid*, who leads the congregation."

Saxon didn't need further explanation. Rempt had already explained the circumstances. The prayer group had been isolated one night by Rempt and elements of his aptly named Viper Cell. Using the same psychotronic neural inhibitor technology that Rempt had used in the rocky mountain passes of the Elburz range to temporarily paralyze the crew of an Antonov transport aircraft, as well as the pilots and WSOs of its two Hind escorts, the cell had gone in and installed the bugs.

These bugs had included, as Rempt put it, "biometric surveillance devices" for the prayer group's leader and one of its principal disciples. These latter were in the form of RIC—

remote intracranial—implants that translated neural impulses from the eyeballs and auditory nerves into encoded audio-visual signals.

According to Rempt, the implants could also be triggered to explode on demand, inducing death by remote control if so desired. Such an execution would effectively mimic the effects of a massive cerebral stroke. Saxon had also gotten a taste of Rempt's penchant for this particular bit of skull-duggery in the windswept crags of the Elburz on One's previous mission.

Along with the real-time audio, there were automatic translation programs that converted the spoken Arabic into English in real time. In case of difficulties, the technicals were also bilingual in Arabic and English and could efficiently translate.

But by this point, it was all academic anyway. Saxon had been in Sa'ana nearly a week since his arrival and initial contact with Rempt. When Rempt finally reestablished contact, the operation at the safe house had already compiled a complete operational dossier on the proceedings at the mosque. Rempt, who could have simply handed over the report, was simply strutting his stuff.

The gist of it was that Sayyid Abulhassan Meshabi, the leader of the prayer group, was also a member of one of the local radical Islamist factions of Al Qadr. This prayer group, as many established throughout the Arab world and elsewhere, including Europe and North America, was as devoted to the politics of violent revolutionary change as it was to religious introspection and prayer.

The group also functioned as a revolutionary cell of Al Qadr. Its main purpose was as a way-point along a weapons-for-drugs route that ran from the southern coast of Arabia to Indonesia, the Philippines, and Australia. The group funneled heroin base from Ethiopia and Eritrea on the northwestern coast of Africa just across the narrow Sunda straits, sent this south, and brought guns, ammunition, and explosives up from the other end of the supply chain.

Rempt's cell had identified two localities as most important for One's hunt for the U.S. hostages. The first was the

hill town of Amram, in the rocky hinterland beyond the Yemeni coastal plain. The other was Socotra, a large, sandy
island off the coast of Yemen in the Arabian Sea. Both would
become operational targets for One, in time.

Hammer felt the tumblers line up, and switched off the
device, instantly feeling the vibration of the black
rubber handle in his palm cease. The electronic pick was
sensitive to the feedback of the interior works of the cylinder
lock.

It had taken under a minute to defeat this one. For appearance's sake, Hammer had kept a plastic punch card similar to the ones used to open the locks of the hotel's rooms
in place while he worked the pick inside the slot for the
emergency passkey. With the lock now disengaged, he removed the card and dropped the burglar tool into the pocket
of his coat.

Closing the door behind him, he donned a monocular
night-vision rig and scoped out the premises from just inside
the entrance. A short corridor with a bathroom to the right
and a small clothes closet to the left stretched in front of him
for a few feet. Beyond was the sleeping area, fronted by a
large picture window. The sleeping area was occupied by
two single beds with a night table between them. Two low-
slung Bauhaus-style chairs were arranged on either side of
the window. The room was unoccupied.

After checking for concealed intruder-detection devices
and audiovisual bugs, Hammer drew the curtains and flipped
on the table lamp on the nightstand. Its shaded bulb cast just
enough light for him to work by and with the curtains drawn,
would not give him away.

A search of the room, quickly made, revealed that Mr.
Bradshaw was in Sa'ana on business for his company based
in Cupertino, California. Not much else, though. Hammer
hadn't expected to find the bloody master plan hereabouts,
but in his trade a bloke needed to be thorough. Still, he wondered what an aerospace firm's business agent would want
in the capital of a country whose gross national product de-

pended on figs, camel dung, and hashish. Well, someone else
had dreamed up Saxon's cover; Hammer's brief was to burn
them both.

Hammer tidied up and left. He would report his findings
to the gov'na and let him worry about that end of the effin'
stick.

As Hammer exited the hotel lobby and lit a cigarette, he
did not realize that he was being photographed from the window of a room on the floor above Saxon's. In the brief few
seconds that his target's face was exposed, Doc Jeckyll got
off a few good digital shots. Enough to secure a positive
check on the subject when he ran it through the unit's remote
database at the Pentagon.

ome two thousand miles to the northwest, across the Red
Sea, and across most of the Arab world, it was an hour
earlier. But it was dark there too, and men worked in secret
and in silence, as they did elsewhere in the world when planning the destruction of their foes.

"You are ready?" asked Dr. Haseeb Muaffaq of his visitor.

"Yes, it can be now done."

Muaffaq nodded and the men fell silent. It was cold in this
remote desert outpost in the Fezzan, and their breaths came
out in streams of vapor. Both of them looked at the large
object that occupied the center of the concrete floor of the
vast underground enclosure.

Technicians on movable scaffolding were busy at work.
The beast had been entombed here since prehistoric days—
or so it seemed, a forgotten relic of another era.

Nearly forgotten, actually, and more precisely. A record
of its existence had remained on military manifests that had
been preserved over time. Now it would be resurrected for
a brief appearance on the global scene. A dinosaur that would
again stalk the earth to strike terror into the souls of men.

"Are the chosen ones well motivated?" Muaffaq asked.

"Yes. They are ready."

"They remain steadfast? They have expressed no doubts?"

"None to my knowledge."

"To your knowledge?"

"None," he corrected himself. "So far none."

The questioner nodded. The answer would suffice. For the moment.

They continued to observe the progress of the work a while longer. Then the doctor left. He would file a report with the Brother Colonel.

The other one, the Iraqi, also returned to his political action cell. It was secret from Libyan security, and reported only to a trusted member of Saddam's inner circle.

The following day was bright and cool, and the last vestiges of the rain that had marred most of the week's clear winter weather was entirely gone. The night that followed was equally mild and clear. The weather was perfect for a stroll about the quaint old Yemeni city, and many of the Sa'anese had taken to doing just that. Women clad in the traditional veil and gown went about their marketing. Men, their cheeks stuffed with the stimulant *qat*, the chewing of which was a lifetime habit for many, attended to business or prayer, or simply lounged about the city's many cafes.

The members of Sayyid Meshabi's prayer group were no exception, and they bustled along with the rest. Although many of them were slated to die this day, none of them knew it.

Not that it mattered.

They would die anyway because they were terrorists and their names were on covert assassination lists. They would die because surveillance on the prayer group had been closed down and all but a few members were now superfluous to the coming op.

If they lived, they would cause more trouble. If they died, less trouble would be caused. So they would die.

Rempt's RIC implants made this job easy, as they were intended to do. All Rempt had to do was flip a toggle on a pocket-sized transmitter unit within a five-hundred-meter range of the subject. On receipt of the carrier wave, the rice-grain-sized explosive squib would detonate, bursting a major cerebral artery. The subject would be dead within minutes. Little could be done to save him.

Rempt saw no reason for cutting anyone else in on the fun. He could pop the six subjects all by himself in the course of a day's work. Suitably attired as a native, his sandy hair died black, his cold blue eyes concealed behind sunglasses, his cheeks puffed out with *qat*—which he actually did enjoy chewing anyway—Rempt whiled away the hours in this manner, keeping the local police, morticians, and mullahs quite busy attending to the several men who had suddenly collapsed with blood gushing from their mouths, ears, and noses from one end of Sa'ana to the other, and then consoling their bereaved survivors.

The boats put out from the harbor and plowed straight across the Arabian Sea. Their destination: outlying Socotra Island. Above the boats, on the windswept cliffs, were outcroppings of whitewashed villas. They clung to the steep ochre promontory like an infestation of fungal sugar cubes. The weather continued to be good. It was good all over the southern littoral of Yemen, and it was good in Sa'ana, except for the men Rempt had terminated, for which nothing was good anymore. It was also good for Saxon and his Marine Force One field unit operating covertly in Yemen. Good for observation of the enemy's movements. Good for many other things.

Saxon and four other 1-Patchers, including Doc Jeckyll and Master Sergeant Death, were set up in one of the villas hugging the heights above the harbor. From this vantage point, they had been watching and maintaining a computer log on all visible boat traffic between the harbor and Socotra Island. Other observation teams tracked regional shipping movements through spotter scopes by day and by night. The safe house also had real- and near-real-time feed from orbital spy platforms covering the sector, which included not only Socotra, but also areas well beyond visual surveillance range, such as the remote hill towns located in the hinterland far north of the coastal strip.

Gradually, a database was built up and the data was processed by Jeckyll. Mission analysis showed clear patterns consistent with the movement of terrorist personnel and weapons between mainland cities along the coastal strip and the island of Socotra and certain key hill towns. There was also movement to and from outlying regions, such as the bandit-infested Empty Quarter of Saudi Arabia to the north and terrorist strongholds in Sri Lanka, Indonesia, and the Philippines reached via shipping lanes from the Arabian Sea into the Indian Ocean.

By this time, a plan of attack had formed in Saxon's mind. Marine Force One, with intelligence support from Rempt's local action cells, would strike first at Amram, a fortified hill town that seemed a likely holding facility for the captured American airmen, and after that would come a larger strike on several positions on Socotra.

The 1-Patchers would approach Amram in a convoy of resupply trucks. Such convoys made regular trips up from the coast, bringing in shipments of food, commodities, and mail from the harbors on the mainland. There would probably be a truck convoy going up to the mountain stronghold within a week's time, Rempt promised. Until then, Saxon's team would continue to observe and firm up its plans.

But until then, there was another pressing issue that needed immediate interdictive action.

"Now, about these wild cards, what do you suggest we do?"

Saxon was conferring with Master Sergeant Death and Lieutenant Balls concerning the rogue operators that had been spotted running surveillance on One. Saxon had set up a countersurveillance detail assigned to stalk the would-be stalkers.

On these subjects too, the 1-Patchers had built up a detailed operational database. The rogues were determined to be part of a motley assortment of mainly British ex-commandos. These were, singly and in groups, known to have hired on as mercenaries in a number of clashes of arms in Africa and elsewhere. It was believed that they were now operating in Sa'ana on behalf of some forthcoming operation to be mounted by Al Qadr. It was further believed that the mercs had been ordered to hit Saxon.

The flat-panel computer screen now showed the faces of the rogue leader, Hammer, and several of the other mercs spotted in the vicinity. Blocks of data on each of them accompanied the photos.

"We should take them out," Master Sergeant Death suggested.

"How?" Lieutenant Balls asked.

"Snipers," Master Sergeant Death replied.

"Maybe," said Saxon. "Anyway, we'll see."

Hammer was dumb, incautious, convinced of his own immortality. Call it what you wanted. He broke tradecraft more times than a dipsomaniac jumped the wagon. Saxon and his crew had been running countersurveillance on Hammer and his freelancer cell since the decision had been made to take them out. Hammer had made it easy. He might just as well have painted bull's-eyes on himself and his mercs. In a way, that was exactly what he'd done.

On the second day after the decision to take down the cell, Saxon was working one of the mobile countersurveillance street teams. He was in the backseat of a late-model Toyota being driven by Zamir, one of Rempt's Yemeni ground personnel. A radio transceiver linked him to feed from a listening post set up across the street from the restaurant.

Jeckyll and another of Rempt's ground crew were in telephone company overalls, Jeckyll perched at the top of a nearby pole by the switching box at the summit. The Yemeni was on the ground at the base of the pole, armed with appropriately forged state papers to ward off the curious or the troublesome.

Hammer's habits made it easy. He came down every day to one of two cafes on the street for an early lunch, and was often joined by other foreign nationals like himself. The listening post picked up most of the conversation, such as the one Saxon now eavesdropped on.

"—orders just came in," Hammer was saying to his table-mates. "We're to pop the bloke anytime we choose. Got it all figured out. Easy as fallin' off a bleedin' log."

"How 'bout payment, mate? Or 'ave you forgotten?"

The second speaker had an Aussie accent. Saxon had seen covert photos and knew all about him. His name was Steven Power. Native of Canberra, where he ran a large auto dealership. Former soldier of fortune in semiretirement. Did odd jobs now and then.

"All arranged. 'Arf wired to yer bank accounts by close of business today. The rest after the job's done."

"Weapons? Logistics? The lot?"

The second of Hammer's tablemates had also been ID'd. He was a fellow Brit, name of Freddie Eastwick. Drummed out of the SAS for insubordination. Good man with a knife and a gun. Not too long on brains.

"Whatever we need, we've got, mates. When we firm up plans, we submit our wants. Plenty of stuff hereabouts, in the city and in the hills, more that can arrive by boat in a jiffy."

Hammer sipped his beer.

"But with the plan I've in mind we shouldn't be needin' much in the way of the hardware, mates."

"How d'ya mean?"

"Well, it's like this. An American businessman is travelin' far from home. He gets lonely, like. Gets to broodin' on things. Maybe his job's not workin' out. Maybe he's had one drink too many at the hotel bar and gets to weighin' the pros and cons of existence. And just maybe this bloke decides to end it all, quicklike."

"And how would he go about doin' that?" asked Eastwick.

"Any number of ways, mates," Hammer replied. "But I was especially thinkin' that a yob what's got himself a nice hotel room high up on the top floor might choose to take a dive out the window as the simplest way out."

"Naturally he'd leave a suicide note," offered the Aussie.

"Naturally," Hammer replied, setting down his coffee *saadeh* and giving his two companions a flint-eyed stare. He fished a folded slip of paper from his shirt pocket. "Got it right here, in fact." He tucked it back in his pocket and went on.

"Figure it'll take the three of us to make sure. No blood. No bruises. Want to make it look as real as possible."

"Break some bones, though."

"Yeah," said Hammer. "Some o' that's permitted. Sure."

"When?"

"Tonight, I think. Maybe tomorrow night. I'll let you blokes know for certain later today."

He drained the espresso cup to its too strong dregs and hailed the waiter for another *saadeh*. The trouble with Yemen was you could get hooked on this bloody stuff, he thought.

The mobile countersurveillance team watched them for a few minutes longer. Then the mercs' party broke up, the bill was paid, and they all left the table.

Saxon wasted no time.

"Green team," he said. "The go-code is Dancer."

Sergeant Freaky's voice came back over Saxon's earpiece. "Affirm. Dancer."

"Blue team. The go-code is Sky."

Sergeant Mainline's voice came back.

"Affirm. Sky."

Saxon got out of the car. He'd just issued termination directives on the Brit and the Aussie. That left Hammer for himself.

The hits took place soon afterward. In the case of the Aussie, Sergeant Freaky was the point man and Master Sergeant Death ran surveillance on the target. Tracking the Canberran was not all that difficult. Although the Aussie took a circuitous route back to his hotel (which was situated in another section of town) designed to expose and defeat surveillance, it was wasted effort since his ultimate destination could be predicted with reasonable accuracy.

In the meantime, Sergeant Freaky had already positioned himself on the stairway that connected with the corridor outside the Aussie's hotel room. He scoped out the corridor through the window in the door to the landing. The hall seemed empty, and that was expected. Freaky had made several covert trips to the hotel floor since countersurveillance had begun, and had noted the maid's schedule. Right now, she'd be on the floor above, working her way down. Sergeant Freaky could expect another fifty minutes until she trundled her cart out of the lift.

A tone sounded in his earpiece.

"Subject approaching." It was Death.

Freaky keyed his comms to acknowledge and got ready to move.

"Subject has entered the lobby."

Minutes passed, and the lift doors trundled open. It was the target. Freaky remained at his position in the stairwell. A bogus maid trundling a cart now appeared from one of the rooms. Freaky heard two clicks in his ear to indicate that the Aussie had entered his hotel room. Still he did nothing.

The Aussie was paranoid. He entered the room with his hand on his gun, whipping it from his belt as soon as the door was shut. He'd also left telltales—stray hairs between the door and jamb, streaks of talcum on the carpet, match sticks under the bedside lamp—none of which were disturbed. Freaky checked his watch. Five minutes passed. Two more ear-clicks over comms. He saw the bogus maid trundle her cart past the door of the stairway.

Holding the door open a crack, Freaky saw her remove the large smoke canister from inside the cart and pull the arming pin. Dense white smoke immediately began filling the corridor.

The maid began to scream in Arabic.

"Fire!" she shouted. "The place is on fire!"

Freaky placed the thermal-imaging goggles on his head and powered them on. By now the corridor was densely filled with billowing smoke. At the same time, the phone in the Aussie's room rang. A voice in Arabic identifying itself as from management told him to get out of the room quickly as his entire floor was now ablaze. The Aussie cursed and opened the door a crack, his hand on the grip of the pistol in his belt. One or two guests were in the hallway, all running toward the elevators.

"Sir, there's a fire. Please go to the lobby," shouted the maid as she passed in the smoke-choked hall.

The Aussie muttered something and shut the door behind him.

At that moment Freaky stepped toward the Aussie with a silenced .22-caliber Walther and pointed it at his head. The gun was bagged in plastic to capture spent cartridges. He fired three shots in rapid succession. The Aussie grunted and collapsed against the doorjamb. The maid was already on her way toward the lift while Freaky ran down the service stairway. Both were out of the lobby as official vehicles, sirens blaring, arrived on the scene.

Almost simultaneously, in another quarter of the city, the SAS renegade was being dealt with by Sergeant Mainline. In the Brit's case it was somewhat simpler, as he was evidently a far less cautious person than the Canberran. As he stopped to relieve himself in a restaurant bathroom, Sergeant Mainline entered and stabbed him in the throat with a Fairbairn-Sykes stiletto. The SAS renegade collapsed to the bathroom floor and Sergeant Mainline exited the bathroom, leaving the implement of death where he'd last put it.

Hammer was another matter. He hadn't returned to his hotel room. Instead, the merc had rented a car and driven up into the hills behind the city. His destination was a secret arms cache in a shepherd's cave from which he would retrieve weaponry for the impending attacks planned by his paymasters. Hammer had never returned to Sa'ana. Learning of his associates' fates, he realized his op had been compromised. For the remainder of the mission in Yemen, he was assumed to be at large and a dangerous unknown factor.

Hammon read his next set of instructions with mounting concern and suspicion. His handlers had never been this bold before. He had not been included in their inner councils, of course, but he had little doubt that the mission he was being ordered to undertake was directly connected with the increasing tempo of attacks against the global oil infrastructure being carried out by Al Qadr.

In the normal course of his activities, Hammon was in a privileged position that afforded him an insider's behind-the-scenes glimpse at the highest level of the U.S. government. Unlike most Americans, Hammon knew that the number and effects of the terror attacks had been downplayed for public consumption, and that much concerning them had been withheld for fear of causing mass hysteria.

For the moment, the president could continue to coyly dismiss the true consequences of the blow being delivered to the West's energy stockpiles and fuel-production infrastructure. This was because of increased Russian output and the quiet use of petroleum reserves from the national strategic stockpile. Both initiatives meant that gasoline and home-heating-oil prices would remain fairly stable. But only in the short run. Within a few months, if the attacks persisted, the true extent of the hammer blows dealt the U.S. economy and social fabric could not be suppressed.

The damage would not just be due to the destruction of oil-production infrastructure. It would also be because of developments described in the Feinmann Group Study of several years before. The study had predicted the depletion of Middle Eastern reserves within a finite period, and the clock had ticked down to a period of less than a year before the zero mark would be hit. It was the belief of the CIA and the White House that the new attack waves were timed to coincide with this timetable, if not hasten its approach. Al Qadr was aiming to turn the lights out on the West, to rob it of its power, to shut off the flow of energy lifeblood to the giant nation. And once the giant toppled, they would close in like ants, gnawing the fallen, helpless carcass to bits.

Hammon would be part of that army of ravenous killer insects. He had selected the code name to help him remember the role he was to play. As Hammon, god of the setting sun, he would light the way to the destruction of the corrupt American empire. He was well aware that the sun itself might also be extinguished, but in its death the enemy would be plunged into the cold, darkness, and savagery of eternal night.

That knowledge, if nothing else, would make his sacrifice bearable.

book two

Chariots in the Smoke

Behold, I am against thee, saith the Lord of hosts, and I will burn her chariots in the smoke, and the sword shall devour thy young lions: and I will cut off thy prey from the earth, and the voice of thy messengers shall no more be heard.

—NAHUM 2:13

chapter *seven*

Headlights doused, the convoy of trucks ground steadily up the mountain road and followed it into the high central plateau. The trucks dogged the highway until it ended. After that, they took a dirt track that climbed the rugged hills that folded in and out of rifts and wadis in a maze of empty, arid high country.

The area surrounding the hill town of Amram has long been a smuggler's Mecca. The location is remote from the major towns and cities clustered along the Arabian seacoast, and is dotted with numerous ruins of ancient towns, caravansaries, forts, and other settlements that were abandoned at various stages of history.

Some of these ruins are ancient, some as recent as the immediate post-World War II years when the British held sovereignty over the Trucial Coast. Some are rarely if ever used, while others serve as regular encampments for the seasonal wanderings of nomadic hill tribes that have lived in the area since Biblical times.

The nomadic Bedouin recognize neither statehood nor transnational boundaries. They range freely between Saudi Arabia, Yemen, Oman, and the interior of the UAE and Qatar. The Bedouin are loyal only to their ancient traditions, their tribal chieftains, and their individual clans. In some cases, they despise their fellow Gulf Arabs as much as Europeans or Americans. Sometimes even more than the hated *kufr* or infidels.

It was their brother Arabs, after all, who conspired with the Western oil cartels to evict them from their tribal homelands once petroleum was discovered on those lands, and who drove them into ways other than the trading and farming that had been their livelihood for untold generations.

Some of those other ways involved smuggling weapons and contraband, including heroin, along the axes of the drug pipeline that crossed the Arabian peninsula in a broad X. The left axis of the X stretched from Central and Eastern Europe, across the Indian Ocean, and into Australia. The right axis of the X ran from the Horn of Africa, crossed India and China, and led into the heartland of the former Soviet Union.

The Bedouin of the Arabian Gulf were important middlemen in the traffic in drugs and arms between groups as disparate as Chechen guerrillas, Basque separatists, militant Indian Sikhs, Indonesian anarchists, and the organized crime cartels of Sydney, Australia. The Bedouin survived on the crumbs dropped from the tables of the major-league players in the international game of dope-dealing and armed revolutionary struggle.

Amram is a small city hugging one of the many craggy, dun-colored hills in the Yemeni hinterland. Stone buildings cluster the hillside, some whitewashed, others weather-beaten, still others in ruins or partial ruins, all watched over by the great ruins of an ancient Crusader castle at the crest of the mountain. Farther out, the countryside is dotted with a constellation of caves and even more ancient ruins. The ruins overlook deep wadis scoured from the hillsides by torrents hurled by the seasonal simoom. Their positions, which command the landscape, make these old fortifications easy to defend and watch over. Any assault, if it's to succeed, must be made by stealth.

Saxon's force quietly positioned itself on the outskirts of a scattering of ruins that surveillance had shown to be frequented by armed men engaged in heavy smuggling of weapons and drugs. The location of the encampment had been revealed to Rempt's intelligence support activity during questioning of members of the Islamic prayer group in Sa'ana. A shipment of weapons was expected within a week from a midnight boat drop off Shuqra on the Yemeni coast.

The weapons had come from Libyan stockpiles, crossed the Sudan, proceeded southward, then eastward across Ethiopia, crossed the Red Sea at the narrow straits at Bab el-

Mandeb by car ferry, and would be clandestinely air-shipped to Iran. The Bedouin would stash the shipment until Iranian go-betweens could arrange for transport by light plane across Oman and the southern Persian Gulf to its ultimate destination. Meanwhile, the ruins had been made ready to receive the merchandise.

Said merchandise, however, would not be transported by its original drivers. Said drivers were now locked up in a subterranean prison beneath the streets of Sa'ana maintained by Rempt's Viper Cell. They had been replaced by a task force of Saxon's Marine raiders. Saxon went over the plan mentally while the trucks followed the last few kilometers of mountain track into the highlands, still weighing pros and cons that only tended to resolve themselves in the heat of action.

The 1-Patcher mortar crews were dug in nearby. At his signal, they would drop HE canisters into the smuggler encampment. Saxon's men were armed with SMAWs, and would use these man-portable ATGMs to further soften up opposition. They would then blitz the encampment from the ground, using small arms and grenades to clean house. The plan was sound and should work, Saxon again decided. The men were good to go. It would happen.

A s the holy days of Ramadan approached, pilgrims from Arab lands, and even from the lands of the *kufr*, began to converge upon Mecca, holiest of the two cities central to Islam. They came to make *hajj*. It is the duty and the desire of pious Muslims to make *hajj* to Mecca at least once in their lives. For in the Great Mosque of Mecca, shrouded beneath its massive cloth covering, resides the sacred Kaaba, or Black Stone, and to circumambulate this holy relic is to achieve spiritual unity between man and his creator.

Ordinarily, the approach of this time is welcomed throughout the kingdom. Prior to the discovery of vast petroleum reserves on the peninsula, servicing pilgrims making *hajj* was a major source of national revenue, and still is. From major hoteliers and restaurateurs, to street peddlers hawking reli-

gious souvenirs, the time of *hajj* normally marks the commencement of a profitable period for many Saudis. These
include the Royal House, whose many state and privately
run businesses interests all reap the benefits of pilgrimage to
Mecca. Normally too, the king himself would journey to
Mecca to preside over worship at the Great Mosque. But
these were troubled times, and the king's counselors had ad-
vised him to remain in Riyadh. They could not guarantee his
security.

Beneath the carefully cultivated atmosphere of peace in
the kingdom, an underground of evil, pledged to uproot the
House of Saud and replace it with rule by armed fanatics
loyal to the one who called himself the Mahdi, was gaining
momentum. Though numerous arrests had been made, security forces knew that many more terrorist cells remained
untouched, awaiting the Mahdi's call to action. The security
forces' intelligence supported the theory that this call might
come during the king's trip to Mecca.

Their warnings fell on deaf ears. The king knew that he
must attend, precisely because the Mahdi wished to paint him
as a coward and discredit his right to rule. Should he die in
the process, then *inshallah*: It would be as the creator willed
it. The king informed his counselors to prepare for his impending journey to the holy city. Nothing, he assured them
firmly, would prevent him from attending the ceremonies to
be held at the Great Mosque.

Marine Force One got into position at dusk, and waited
until the fall of complete darkness. In the early hours
before dawn, they hit the target encampment. The commando
fighting cell made up of Saxon's Marine squadron in Yemen
and Rempt's ragtag cadre of urban guerrillas swept into the
mountain stronghold, quickly taking it.

They discovered a drug-manufacturing laboratory, complete with tanks of ether and other materials for the produc-
tion of heroin paste. They also discovered an ammo dump
and warehouse facilities. These they blew up. All prisoners
captured in the raid were taken away for interrogation.

The American hostages were not found at the mountain encampment. This left only Socotra as a likely site for the captives. But a strike on Socotra could not be a mere raid. Because of the size of the island and mission logistics, including transport from remote staging bases to the island, the op would have to be a major military engagement. This would involve an assault at the brigade level, and considerable planning before it could commence. Finally, the obvious: They would have to be reasonably sure that on Socotra they would find what they were looking for. This meant continued reconnaissance.

Then, should the results warrant it, the fire.

N o effort had been spared for the operation. Complete secrecy was assured by numerous cutouts between the inner core of mission personnel and the multitude of personnel and corporate entities occupying the rings that radiated out from this operational nucleus.

An elaborate system of interlocking cover stories had been carefully crafted by an isolated intelligence planning cell for months prior to the acquisition of the full technology complement. Even the desert installation at which the weapons were being developed and prepared was part of a double blind. All workers, except a handful with the highest security clearances, were brought in from a separate staging area ten kilometers distant in a bus with opaque windows, then bused out the same way at the ends of their shifts.

These personnel included the technicians from the German-French industrial consortium that had been contracted to retrofit the aircraft and to set up the mission simulators. The Europeans had proven difficult at times, especially the French, but fortunately, no harsh measures had proven necessary. The inner core at the installation had been given plenary powers to execute any problem individual without trial if they were deemed to jeopardize the mission.

Still, the mission-control cell breathed with relief only after the last of the foreign technicians had left. From there on in, the Libyan-Iraqi staff that they had trained in the operation of the simulators could fully take over. The simulators were key to the entire operation. The combat personnel had been handpicked because of their inborn skills, but those skills would have to be honed to a far finer edge for success to be truly within reach.

It would not be technology, but the fighting *mujaheed* that would win the day. The West had lost the awareness of this fact. Its soldiers were weak, pampered. They had so lost their manhood that they now competed with women for pride of place in the ranks. This was what came of building machines to fight one's wars instead of fighting them with warriors, as it was ordained to be.

But the *kufr* in the West would be shown their error. They had already been shown this one September morning by Allah's brave warriors, who feared failure more than death. They would be shown this unpleasant truth of their impotence yet again, on a scale they had never anticipated.

Inside the simulators, the four *mujahideen* chosen for the mission practiced the mission over and over again. By the time the actual operation commenced, it would be as if they had lived it a thousand and one times already. Moreover, the simulator trials had already shown up numerous small but quite important weaknesses in the overall plan. As the simulator trials progressed, these weaknesses were corrected.

The mission controller, a full colonel, now watched from the observation and control suite above the central pit that housed the huge simulation machines. Beside him, the technical officer flipped a series of switches and nodded. The simulator mission had concluded. Now the personnel would be debriefed by the installation's psychologists.

The colonel observed the debriefing, as he frequently did, from an adjoining room through a one-way mirror. His eyes, ears, and mind were, in his own opinion, as accurate gauges of the inner dynamics of the human brain as any lie detector. He personally interviewed the psychologists as well, for he did not trust those soft products of Western universities and their Zionist-invented notions of the workings of the psyche. The colonel knew that it was nothing less than Allah that inspired all human activity, this and nothing else. Allah knew and saw all, Allah guided all endeavors.

The colonel smoked his cigarette down to the filter and turned from the one-way window, flipping off the room's intercom speaker. He had seen and heard enough. Perhaps he should rest, after all. He was perhaps driving himself too hard. Yet the mission must not fail, and he would permit no detail to contribute to this failure.

The colonel switched off the light and left the room. He had other matters to attend to. Before he had taken but a few steps, his mind was already on these and the simulators forgotten.

W hite House Chief of Staff Marvin Lacy sat in his accustomed position on the fireplace-side couch, one of two set face-to-face near the entrance to the Oval Office. President Travis Claymore sat facing Lacy on the opposite couch, paperwork spread out beside him.

Claymore preferred conducting conferences with his inner cabinet members this way, believing that it kept things up close and personal. In the case of Lacy, their long political relationship left no room for pretense or posturing of any kind. Lacy had been Claymore's right-hand man since Claymore's bitterly contested run for California governor some twenty years before.

Lacy's organizational skills, selfless dedication, and unerring political acumen had more than once helped make the crucial difference between success and failure. When there was a sound bite or photo op to be had by the candidate, Lacy had made sure the stage was properly set, with placard-carrying supporters and all the trimmings.

Lacy had shown the same qualities as chief campaign manager on Claymore's bid for the presidency after two terms as governor, and they had served Claymore as well on a national level as in the state races of yesteryear.

As chief of staff, Lacy worked closely with the president on all matters of presidential business, including the most closely held matters of national security. Lacy was the first and often the last person to whom the president turned. He used Lacy as a sounding board to field new ideas and as the last word on done deals.

This morning, Lacy faced a haggard man, one who obviously had not slept well the past night nor, he well knew, on previous nights. Lacy knew Travis Claymore like a book, and he was well aware of the demons that were haunting the president at the moment.

No member of the White House staff, however menial, would doubt that the recent spate of Al Qadr attacks on oil infrastructure, including yesterday's suicide bombing of an oil refinery in Ohio, were behind the president's haggard look.

Only Claymore suspected that there was another reason, a personal one. Chuck Hobhouse was an old Claymore supporter who went back to the California campaign days, and who even predated Lacy's appearance on the scene. Hobhouse, though loyal and politically savvy, was a man with problems. His tour in Vietnam, where he had been several times wounded in action, had left him with deep emotional and physical scars.

Many had never healed. One of Lacy's jobs way back when had been to bail Hobhouse out of jail after one of his notorious booze and drug benders. Recently, he'd cleaned up his act, but there had been episodes of backsliding. In the end, the split between Hobhouse and the president had come after the campaign. There had been an incident during the campaign that, if not covered up by Lacy, might have seriously hurt the president's chances to win.

Hobhouse had been the cause. He was an embarrassment. But he was also Claymore's oldest and closest friend. Claymore knew he had to go, but couldn't bring himself to cut the umbilical. As a compromise, he'd squirreled Hobhouse away in a State Department back office to work on a national security white paper nobody cared to read. In a few years, Hobhouse could retire with pension. But some days ago, Hobhouse hadn't shown up for work. He had gone missing. Claymore had asked Lacy to make discreet inquiries. This meant: check the hospitals and jails.

"Nothing yet on Chuck," Lacy reported in answer to the president's question.

"I don't know if that's good or bad."

"Take it as a good sign, Trav," Lacy said. "He hasn't been arrested anywhere in the country—at least not under his real name. He hasn't turned up in any drunk tanks or hospitals."

"Did you check that cabin in the woods?"

"Yeah. He's not there either."

"I don't like it."

"It's probably nothing, Trav," Lacy said soothingly. "You know Chuck. He's probably sleeping off a bender in a motel somewhere in Podunk. You're forgetting that he doesn't have to punch a clock. Unlike you and me, he sets his own hours. No wife, no kids. Listen to me, Trav. You're overreacting."

"Yeah, maybe, maybe . . ."

"You are. It's the stress of all that's been happening. We're under attack—again. The war that began on September 11th of 2001 is far from over. Years have gone by, but the enemy is like a hydra. We chop off ten heads, twenty more grow back. From Al Qaeda to Al Qadr, how many other terrorist organizations have we had to deal with?"

"Ten, a dozen."

"At least that much. All with different names, led by different leaders, espousing different goals, but all linked, all part of a single war plan. Let's focus on that, Trav. Chuck can wait."

"You're right," said the president. "Hell, I'm probably making a mountain out of a molehill anyway."

"Right, Trav. Chuck'll turn up. He always does."

The president nodded and turned to the manila file jacket beside him on the couch. It contained the prepared speech for his evening's televised address to the nation. Claymore was to give his assurance that the recent escalation of terrorist warfare would not forestall ultimate victory. Americans had nothing to fear. Their oil supply would not run out. They would be able to heat their homes in the winter. Live their lives normally in every way.

But there had been many speeches, by himself and his

predecessor, since the war had begun, and he did not know
if he believed them himself anymore.

"Okay, pal, let's get on with it," said the president to Lacy,
and pulled pages from the folder.

It was late when he returned home that night, and his mind
burned with the recollections of the past hours. His handler had insisted on a face-to-face meeting. At first Hammon
had balked at this serious security breach, but the handler
had been clear about its necessity. A meeting was required.
Hammon was to attend.

Hammon had followed his orders to the letter, relieved at
learning about the intricate planning that had gone into the
meeting arrangements. At the shopping mall in Leesburg,
Virginia, where contact would be made, a double awaited
him in the men's room. The double had been well selected.
Hammon could see right off that he was a close physical
match. Hammon's hat, trench coat, and eyeglasses were
traded for the leather coat, ball cap, and aviator-style sunglasses worn by the double, as well as a set of car keys.

As instructed, Hammon waited five minutes after the double left the men's room, then proceeded to the third level of
the mall's car park. He found the Toyota sedan where he had
been instructed to look for it, climbed inside, and gunned the
ignition. He found that his hands were shaking, and he des-
perately wanted a drink to help steady his nerves, yet he
knew that this was impossible.

Hammon drove several miles outside Leesburg via the circuitous route he had been instructed to use. He parked the
Toyota on a side street and, leaving the keys in the ignition,
walked around the corner. Before he reached the van whose
description matched that which he'd been given, its side door
had slid open and hands beckoned him inside. There, Hammon met his new handler for the first time.

"Our journey will take another hour," said the handler,
whose code name Hammon already knew as Arthur. "Of
course our destination is quite near, but we must not break
tradecraft."

Hammon understood. The driver would drive a surveillance-evading route before proceeding to the safe house. Hammon judged that this would be one of the numerous private homes in the suburban enclaves off the highways.

Later, ensconced in the cozy living room of the safe house, Arthur poured them both cordials and they discussed the mission.

"I will explain everything," Arthur began. "You have a new mission. The culmination of your career."

When Arthur told Hammon what the mission was, Hammon almost dropped his drink on the carpet.

"I don't think . . . I mean . . ."

His self-control had lapsed and he had begun to splutter.

"You must," replied Arthur, leaning forward, his eyes suddenly cold and hard. "All these years you have been a sleeper, you knew that one day you would be called upon to perform this act. To refuse now would be to cast doubt on everything that has come before. All your training, all that we together have worked for in common cause. It would all be tainted."

It was true. He knew this despite his reservations as the shock began wearing off. And Hammon also knew that if he refused, or if Arthur entertained even the slightest doubt of his trustworthiness, then he would not leave this place alive.

"If all goes according to plan," Arthur went on, "you will not be suspected of the assassination. Another will take your place. Do not forget that it is not the first time that we have done this. Sirhan is living proof of this.

"As Sirhan was a surrogate for another, so yet another will be your Sirhan. Indeed, you will retire wealthy and honored as the avenger of a great wrong. Another will die, and die willingly, in your place. Of this rest assured."

Arthur continued to speak, and Hammon grew calmer. His last doubts were evaporating and a serene conviction, even a mounting sense of excitement, had begun to take hold of him. Yes, he realized, it would work. It had been planned with the same meticulous attention to detail as all the other ops in which he'd played a part. Fail-safes had been built in to the mission. False trails. Cutouts. Backstops. And it was true what Arthur had said—they had indeed done it before, more than once, in fact, and Sirhan had been but the second of several patsies.

"Here is the weapon," Arthur said, and placed it on the coffeetable between them. Hammon studied it for a moment. Then he picked it up and held it in his hands. "It gives one a sense of power, this weapon, does it not?" Arthur asked, pouring more whiskey for them both.

"Yes," Hammon said, studying the instrument of death. It was extremely light, yet there was no doubt of its lethality. "Yes, I almost believe I can feel a sort of heat from the thing."

Arthur smiled at Hammon's fanciful notion, and picked up the cut-crystal goblet from the low table between the two men. Otherwise, he said nothing more about the death instrument, nor did Hammon realize that Arthur's smile had been condescending. Hammon was a useful tool, nothing more. If his foibles served operational ends, Arthur would suffer them.

"We have much to talk about, much to go over. You will soon be missed." Arthur sipped from the goblet. "This cannot be helped. But the sooner you return, the better. For all of us."

Hammon nodded, and placed the weapon on the ornamental glass surface of the antique table. He sipped the golden liqueur, and watched Arthur put on a pair of eyeglasses in order to better consult the folder on his lap. When Arthur spoke, Hammon's initial fear was a thing of the past.

He was now all eagerness, all attention.

chapter *eight*

Dahlak Island sits some twenty miles off the southeastern coast of Eritrea, to which North African nation it belongs. It occupies a position just above the Straits of Bab el-Mandeb, the narrow bottleneck between the Red and Arabian Seas, which straddles Africa and the Middle East. Nothing grows on Dahlak Island, which is a brown piece of the earth's mantle thrust out of the sea like the tip of an accusing finger, and nobody lives on Dahlak Island either.

Nobody except spooks, that is, who run a farm of a kind in an earth where nothing else grows except antennas. The spooks come in two flavors. The first is a combined detachment from Israel's Mossad Section W, its Signals Intelligence Directorate, and the Israeli Defense Force's equivalent SIGINT department, Unit 171. The second flavor of spook is from the American National Security Agency or NSA, whose personnel are culled from the NSA's electronic intelligence facility based at Camp Peary, Maryland.

The operation is one of many similar listening posts on foreign soil run jointly by the NSA and intelligence agencies of other countries, such as the aptly named Japanese Nibetsu or "Rabbit Ears" listening post on the island of Okinawa. The arrangement has great appeal to foreign nations because of the NSA's enormous and clandestine budget, a budget not controlled by Congress nor subject to the approval of anyone besides the circle of five men who run the NSA, who are themselves answerable to nobody and who are not any of the "official" heads listed on the NSA roster or anywhere else.

In essence, the NSA runs itself and can therefore spend as much as it likes, which, to a country like Israel, which holds a hundred-year lease on Dahlak Island, is very good news. Countries that permit the NSA to liaise with their intelligence-gathering bases can look forward to a blank check for equipment they could never hope to acquire on their own. They also gain use of the array of ferret satellites nobody but the U.S. orbits, and ELINT aircraft, such as RC-135U, AWACS, Joint STARS, and other airborne surveillance assets, including TR-1 and SR-71 spy planes.

Such was the case at Dahlak Island, where the joint U.S.-Israeli listening post monitored telephone, radio, and other electronic communications traffic and telemetry originating from a broad territorial swathe that covered most of the northern half of Africa, including Somalia, Libya, Eritrea's neighbor Ethiopia, and the lower half of the Arabian Peninsula, including the Gulf states of Yemen, Oman, Qatar, and the United Arab Emirates to the east, around the clock.

The spooks worked in joint shifts, teams of electronic surveillance officers manning consoles similar in appearance to those found on AWACS aircraft or air traffic control towers. The consoles displayed information from rack-mounted arrays of classified black boxes. A mainframe computer processed the complex assortment of signals gathered by the network's far-flung air, land, sea, and orbital assets, funneling raw intelligence into the installation.

A sprawling antenna farm, made up of several large, swiveling dishes and an acre of Yagi-type stationary antennas, collected the massive amounts of electromagnetic signals intelligence that pulsed down the throat of the funnel into the computers and processing modules within the geodesic domes of the base. The men and women in the loop sifted the finished intelligence and extracted those nuggets deemed of interest to their masters.

The spooks enjoyed their trade, and like all accomplished tradesmen had their stock jokes for insiders. One of the jokes wasn't a joke at all, but a kind of story. The story, so the spooks told it, was that right now there was so much eavesdropping hardware trained on Yemen and Oman that if the sultans who ruled them farted, the president, at his desk in the Oval Office, would be knocked clean off his wingback chair.

Like many jokes, this was only metaphorically true, because only the tiniest fraction of the reams of data generated by the listening post found its way into the Oval Office. In fact, most of the downstream data from Dahlak Island would wind up in a large room on the third floor of the Pentagon that was part of the National Military Command Center or NMCC. There, first via satellite, and then via secure landline fiber-optic cable, the processed intel product from Dahlak Island would be scanned by a joint group known collectively as Task Force Bravo.

Task Force Bravo had been created less than a month before to act as an ad hoc intelligence-gathering unit to produce and refine intelligence product relevant to potential military strikes on Al Qadr terrorist bases in the Persian Gulf and Mideast and other countries known to harbor Al Qadr cadres. These included Iran, Iraq, Syria, and African states such as Somalia, Ethiopia, the Sudan, and Libya.

Task Force Bravo had been created by presidential finding, although this did not make its establishment all that special. During the Carter, Reagan, or even the first Bush Administrations, such findings were few and far between. After the 911 strikes, they increasingly became rubber-stamp affairs as common as search warrants signed by bored county judges.

Bravo's job involved sifting through data generated by the Dahlak Island listening post, and also from the U.S.-Turkey post at Incirlik, from the Okinawan Nibetsu, and from the U.S.-Australian facility at Alice Springs, as well as a host of other sources. It was staffed around the clock by a joint team culled from the CIA, NSA, DIA, and intelligence branches of Delta, the Marines, the Air Force, and the Army. Its intel product was the be-all and end-all, the holy of holies.

From Bravo, the finished intel found its way to a tight-knit bigot list that included the president, vice president, the CJCS and joint chiefs, the directors of the alphabet-soup spy agencies whose personnel ran the operation, and the senior cabinet advisors of the National Security Council.

After that, it ended up as policy, and after that, as bullets from the barrels of a million guns.

The black discoid aircraft came hurtling out of the bright morning sun. It was the so-called golden time, the witching hour of airborne surveillance, when the air is clear and free of dust particles and the slant of the ascending sun creates contour-defining shadows and highlights the shape and color of objects on the ground.

In its Mach two-plus transit of the skies above southern Iraq at eighty thousand feet, the SR-71 spy plane flew what its pilots called the black line. The black line—so called because the SR's airframe is not designed to do much serious maneuvering and so must fly a relatively straight track—in this case a vector slanting from Diego Garcia to the southern end of the Zagros mountain range in Iran, where the Blackbird would execute a turn-and-burn and head back to Diego.

For most of its surveillance overflight, the SR's multispectral imaging array—the mix of cameras and conformal synthetic-aperture radar modules whose configuration depends on the mission and the block version of the plane—would be turned off. Searching for hostile aircraft and SAMs and the performance of routine maintenance tasks would occupy the SR's backseater and RSO, or reconnaissance systems officer, throughout most of the flight. (The range, altitude, and lethality of surface-to-air missiles has increased radically since 1964, when Lyndon Johnson first publicly announced the existence of the SR program, and the Blackbird, despite upgrades, has grown more vulnerable as a result.)

The RSO would activate the Blackbird's imaging array for a relatively brief period about midway through the flight when the SR's black line brought it across the southern tier of Iraq. At that point the half-dozen sensors clustered along the aircraft's underbelly would begin transmitting data in real time to the nearest of the web of relay satellites orbited by the Department of Defense. In the old days, the Blackbird could only shoot conventional film. The film canisters would be bucket-dropped above remote retrieval sites, usually over open water, and it could be up to twenty-four hours before military analysts could inspect the intelligence take.

Not so today. Telemetry from the Blackbird would be available on computer terminals and recorded on disk drives at the Pentagon within a matter of minutes after being recorded. As the SR-71 streaked across the deserts of southern Iraq, its sensor array began transmitting data that was of great interest to certain analysts at the Pentagon's National Military Command Center who had seen things in the desert from previous satellite overflies that seemed to merit a closer look. As the sun rose on Iraq, it was a little after ten P.M. on the western shore of the Potomac River. The first images from Iraq arrived at the NMCC at about the same time as a large pizza from Antonio's in the Pentagon Mall.

Both were hungrily consumed by those who had awaited their delivery for hours.

Captain William Clinton still got kidded about his name, but mercifully not as often as when he was Lieutenant William Clinton just out of the Air Force Academy. Clinton, who was black, didn't mind the comparison. He still remembered Chris Rock's line "I am Bill Clinton," as another generation had remembered Nixon's "I am not a crook." The presidential administrations had changed from GOP back to Democrats again, but Captain Clinton still had Clintonesque problems. His woman suspected he was cheating on her, which he was, but it didn't mean anything. Clinton's job as an intelligence analyst for the Air Force's Special Operations Division was his main interest.

After his second kid, Clinton's wife Roberta stopped being interested in sex, or maybe not the kind of sex Clinton wanted from a woman. Or maybe it was that Clinton didn't get the same kind of thrill out of the same kind of sex from Roberta anymore that he got from other women. It didn't matter. Clinton's job sometimes made him so uptight he had to have a little sport-fucking to let the steam out of his system.

Finding partners was no problem. There were plenty of available women on the Internet. They weren't exactly ho's; they were more like fringe ho's or maybe part-time ho's. It would be called a date, but it would be understood that a little something extra had to change hands at the end of it. Call it a little present. If the lady could arrange for her girlfriend to come along, which Clinton sometimes liked, then both got presents. Well, shit, how much different was that from the way it worked otherwise, Clinton asked himself. Not much really. It always cost a man with a woman, one way or the other. No way around that.

Captain Clinton considered it a kind of health-club membership fee for horizontal gymnastics and floor exercises. The expense was justified. Clinton's workouts got his head clear, and he needed that space to deal with the stress of his job. Being seconded to the NMCC's classified Task Force Bravo program involved the longest hours and hardest work that Clinton had ever put in during his entire career.

Clinton headed the Iraq section of the global surveillance initiative. The surveillance product of dozens of assets converged on him and his staff in an avalanche of data that, already refined and culled out by computers, was still almost overwhelming for Clinton and his staff of junior officers.

The knowledge that his assessments would have influence on a global effort to take out Al Qadr terror bases, training camps, weapons depots, and other infrastructure, and that an incorrect assessment could cost the lives of friendly forces, was an added burden. There was also peer competition. The posting was an elite one, and it was an important milestone in Clinton's career in the Air Force. He knew a lot rested on his shoulders. He couldn't afford to be wrong. Not even half-right. No, the least he had to be was dead-right. That or nothing.

As the intel feed from the SR-71 overflight of southern Iraq became available, Clinton and his staff immediately tuned out everything else and got into photo-analyst mode. What they were especially interested in was what had been identified as a training camp at Salman Pak. The camp had been known about for some time—it occupied several square miles of remote desert distant from military outposts and major road networks—and its changing activities and physical layout were a source of regular interest to U.S. intelligence.

Recently the old Boeing 707 that had been set up next to a railway spur on the northeastern edge of the base had been removed and two 747s installed about five hundred feet apart from each other. That the aircraft would be used to train potential terrorists in hijackings and suicide missions was not a surprising conclusion to draw.

What had caught the attention of Bravo's analysts was what had begun to appear upon the surface of the desert not far from the parked aircraft. Gradually, over the course of several weeks, orbital imagery had shown a series of large squares, circles, and rectangles being etched across the flat, tawny brown crust of the desert floor. The figures had been fashioned of some black or very dark material, possibly painted lengths of locomotive rails that had been emplaced by teams of combat engineers, it was surmised.

Later on, posts of iron and cement had been added here and there along the perimeter of the geometrical designs. To intensify the mystery of precisely what these figures represented, it was immediately noticed that they were close, if not identical, to similar geometric patterns detected in Libya on overflights of some months previously, patterns that were now no longer visible on the sands of the Libyan Fezzan, an equally remote stretch of North African sand desert also used for the training of unconventional-warfare cadre, and in this case supported by the regime of the Brother Colonel.

It was obvious that the patterns held some relationship to some other place or location in another part of the world, and that they were a kind of training template for a terrorist strike presumed to be in the planning stages. This much was plain from isolated reconnaissance images showing terrorist troops conducting training exercises within the confines of the geometrical patterns. Those who planned such maneuvers were always careful to avoid known overflights of U.S. surveillance satellites, but they had no way to know when a

TR-1, SR-71, or still more exotic spy aircraft might pass overhead, and so, over the course of time, some of what they were doing had been seen by the U.S. and its allies.

What Clinton and his section needed to discover, if they could, was what those shapes represented. Advance knowledge of this might stave off a terrorist attack elsewhere in the world. Because the geometric design was spread out over a large area, and one of its sides was directly adjacent to the two parked 747s, the consensus was that it represented an airport. But if so, then which airport? And what was the intended outcome of the training?

Clinton hoped that the new SR-71 data, much clearer in definition than earlier imagery, might shed light on the question. His computer terminal gave him access to programs designed to compare the patterns to known commercial, private, and military airports and airfields around the world, and his analysis section had booked enough processing time on the huge Qube megacomputer server on the Building's fourth floor to give the operation a serious chance of success.

All that Clinton needed was a few clean pictures of the geometrical installation to start the process going. Once they were converted into vector graphics showing different views of the installation, the data could be compared against the vast number of airports and airfields stored in the database.

There was only one thing wrong, but it promised to become a major hitch. To Clinton, there were aspects of the airport theory that just didn't click. He couldn't quite put his finger on the sticking point. A gut instinct told him that they were following a red herring, that it was something else, something else entirely, that those patterns actually represented.

K rieger highballed the Jeep across the desert crust, bouncing in his seat as the dual-wishbone suspension and oversized steel-belted radial tires soaked up the punishing impact of driving fast along extremely rough terrain.

The smell of the hot wind in his face, the scalding bite of the sun on his bare, muscular forearms, the flat, empty vista of the southern Iraqi desert all around him, and the challenge of tough combat training for an imminent mission—all of it exhilarated him, gave him a euphoric high that no drug, no piece of ass, nothing else in the whole wide world could ever halfway touch.

The safe house in Ahazar, Spain, had been nice and cozy. But a cage, even a gilded one, was still a cage. The companionship and overstimulated libidos of Paloma and Marissa had been a dependable source of diversion for a while, but after a few weeks the thrill was gone and Krieger wished the both of them gone.

He would have sent them packing, except for the fact that his cock needed regular exercise and the girls were reasonably discreet professionals. Without them around he'd wind up recruiting bimbos from the local cantinas, and they would talk, and talk would lead to exposure, and exposure to various unpleasant outcomes Krieger would prefer not to consider, and so the twins had stayed on to the end.

When the time came to leave the villa Krieger had entertained no regrets. The twins were shot and, after being stood on their heads in the bathtub to drain their blood through the ugly gashes in their formerly flawless white throats, cut into chunks with a buzz saw, then boiled in pots late at night. The cooked flesh was deposited in plastic bags and dumped over the side of a boat by Krieger the following morning, to be eaten by sharks far enough out of sight of land to attract no undue attention from the few walkers and joggers that might be out at that early hour.

The bones were burned in the stove until they either flaked apart or became brittle enough to shatter with a mallet. The fire produced by the stove wasn't hot enough to burn the bones to ash, but when mixed with sticky dog food, the fifty-odd pounds of bone flakes were also highly tasty to the many ravenous sharks that swarmed through the reef-infested waters outside the island.

It took the better part of the week to erase all witnesses to Krieger's presence on the island, but patience was its own reward, and Krieger could now answer the call from Libya with a light heart, leaving nothing but fat sharks behind to tell the tale.

He had liked Tripoli, just as he had liked Baghdad during his stays there. He liked the brogue of Iraqi Arabic, the curious compound words those fuckers used, like the one for ice-cream cone that sounded so strange and mysterious that a foreigner would never think it meant what it meant, and the courtesy of Baghdadis juxtaposed against their propensity to get into bloody street fights at the drop of a hat; the boatmen who waited at the ends of narrow streets in odd quarters of the city, ready to ferry you across the Tigris like shabby versions of Venetian gondoliers; even the rows of shabby little restaurants along Rasheed Street, Baghdad's seedy main drag, where you could never be sure what kind of meat wound up on your plate, no matter what the menu said.

Krieger had sojourned in Tripoli for several weeks, during which time he met with agents close to Qaddafi. Unlike Baghdad, Tripoli was not under any current embargo or blockade, and the regime under Qaddafi still had plenty of petrobucks left in the national coffer to spend. The Al Shatti hotel district wasn't up to Cannes, or even some of the better stretches of prime Florida beachfront, but it was clearly on a par with the best the Arab world could offer.

There was plenty of nightlife, casino gambling, and world-class whores available if you had the cash to afford it, and Krieger always did. After hard days of working with the Libyan spooks and military types, who were always pains in the neck to deal with, he could look forward to unwinding completely with drugs and an understanding woman or two.

Finally, all arrangements had been made and he had commenced training the first section of cadre at a remote outpost in the Fezzan. The Iraqis had better facilities, so this camp was struck and the new camp at Salman Pak established. The final phase of training would take place here. After that the mission would either get the go-ahead or be aborted.

Krieger swung the jeep around hard and killed the engine. Flinging the cigarette he'd been smoking to the sand, he arm-vaulted from the cab and faced the men assembled there.

"At ease," he shouted as they saluted him crisply, just as he had trained them to do.

Krieger consulted his wristwatch. It was almost time. In a few minutes the regular transit of an American Improved Crystal imaging satellite would bring it overhead on a reconnaissance flyby. There were things Krieger wanted the CIA, NSA, and the Pentagon to see, and things he didn't. What would follow was one of the former.

"Bring the prisoners."

"At once, sir!"

Krieger's executive officer, Fahdlalah, in turn gestured to his two orderlies, who double-timed it over to the back of a parked deuce-and-a-half. Soon they had pulled three captives from the truck's rear and were frog-marching them toward a patch of ground in which a shallow circular pit had been excavated. Their wrists tied behind their backs, the prisoners were tossed pell-mell into the pit, where they fell to their knees.

Krieger again consulted his wristwatch. Show time.

"Put on your masks."

Krieger untied the bandana from his neck and shook it open, then rolled it so that a triangular section of cloth was left exposed. He then tied it around the back of his neck so that his face was partially concealed. The others under his command did the same.

The condemned were asked if they had any final words. None did. One of them was an American. All, Kreiger had determined, were CIA contract agents. Spies in his midst.

Krieger stepped to the edge of the crater and shot each of the traitors in the head at close range, raking them with automatic fire from his Skorpion machine pistol until the forty-round clip was emptied. A wave of exultation swept over him like a fiery surf. He felt like a god, a god of death. He was fucking unbeatable. But this was nothing. There was much more to come. More and even better. Kreiger checked his watch again as the hot wind blew away the last acrid wisps of cordite smoke.

Perfectly timed.

He had taken his act and had put it on the road. The recon

sat had surely recorded everything, and it was now a matter of public—or maybe not-so-public—record.

Ejecting the spent clip and tossing it into the pit with the corpses, he palmed a fresh one into the Skorpion's receiver, charged the weapon by pulling back the slide, then turned triumphantly to face his troops.

Hundreds of miles to the south, the visitors that the brothers had quietly received in the dawn withdrew to the hiding places in which they would spend the rest of the day. From these base camps patrols would walk the land of the brothers, sending back regular reports.

Old al-Kuri, next door, would also receive uninvited guests who would conduct identical operations. The interlopers' sojourn would be short, however. By nightfall they would break camp, sanitize all traces of their presence, and leave by the same route from which they had come.

The reports of the SEAL teams, and the mission data they had collected, would determine what future visitors these old-timers might next receive.

chapter *nine*

"**D**addy, the bad man's on the Web again."

"What bad man?"

Timothy Lomax was busy doing other things, and hadn't been paying attention to what his eleven-year-old son, Timmy Junior, was up to. By the time he realized what was happening, it was already too late.

"Didn't I tell you not to download any e-mail attachments without asking me first, Timmy?"

Lomax could hear as well as see that the damage, however much or little, had already been done. A familiar face, bearded below and turbaned above, filled the screen, and a familiar pair of deep-set eyes glowered balefully at Lomax and his son.

Hassan Ramad Ali, who called himself the Mahdi, was at it again, and the Lomax PC had just been hit by what the street had taken to calling "Islam spam," "evil-mail," and sometimes "mail from e-thiopia." Lomax tried to stop the rogue program from executing, but nothing on the desktop worked, not the keyboard, not the mouse, nothing at all—not even the power button.

Lomax figured he couldn't even turn the damn thing off without pulling the plug, because these days the power button only sent a signal to a microchip inside the PC, which the Mahdi's virus, or whatever you called it, obviously controlled. Afraid to pull the plug for fear of damaging the machine he'd saved up to buy from his veteran's benefits, Lomax stood behind his seated son, watching and listening to the Mahdi's message.

"Do you think the long arm of your godless technology will give you dominion over the earth forever?" the Mahdi said, the words clearly overdubbed by a translator because they didn't match the movements of the lips. "Or that it can prevail against the power of Allah, the mighty one? His holy *mujahideen*—those we call freedom fighters—are countless in number. Down through the generations, should it take even a thousand years, we shall destroy you utterly. . . ."

At this point Lomax decided to phone his ISP's tech-support number, figuring maybe there was something they could suggest, but the line was busy. Cursing, Lomax hung up, figuring there must be millions of people burning up the phone lines with similar questions.

". . . Because we are like the oil which you crave as addicts crave the needles in their veins. For as petroleum is the distillate of numberless billions of dead organisms into a source of energy, so too the distillate of the anger and holy rage of a sea of abused Muslims, whose numbers dwarf you, and which grows daily, is a force more potent than any on earth. And as the precious supply of oil dwindles and is soon gone forever, so your evil nations will fall and your great cities become dark and cold, fit only for angels of death to tread over the corpses of millions.

"But the fire of our hatred is eternal. Grow it shall, and we in turn shall sweep over you like locusts and devour you until you are consumed and wiped clean from the face of the earth, as were the towers of the World Trade Center in New York and the mighty span of the Golden Gate Bridge in San Francisco, and as other works you cherish, which shall also soon be annihilated. . . ."

The message went on a bit longer with more terrible prophecies of doom, heaven's vengeance, and the corrupt West's imminent destruction. Then the Mahdi's glowering visage faded from the screen, which flashed a message:

**WE COULD HAVE DESTROYED YOUR COMPUTER
BUT CHOSE TO GRANT YOU PEACE.
READ Q'URAN TODAY!
PRAISE ALLAH THE ALL-WISE,
COMPASSIONATE, AND MERCIFUL!**

After these words too had finally faded from the screen, Lomax was relieved that his brand-new, hard-earned computer returned to normal again. After running one of the antivirus programs that had come with it, and getting a clean bill of health, Lomax let Timmy go back to his Web surfing, but with a strong admonition not to do anything like that again.

Some of the Islam spam that people had gotten in the past hadn't been this benign, according to the media. A couple of the messages had resulted in monitors that blew up or caught fire, or disk drives that were permanently damaged. There was also Hitler spam and "virtual anthrax" to worry about; the neo-Nazis were on the bandwagon too.

What the hell was the damn world coming to? Lomax wondered. When he was a kid there was Vietnam, the Cold War, and later there were plane hijackings and stuff like that. But this . . . this was a nightmare that never seemed to come to an end, a war that went on forever.

It was as if the sky were falling, as if everything was coming apart and nobody could do anything to stop it from happening. The economy had been in a downward spiral for years since the 911 attacks, and whether or not the terrorists had anything to do with this, it was plain that with each year more and more Americans were out of jobs and less and less of the good life was available to those who had jobs.

The thin facade of national unity and determination had dissolved, and in its place there was now violence gathering in the air like electricity before a thunderstorm. Lomax could see it, hear it, feel it, sense it, everywhere. People were getting fed up with being victimized by terrorist attacks, and were ready to lash out at any convenient scapegoat. In the course of logging highway miles in his truck, he'd seen numerous examples of insanely explosive and totally senseless road rage. Sometimes cars would cut so close in front of his truck, it was like they were intentionally courting suicide. Other times they'd tailgate you, leaning on the horn for miles, then abruptly change lanes and jackrabbit away.

Lomax lit a cigarette and went back to repairing the lawnmower in his backyard. Fixing things out by the tool shed used to give him pleasure, because he enjoyed working with his hands. But now nothing did anymore. Inside him a malignant fear had sprouted and had sunk down its roots. Now it was spreading like a cancer, and there was no way to stop it.

It was the fear that the world was going to end one day soon, and that all of this, the old tool shed, his house, his son, his job, his country—everything—would be no more, and darkness would cover the earth, just like in the Bible. The word might not have been in Lomax's vocabulary, but he was thinking about Apocalypse.

Courtesy of the Mahdi.

In the cramped meeting room, men sat grimly around the rectangular conference table of polished mahogany, fluorescent squares set in acoustic ceiling tiles casting a pale light over the meeting. The National Security Council had been convened for a special session (the word "emergency" was frowned upon by this Administration in the context of such gatherings), and indeed virtually any meeting held in the NSC chamber with the president and cabinet chiefs in attendance was special, since President Travis Claymore preferred the Yellow Oval Room or the Map Room or his office, or weekend sessions at Camp David, for the transaction of most presidential business.

Claymore found the small meeting room in the White House basement claustrophobic and filled with the tired, gray-flannel ghosts of the Cold War era. In the several months of his Administration less than five percent of meetings involving the NSC chiefs had been held in the NSC chamber.

The basement conference room was instead relegated to the NSC deputies and their working groups, made up of subdeputies and assistants who participated in NSC meetings held elsewhere by secure video teleconference (SVTC). The procedure that evolved was to keep the SVTC line open for the first twenty minutes of any given conference so the deputies could have their say, and then leave the rest of the proceedings entirely to the cabinet honchos, the president and the vice president.

But not at this meeting. It was one of the rare five-per centers at which both senior cabinet members and the president were all present, and the row of chairs for "backseaters" was filled to capacity by the deputies who normally had the table, and the room, all to themselves.

Today the ghosts of the Cold War, and of starker apparitions, seen through a glass darkly, had arisen to haunt the nation.

"On closer examination the pylons have numbers in Arabic characters on them, so they're likely some form of marker or guidepost; as if to say, 'Here's objective one or objective two,' that sort of thing."

General Buck Starkweather, chairman of the joint chiefs, was speaking. The subject of his brief had been the aerial surveillance of Salman Pak. The CJCS had referred to the pylons first detected by satellite at various intervals amid the geometric patterns etched upon the umber sands. The ensuing SR-71 telemetry had revealed still greater detail, including the Arabic markings to which the chairman had referred.

"As to the nature of the geometric figures, or patterns if you will, our people at the Pentagon believe the best guesstimate is that we're looking at the schematic for a major commercial airport, commercial or government airfield, or portion of a U.S. military base, in that order."

"That's a little general," someone ventured.

"Napoleon was a little general," Starkweather retorted, eliciting a laugh. "And I haven't finished yet.

"We've had our best people working on the problem," the CJCS went on. "We've taken the imagery we've collected and compared it with an extensive database of all known matching facilities in the world. Military bases, airports, you name it;, every facility fitting the criteria from Washington to Kuala Lumpur has been compared to the surveillance data."

Starkweather half-turned and gestured toward his aide. "Lieutenant . . ."

The mahogany wall panels covering the sixty-inch flat-panel display at the head of the table before which the CJCS stood slid suddenly aside. On the windowed display were a series of overhead images of geometric patterns on an expanse of high desert thousands of miles distant.

"The central image is of the figures imaged by airborne photo-reconnaissance assets over Salman Pak, Iraq," narrated the CJCS. "The others, comprised of space images of other locations, are what we consider the best matches for what that central schematic design may represent."

Starkweather unclipped a laser pointer from the breast pocket of his uniform jacket and nodded at his aide. One by one the smaller images were resized and overlaid on the central Salman Pak image. The CJCS switched the pointer on, and a red dot darted onto a portion of the screen.

"This, we believe, represents the closest match. Newark International Airport in New Jersey, gentlemen. For those of you unfamiliar with it, Newark's the second of the two international airports that service the New York metropolitan area, the other being JFK Airport in Long Island."

The CJCS played the red dot of light up and down various axes of the multiple images, citing correspondences and points of convergence revealed by the overlaid patterns. The training ground at Salman Pak did, in fact, seem to correspond with the sprawling grid of runways and taxiways adjacent to Newark International's main terminal building. In descending order, Logan Airport just outside Boston, Chicago's O'Hare, and LAX were also close matches, though not as close as Newark.

The president asked some questions, and it was decided to mount tight security at all those airports while continued investigations of the enigma of the patterns on the desert were made. As to the follow-up action, the president would decide when more was known.

Starkweather next addressed the issue of the U.S. hostages.

"Now to Yemen," he began, nodding to his aide to prepare the audiovisuals showing plans for operations to be conducted on Socotra via the Brothers and Al Kuri.

"Just a minute," interjected White House National Security Advisor Ross Conejo. "Before we go there, I'd like to briefly get back to the issue of further study and follow-up action on the Salman Pak findings. I was of the understanding that we've got intelligence assets in the vicinity, if not at Salman Pak itself. You said nothing about them or how they might be able to help clarify this matter."

Starkweather's face became pinched.

"You're wrong, Ross," he replied. "It's true we *had* intelligence assets at Salman Pak, but not anymore." His gaze swept across the assemblage, falling at last on the director of the CIA. "Past tense, gentlemen. They were all executed. Machine-pistol bursts to the head. Point-blank. It was yesterday, right after we got the imagery I've just shown you."

The room fell silent. With no further pause, and not a word concerning the fact that the executioner was most likely a former non-operational contact for Langley, Starkweather nodded to his aide and went on with his brief.

Colonel David Saxon had put the brigade through its paces. Marine Force One's operational elements, much of its planning and logistics staff, and virtually all of its intelligence platoon had been moved lock, stock, and barrel to the Marine Corps Mountain Warfare Training Center (MWTC).

The center, located about twenty-one miles northwest of Bridgeport, California, occupies 46,000 acres of the Tolyabe National Forest. Leased in 1951 from the Forest Service, the MWTC is used to train U.S. and international military forces in mountain and cold-weather combat operations.

The area is located in a rough part of the western Rockies. It takes up mile after mile of rugged country, with elevations as high as 11,400 feet, where winter storms can dump up to four feet of snow in as little as twelve hours and where temperatures can drop to minus twenty degrees Fahrenheit. It's considered the premier facility of its type in the world—or the biggest bitch—depending on who you talk to.

Saxon now reflected on the differences of weather and terrain from his point of origin. Six hours before, he'd stepped onto a military transport plane from Vieques Island,

Puerto Rico, where two 1-Patcher companies were engaged in training for another operation. At Vieques he had been informed that orders had been cut for a coming mission.

This was not much of a surprise to Saxon, as unofficially he had been tasked with training his force to play its part in a series of major, coordinated military strikes against Al Qadr bases in as many as ten countries in the Middle East, Europe, and the Horn of Africa that was to involve U.S., U.K., and other NATO forces.

According to General Patient K., Saxon's boss at the Pentagon, and the champion of the Marine special ops brigade, Marine Force One was to play a major role in the coming multinational engagements. The orders Saxon had just received merely confirmed everything the general had briefed him about verbally.

When Saxon got off the plane in California, he was relieved to find his XO, Lieutenant Butch Williamson, waiting for him in a Hummer.

"Hop in, Boss," Williamson said.

Saxon got into the Hummer and Williamson took off.

"What's been happening while I was in P.R.?"

"Been going good, Colonel," Williamson said. "The training schedule's up to speed. Couple of minor injuries, nothing critical. Only one thing, but I'm not supposed to tell you."

"Yeah? And what might that be?"

"Well, sir, it's like this. When you made colonel, the men were gonna throw you a little party at Lejeune, but then there was the mission, so it never happened. So we got a little surprise party planned. I figured I should tell you in case, ah, you had any problems with it."

"Why would I?" Saxon was beginning to get the lieutenant's drift, but he might as well hear it all.

"Colonel, they smuggled some strippers in last night. Three girls. They're supposed to jump out of a big cake. They got a million cases of beer. No hard liquor, mind you, but enough beer to float a carrier."

Saxon was silent for a while.

"Well, sir?" Williamson put in diffidently. "We're kinda getting close to camp."

"I'll try to act surprised," Saxon said.

* * *

The sun shone out of a clear, cobalt-blue sky as the tankers rolled along a curving stretch of State Route I-20. The convoy of six gleaming cylinders on wheels, each containing twenty thousand cubic gallons of fluid petrochemical product, was about forty minutes out of the sprawling Mobil tank farm on the outskirts of Culver City, and was now midway along its route.

In about a half hour the convoy would reach its destination, Metropolitan Boulder, where the tankers would split up and offload their cargos of home heating oil and gasoline to the storage tanks of two major local heating-oil suppliers and a string of Mobil service stations.

Security was part of the rationale behind the convoy, but only a part of this rationale. The main reason for the convoy was efficiency. In the trucking business, as in all other businesses, time was money, and it made more sense to bulk-haul a large load rather than break it up into several smaller trips. The customer didn't want some of his delivery this week and some next week. He wanted it all at once or he'd find himself another supplier.

In the cabs of the convoy, the drivers communicated with one another and other trucks via CB radio, mostly small talk, and also with the company's base station in Culver City. At about the halfway mark in their short journey, the base station called the lead truck to check on the convoy's status.

"How's it going there, buddy?" asked the base station.

"Five by five, so far anyway. We're about—*Oh, shit, there's a—*"

A series of explosions cut off the driver's words and abruptly ended the transmission. The detonations came in rapid pulses, each thudding report separated by short intervals of total silence. The base station operator immediately called the state police while trying to reestablish contact with the convoy. Sweat had broken out on his face and his pulse was racing.

In the second that he picked up the phone to call the police, the first shock wave from the multiple explosions from the fireballs that had moments before been six tanker trucks reached the petrochemical tank farm located just outside of Culver City. The base station operator uttered an oath and said no more. An instant later the tank farm itself went up in an enormous fireball and blast front many force factors greater than even the tremendous explosion on the highway that was audible in five counties.

The explosions that destroyed the four storage tanks and the massive fireball produced by the explosion were so great that they caused seismic wave detectors across the Midwest to react with a series of sharp spikes. DSP infrared detection satellites used to detect missile launches and nuclear explosions also registered the violent shock waves, and for a tense moment the Pentagon was under the false assumption that a nuclear weapon had been detonated in heartland America. The status of the single integrated operations plan for nuclear war and defense, or SIOP, automatically rose one defcon level, ratcheted up by the automated SINDAS computer system that had been installed years before.

In fact, the blast effects of the two explosions were equivalent to low- and medium-yield nuclear detonations. The aftermath of the strike on the convoy was also similar in many ways to a tactical nuclear airburst. The hard macadamized surface of the highway served to reflect a sizable percentage of the blast waves up into the air, leaving only light cratering in the explosions' wake.

The comparatively soft and unstable soil foundation of the tank farm was another matter. It absorbed the kiloton of explosive force as the entire complex vaporized in a fireball and began to liquefy. As the fireball rose, creating a towering mushroom cloud, it drew up tens of thousands of tons of loose earth and pulverized detritus that had once been a twenty-acre facility.

A toxic plume of fallout comprised of petrochemical fractions, asbestos particles, metal dust, PVC residue, and many other carcinogenic substances, slowly began to drift into the stratosphere. Picked up by the winds, the cancer cloud began to migrate over the farms and towns that made up the tristate area of Nebraska, Iowa, and South Dakota.

Later they would call it the Oil Attacks, Smoky Wednesday, Stinking Wednesday, Day of Wrath, and several other names besides these. In the immediate aftermath of the attack, there was only shock and a numbing sense of panic that was all too familiar to a nation under continued attack for years.

It had happened again. And it had been worse than when it had happened before. A nation shaken to its core now lapsed deeper into shock.

chapter *ten*

"That's right, Marcy, the old Bush remark from the Gulf War about it being all about oil and jobs. Blunt but true. What a genius that great American statesman had with words."

"Yes, Brad. He had a gift for boiling it down to a few short but poignant statements, didn't he? Like his famous remark about broccoli, for example."

"You are so right, Marcy. But getting back to oil—"

"And jobs, Brad."

"Jobs, right. They're the lifeblood of society."

"And there's so much most people don't know about oil, Brad. I mean, I was amazed at all the things that come from it. I mean it's not just—"

"—not just gasoline and home heating oil. Yes, I know, Marcy. There are literally hundreds and hundreds of products that all of us use every day without thinking of where they come from that would not exist if there was no oil. Take my wife's—"

"—or if oil prices were so high we couldn't afford them—"

"—hair spray, for example. Exactly, Marcy, exactly."

"Now, what about—"

"And when the president just spoke about why we need to take whatever action they're contemplating against the Al Qadr terrorists, I think he had all this in mind."

"Right, Brad. The president made it very clear that the attacks on the oil and petroleum industry, in the U.S. and abroad, are all linked, are all part of a new strategy by Al Qadr to starve us of many of the products that make our nation great."

"That's an interesting way of putting it, but yes, I suppose our products, our commerce, millions of goods on millions of shelves, do make our country great. They're symbols of our national greatness. Including the hair spray many of our wives use every morning."

"Exactly, Brad. Like the World Trade Center towers used to be. Symbols of America's economic power, of its greatness if you will."

"For those of you who've just tuned in, we've been talking about a major new military offensive against the terrorist organization Al Qadr that was launched earlier this morning. The Pentagon has reportedly sent a division, including a brigade of Marine special forces, into parts of the southern Arabian Peninsula. They are supported by warplanes, including F-16 bombers and B-52 fighters, and by Tomahawk helicopters from our many battleships offshore."

"How many soldiers are there in a brigade, Brad? I always wondered."

"I'm afraid I'm not up on all that military stuff, Marcy. But a brigade would have lots of them, and as you know, many are special forces, which means they'll parachute in from whirlybirds, eat snakes, and do exciting stuff like that.

"Anyway, we've got to go to a commercial right now, but we'll be right back with our special guests, Tracy and Rick."

"And don't forget Bonzo, the singing turducken."

"I was just about to mention that, Marcy. Anyway, stay tuned, folks. It's gonna be an exciting show this morning, one you don't want to miss."

Mud in his face. PETN fumes in his nostrils. Explosions and shouts in his ears. Pain in his legs, shoulders, back, chest, neck. Bullets whistling past.

And he hadn't even gotten started.

The LCAC carrying a Marine company including Sergeant Nasty Breath of Marine Force One, skimmed the wake-crossed surface of the Arabian Sea. Its destination, five minutes away, was a stretch of sandy coastline between Ash Shibur and Riyan code-named Chicago Beach.

Strung out along the coast of Yemen and Oman were a series of other sandy beachheads, bearing code names such as New York, Alexandria, San Francisco, Los Angeles, and Detroit. Approaching those beachheads was a mixed force of landing and assault craft, including LCACs, amphibious tank and personnel transporters, DD21 Zumwalt-class stealth destroyers, attack submarines, and Aegis missile cruisers.

The coordinated landing operations, collectively falling under the code name Operation Valiant Echo, was to be the first amphibious land-and-stay operation conducted since MacArthur's landing at Inchon. It was planned to involve a division of combined-arms military forces and secure an area roughly equal to the size of Texas in a matter of hours.

But Valiant Echo was only one element of the multilayered, simultaneous operations that were taking place everywhere in the theater. Coordinated with the landings from the sea were cruise-missile strikes, airborne assaults, and parachute and heliborne troop landings throughout the theater.

In North Yemen, South Yemen, Oman, Iraq, Iran, Ethiopia, and the Sudan, an offensive involving the United States, Britain, Germany, France, and numerous other nations was now unfolding. The massive coalition assault was designed to root out and destroy terrorist bases, training centers, transshipment points, arms depots, and troop encampments that had grown to infest those countries, and then to bring captives back for trial before international war tribunals.

Other objectives were to capture Hassan Ramad Ali, the Al Qadr terrorist chieftain who called himself the Mahdi, and to recover the American hostages that had already been held captive for several months.

As part of these latter objectives, two locales in particular were considered especially significant.

One was the Hajar mountain range, a rugged series of stony escarpments (hence the name Hajar, which means stone in Arabic) beginning midway from the coastal plain. Behind the Hajar lies the Jabal al-Akhdar, a moist belt of green mountain country, whose terrain also gave rise to the Arabic name for the place.

Behind the Jabal al-Akhdar, and separated from it by a

stony desert whose surface is a hard, gravely crust, begins the Rub al-Khali, the aptly named Empty Quarter. This is a sea of tawny yellow sand that takes up most of the southern quadrant of Saudi Arabia and whose ill-defined lower reaches afford jurisdictional protection to the nomadic outlaw bands that inhabit it. It was in the rugged country of the Hajar, and its environs, that surveillance and intelligence had pinpointed a likely hiding place for the Mahdi.

Yet another objective and possible hiding place was the island of Socotra, a large outcropping of sand and rock in the Arabian Sea not far from the Yemeni coast. Satellite imaging had revealed signs that the American hostages might be held on the island's central plateau, prisoners of Al Qadr.

Close by Socotra island were three far smaller islets, Darsa, Samha, and Abd al-Kuri. The first two, in closest proximity to Socotra, were known collectively as the Brothers. In the weeks prior to the attack, friendly bases had been established on the Brothers and Abd al-Kuri, the latter of which had been the scene of helicopter landings of Seabees. These famed naval combat engineers had gone to work bulldozing a landing strip able to support heavy bombers, intercontinental transport aircraft, and fighter planes, as well as the infrastructure needed to maintain a round-the-clock schedule of arrivals and departures of several months duration.

On Darsa the Marines task force had established COMCENTs and FARPs at various points. The FARPs, forward area rearming points (what an earlier generation had called "ammo dumps"), were situated at localities affording shelter from overhead observation and from enemy attack.

The theater CINC was General Randolph Hallsey, a Corps veteran of many regional conflicts including the Grenada assault, the First Gulf War, and the war against Al Qaeda and the Taliban in Afghanistan. Hallsey was a hard-charging general of the old school who viewed the Corps as elite infantry rather than special forces, and anyone who thought differently be damned to shine Chesty Puller's combat boots in hell.

While Hallsey was a pragmatist, and realized that certain

objectives called for the use of scalpel forces skilled in low-intensity combat operations, he would nevertheless use his snake-eaters only should there be no alternative to conventional forces. Until then Marine Force One would hump the boonies with the rest of division's jarheads. Hallsey made it so with a stroke of his pen, and tossed the orders into the out basket on his desk.

"**S**tabilize the launcher, ass of an ass."
    "I am trying, my captain, but the hydraulic pressure is too low."
    "Don't give me that, son of a donkey. I ran a check on all systems."
    "I do not lie, my captain. Come and see for yourself, if you doubt my words."
    The captain slapped his thigh in exasperation. Shaking his head, he strode over to the launch vehicle, a GAZ truckbed on eight heavy, oversized tires painted in a desert-camouflage color scheme, technically called a TEL or transporter-erector-launcher. He was in a foul mood and the fingers of his gun hand itched. A bad sign for the corporal should the corporal continue giving him trouble.
    Sweat was already beginning to break out on his forehead, for with the rising of the sun the pleasant cool of the morning was giving way to the humid heat of day. Reaching the rear of the TEL, Captain Jarmoosh shoved the corporal aside without a word and studied the bank of levers, dials, and readout panels exposed from beneath a protective steel cover, which was now flipped back.
    "Damn this piece of shit," he snarled as he saw that what the corporal had claimed was in fact the truth.
    "You see, my captain, I did not speak a lie."
    Corporal Hussein had sidled up beside the taller, broader-shouldered man and addressed the side of his head.
    "It is as I have said. Just as I have said."
    Captain Jarmoosh's response was to lash out with his right hand in a sweeping backhand blow that knocked the corporal to the ground.

"Fix the damned piece of shit, son of a harlot she-camel," he shouted, and without looking at his subordinate, stalked off to find some shade. "And heaven help you if it is not working when the orders come."

The mobile SCUD unit had its orders, and those orders were to be carried out.

The SCUD crew was to be ready to fire its missile equipped with a chemical warhead at the NATO invasion forces. Though the captain had not been informed of the intended target zone for the missile strike—he would receive coordinates by secure radio if and when ordered to fire—the missile's limited range gave him a fairly good idea.

It would surely be the regional CINC's headquarters on Darsa. He would bet a month's pay on it.

The beachheads had come under intense fire.

Los Angeles, San Francisco, New York, Detroit, Chicago, Alexandria, Boulder. Symbols of places where the enemy had struck. Symbols of the payback they were due.

Strung out along the narrow coastal strip that fronted the Arabian sea to the south and the Gulf of Oman to the east up to the mouth of the Persian Gulf, coordinated attacks on a heavily entrenched enemy force were being carried out.

Inland from the beach zone, TLAMs blasted concrete bunkers, machine-gun embrasures, mortar pits, and other fortified defensive positions with repeated conventional high-explosive strikes, FAE airbursts, and cluster-bomblet saturation. Tube battalions had also set up by now, adding artillery support to the offensive.

Sandwiched between the beach zone and the inland defenses now being pounded by missiles and big guns was a division-sized formation of Al Qadr soldiery.

This terrorist force fielded no tanks or heavy artillery. The largest gunnery tubes that it possessed were eighty-millimeter mortars and twenty-millimeter antiaircraft guns. Although some of these were relatively advanced French or German models with computer-calibration and laser-ranging features, the bulk was manually operated surplus gear, such as the handful of radar-directed twenty-three-millimeter ZSU-23-4 Shilkas, quad-barreled flak guns mounted on a tank chassis. These were older models, sold to the Nexus from aging Cold War-era Iraqi stocks, as were the motley assortment of armored personnel carriers, mostly BMPs and BTRs, that had come from the same source.

This force had no offensive air, or so little that it was tactically irrelevant. But the Al Qadr had well-trained mobile squads equipped with a variety of man-portable weapons systems, including TOW, Stryx, and MILAN, and all platoons had men with Singaporean-made Ultimax 100 light machine guns, in addition to the AK-47s and AK-74s that the rank and file had been issued.

The Al Qadr troops had had plenty of time to prepare the battlefield as well, siting their defenses for maximum effect in the event of an invasion. They had created a layered defense in depth, and it was composed of trench and foxhole emplacements surrounded by sandbags on the palm-lined dunes overlooking the beach, and concrete pillboxes and bunkers behind the dunes and below the coastal highway. In between, lines of antitank ditches had been excavated, most festooned with rings of razor wire, fringed with fields of antiarmor and antipersonnel land mines.

This wouldn't be a land-and-stay operation, as it had been at Normandy, Anzio, Gaudalcanal, or Inchon in the last century. Valiant Echo's mission objectives were far more limited and the enemy was far less able to mount a credible defense, much less hurl the attackers back into the sea, the way the divisions under German Panzer and army group commanders had hoped to do to GIs storming European beachheads.

The OPPLAN developed by the CINC and his staff called for a beach landing as the simplest means to quickly build up and pre-position sufficient troops and war matériel necessary to launch a multi-pronged strike into the interior of Yemen and Oman. The only other alternative would have been a heavy airlift from Saudi across the baking sand sea known as the Empty Quarter. This plan had posed operational problems of its own, and had been abandoned in favor of an amphibious landing from the Arabian littoral.

In the end the OPPLAN proposed by the Navy won out with the CJCS, the president, and the SecDef. A "from the sea" landing would likely be faster, simpler, and doable at less cost in human life, despite the entrenched enemy forces, than an airlift. The Al Qadr forces could be quickly isolated, bypassed, and neutralized by waves of coalition air strikes.

The defenders were essentially postured to fight a World War II-style battle against a fifth-generation military force, much the same mistake that Saddam Hussein had made in the First Gulf War. Even as the troops, tanks, APCs, artillery, and other combat resources began piling up on the beaches, the enemy was being whittled down by missile strikes and overwhelming air superiority.

As the heavy-lifters, the LCACs and the amphibious tank carriers, came barreling in under the protection of F-22 top cover and TLAM strikes launched from the carrier battle group in the Arabian Sea, the enemy threw everything it had at the Marines storming the beachheads.

The deadly semaphores of white and red tracers crisscrossed over the sands as troops on both sides traded automatic-weapons fire. Marines hit the dirt, dived into shell craters, or ducked behind the protection of mobile armor as mortar rounds came dropping in with the characteristic sound of ripping silk. The stuttering of quad-barreled Shilkas, the coughing of cannons, and the wheeze of ATGW rockets fired from Al Qadr Bimps and BTRs was answered by the rolling boom of the heavy cannons of friendly MBTs, with a choir of Chaparral rocket launchers, heavy coaxial machine guns, and TOW launchers from Bradleys on the beach, singing counterpoint like Valkyries in a Wagnerian opera. All hell was breaking loose in a paroxysm of fire and steel as waves of soldiers and war machinery clawed, tore, and busted their way onto the enemy's bitterly contested home ground.

Now, as the LCACs—the hovercraft disgorging their burden of Marines onto the beachheads before heading back out into the Arabian Sea to pick up more—screamed in, the air overhead was rent by the sonic booms of fighter aircraft streaking inland to take out entrenched positions beyond the coastal highway.

The F-22s, Joint Strike Fighters, FA/18s, and friendly aircraft, including British Tornados, EFA 2000 Eurofighters, and French Rafales, would vanish over the heights above the beach, followed minutes later by the multiple thunderclaps and snake-headed mushroom clouds created by air-to-ground munition strikes hitting enemy targets.

The humid salt air was soon filled with the mixed stench of modern combat, an odor made up of diesel fumes, cordite smoke, burnt aviation fuel, and the sour stink of blast debris and high-explosive bomb residue that blew over the beachhead on seaborne winds.

Everywhere on the beachheads Marines dug in, waiting for the preliminary air strikes to end, and for the order to move out to come down to them.

"Yeah, baby, you know I be thinkin' of your fine ass right about now."

Corporal Frisky was on his satphone, putting in a long-distance call from Chicago Beach to his girlfriend in Houston, Texas. The NCOs had confiscated all wireless phones, but a lot of guys had risked court-martial and kept them handy anyway, just in case.

It was an hour since the Marine invasion force had been ordered to dig in on the beach while the fast-movers, heavy armor, and TLAM batteries of the CBG offshore softened up the assholes dumb enough to fight the U.S. Marines and think they could live. A lull had now fallen over the battlefield. Frisky, bored like the rest of his platoon, figured he might take a hit or even get his dick shot off before the end of the day. He at least wanted to get in some phone sex.

"Yeah, that's right, girl. Even with the bombs burstin' and the bullets flyin', I can't get you off my mind. What's that? No, honey, nobody else is listenin'. Just you, me, and a couple' a million bullets. So come on, tell me what you'd do if I was layin' up in your crib right now."

Corporal Frisky had to fend off a sudden grab for the phone by his equally bored buddies, fortunately managing to bring it back to his ear as Shakeena warmed to her task.

"Oh, yeah, baby, yeah! That's just what I wanna hear. Man, I can almost see you doin' it. Yeah, baby, me too. I'm working on it. Yeah. I'm just about to—"

Just then the order to move out was passed down to the troops, barked out as only a Marine NCO's well-trained lungs are capable of barking out an order. Corporal Frisky, a Marine to the core, immediately stopped thinking of his girlfriend, or anything else save getting his ass in gear, and found himself trying to climb out of his foxhole with his M-4 in one hand and his satphone in the other. In the course of these actions, the satphone toppled into the hole while Frisky ran on through the smoke of battle, leaving Shakeena hanging on the line. Soon even Frisky's lost phone was missing in action. An incoming mortar round soon scored a direct hit on the hole in which Frisky and his buddies had been dug in only a few minutes before.

Further inland, Blue, Gold, and Red Forces were charging in under heavy fire from enemy forces dug into seaward bluffs rising above their respective beach zones. Even with Whiskey Cobra air support, the V-22 converti-planes that had ferried the Marine Force One commandos to the mission's LZs were being confronted by a determined enemy defense.

So far, though, with the LZs looming into visual range, the biggest worry faced by the Osprey pilots—SAMs of various types, from shoulder-launched SA-7B tail-chasers to the bigger, mobile, radar-enhanced versions like SA-10s—had failed to materialize.

The enemy was engaging the airmobile force with mostly automatic small arms, including heavy machine guns, and twenty-three millimeter fire from mobile and revetmented Shilka emplacements, Bimps, and weapons platforms of similar types. The Ospreys were capable of soaking up a fairly heavy ration of fire of that order, and vulnerable points such as engine nacelles and bulkhead areas sheltering fuel tanks and lines were especially protected with lightweight armor at hard-points on the V-22s hull.

Still, knowing about this and training for it was one helluva difference from actually flying into a combat hot zone. The V-22 pilots had a lot on their minds and were shouldering a big responsibility. For one thing, there was the Osprey itself. The converti-plane program had been launched under stormy beginnings and had been near to cancellation on several occasions.

While the Osprey had been fielded for several years, these landings marked the first time that the V-22 had ever been flown under actual combat conditions. How the aircraft performed now would likely determine if the Osprey became the dream machine the Marines had doggedly sought for decades, or whether the entire program would be scrapped by its many opponents in Congress and elsewhere.

There were also the men and military hardware on board to consider. Each of the three Ospreys in the first squadron into the fire zone was carrying a company-strength Marine contingent and an assortment of gear including APCs, FAVs, HUMVEEs, and other troop carriers. None of the pilots wanted to go down in history as the schmo to blow it at this critical instant.

The AHW-1 Cobras escorting the Ospreys worked the emplacements while the Ospreys hung back, flying holding patterns. Finally the word came back to the V-22 pilots: The LZ was no longer hot.

One by one the Ospreys came sweeping in, translated to helicopter mode, and made vertical landings. The Marines inside their hulls were now ready to play their own parts in the battle to take Yemen and Oman.

chapter *eleven*

Captain Michaels felt the familiar blunt pressure of metal against the back of his head, right above the knot of his blindfold.

"You are a brave soldier, Captain, and a loyal citizen of your country, but this time I am afraid that the gun is loaded."

By way of emphasis the raghead they called Puke Face—a particularly brutal bastard whom Michaels recognized by voice—dug and twisted the muzzle painfully into Michaels's occipital bone. The pressure on the rear of his skull was momentarily relaxed as Puke Face thumbed back the hammer and cocked the weapon.

"I will count to three. If at the end you remain uncooperative, I will blow off your head."

Michaels had been here before. Puke Face and other ragheads had claimed the gun was loaded before too, but it had always been empty. Odds were it was the same now. But logic was one thing, and having the weapon flush against your head was a whole 'nother story. Sweat began to soak the blindfold. Michaels felt sick.

"One."

"Be reasonable, Captain," another and more sympathetic voice put in. This was Sob Sister, the better half of the good guy-bad guy routine that he and Puke Face had going.

"It is only a video you are being asked to make," Sob Sister went on. "Nobody will care at this point. Your leaders expect you to be cooperative. Be reasonable. Save your life. If not for yourself, then for your wife, or perhaps it is a sweetheart?"

Sure. Nothing but a video that would make him into a

shitty little fart of a traitor. Michaels could never live with himself afterward. Even if it amounted to nothing, at the very least Michaels knew that making the damn DVD would haunt him for the rest of his life.

"Two."

Michaels heard the second guy in the room walk over and speak. This time Sob Sister's voice was close by his ear.

"Please, Captain. I am a religious man. I believe in the sanctity of human life, just as you do. As a soldier, you are worthy of my respect. I do not want to see such a man die, or know that his children are to be without a father, his wife without a husband. Reconsider. You have little time left."

Michaels clenched his teeth and still said nothing.

"Three."

A thunderclap drowned out reality and Michaels's head exploded. With this crack of doom there came a short fireworks display, and he pitched forward into nothingness and blackness wondering, as he fell into the bottomless pit, if this is what it felt like to die.

A warm, gentle rain—smelling of death and the sea—fell as Marine Force One's light armor company, designated as Task Force Tiger, penetrated into Operations Sector Ripcord.

Tiger was now entirely on its own. The Ospreys that had shuttled the mobile recon company into the sector were long departed, and the Whiskey Cobras that had cleaned out the hornets' nest at the hot LZ had returned to the sector FARP for refueling and rearming.

Tiger's mission, which was to search for and rescue the downed American airmen and to capture Hassan Ramad Ali, the Mahdi, if found, was complicated by terrain, weather, and the opposition of a cunning and ruthless enemy. A modern highway system with primary and secondary roads made navigating the flat, low-lying coastal belt a simple matter, but once beyond into the highlands, the going became far tougher.

Here the main roads—and good ones at that, built by European and American contractors—began petering out into narrow mountain tracks twisting and switchbacking up the sides of steep, barren hills where the going was treacherous.

To complicate matters, Al Qadr forces infested the hill country, where they were set up in excellent positions from which to launch ambushes and guerrilla attacks. Although Tiger had overhead assets such as UAVs and UCAVs at its disposal, and could call in top cover in the form of F-22 or Cobra support if necessary, the force had to live with the expectation of danger around every bend in the road.

In order to get the big picture on the battle space, Saxon had sent out motorized scout patrols. While Task Force Tiger also had a Global Hawk UCAV orbiting at thirty thousand feet that was sending down real-time imagery, there was no substitute for surveillance coverage on the ground.

The three Humvees with their contingents of Marine scouts, which were now somewhere in the hills surrounding the main force, could not only go in close and check out what the UCAV saw from up above, but were also running flank and rear-guard security for the main salient of the strike force.

"Possible contact, Boss."

Saxon heard Doc Jeckyll, One's chief technical specialist, sing out from inside the modified M-2 Bradley that was the recon force's mobile command vehicle. Saxon dropped the field glasses through which he'd been scouting the bleak desert terrain surrounding the roadway from the turret hatch, and ducked down inside the armored vehicle's crew compartment, where Jeckyll was seated at banks of rack-mounted signals-processing equipment, display terminals, and miscellaneous tactical communications gear.

On a bank of rack-mounted flat-panel displays Jeckyll had a bird's-eye view of the terrain up on screen. Jeckyll pointed to what at first seemed an otherwise nondescript section of hill country. When he'd enhanced the imagery, Saxon could clearly see evidence of a well-concealed bunker complex hidden in the craggy sides of the adjacent bluffs.

"Does look like a possible to me," Saxon commented as he took in the overhead imagery.

"Yeah, I'd say it's a real good candidate," Jeckyll added.

Saxon told Jeckyll to get more imaging from the UCAV. Then, grabbing a chair at one of the free consoles near Jeckyll, Saxon sent a secure tactical e-mail message to Surveillance Team Alpha, whose blue icon on the on-screen map display before him indicated that it was closest in proximity to the hide site Jeckyll had identified.

Saxon typed out his orders and sent them to Alpha, in minutes receiving a confirmation that Alpha had received the orders and was acting upon Saxon's instructions. Via global-mobile communications, the same tactical data that Saxon had access to inside the Bradley was available to the portable computer systems mounted inside the mobile team's Humvees. These included enhanced GPS satellite coverage that enabled Alpha's crews to pinpoint the best possible routes to the target.

Unfortunately nobody had seen the enemy equipped with shoulder-fire weapons on the perimeter of the mobile CP. When the ambush struck it was without warning. Saxon heard the first explosions, and grabbed at the handholds mounted on the ceiling of the APC for support as a detonating warhead rocked the armored vehicle.

Then the lights went out and everything seemed to suddenly tilt over, like a ship capsizing in a storm. A second explosion followed hot on the heels of the initial burst. And with the darkness there came a deathly stillness.

Captain Craig Michaels came back to his senses on a hard, dank stone floor of a subterranean prison. There was a hollow, rushing sound, like water surging through a cave or a tunnel, in his ears, and a steady, painful throbbing near his right temple. He gingerly touched the side of his head with the tips of his fingers. The hair and flesh on the robin's-egg-sized lump were singed.

Powder burn, he thought. Puke Face had fired his pistol close to his ear and then sapped him with the butt, or vice versa. It was a wonder his eardrum hadn't been punctured or his skull fractured.

Michaels suddenly felt a familiar softness against the side of his face. He recoiled reflexively in horror in the near pitch darkness at the sensation of tiny feet running swiftly across his chest.

"Sorry . . ." he muttered, remembering, "little friend."

He had taken to feeding his prison's seemingly lone rat with crumbs from the meager rations he was given. The rat had become sort of a pet with Michaels, reminding him of the kangaroo rat his kids had named Matilda. He'd be sad to leave it behind when his day of freedom came. Correction, *if* it ever came. Michaels was a pragmatist and didn't want to con himself. He might never make it out of this. It was all too possible.

Michaels idly rolled a piece of stale bread into a tiny pill, and felt the rat gently take it in its jaws, then the rubberlike touch of small padded feet was gone. Somewhere in the darkness he heard a faint rustling, and he knew it was turning its prize around in its nimble little forepaws, whirling and nibbling as rats did when they ate, the way his kids' rat did.

Michaels sat up with difficulty, propping himself against the cold, dank wall. Faintly, there was a series of short, hollow knocking noises. He listened intently, straining to hear.

Tap code.

It was from one of his aircrew, Sergeant Rodney Strozzapreto. Michaels could tell from the unique signature each sender gave himself so he could be identified. Michaels's pulse quickened as the taps spelled out a coherent message.

One of the friendlier guards had let slip that an American attack had begun. Rescue forces were out looking for them. But there was something else. Word that they might be moved elsewhere by their captors. Moved soon.

Michaels thought for a moment. The time might come when the plans he had made with his crewmen might need to be realized. Their lives might depend on what they did within the next twenty-four to forty-eight hours. Come what may, they had to be ready to act if and when the opportunity presented itself. Michaels composed his message in his mind and began to carefully tap out his reply.

It was more than just an answer. It was an order.

*   *   *

Enemy fire suddenly exploded all around Task Force Tiger.

The staccato report of multi-barrel guns, the hiss and boom of rockets, and the banshee wailing of incoming mortar rounds shattered the morning silence. Excited voices were now on the radio net, as elements of the mobile force reported multiple enemy contacts and actions being taken to counter or overwhelm the unfriendlies.

Saxon paid close attention to the chatter over the comms net. So far some of the mobile CP's vehicles had been hit, though none seriously damaged, and there had been no friendly casualties, not serious ones at least. As to the rocket salvos that had struck his own headquarters APC, Saxon's pickets had made short work of the Al Qadr who'd fired on it. The damage sustained by the strikes had been thankfully minor, and all systems were now powered up and back in action.

The tactical picture had clarified too. There were apparently some diehard Al Qadr dug into positions and armed with heavy-caliber weapons and man-portable antiarmor missiles of the MILAN variety. There was also a mortar crew on the high ground on the north tangent of the operational sector, dropping HE cans down on the column. It was these scattered forces that had launched the attack on Saxon's HQ.

The AHW-1 Cobra helos available to the force were kept at the ready, but Saxon didn't think this was necessarily a threat that the force itself couldn't handle on its own. Marines were already debarking the Bradleys, fanning out through the surrounding terrain while their armor gave them cover.

The Marine search-and-destroy ops were directed by overhead imaging from Global Hawk, far too high up for any of the SAMs in the vicinity to reliably target and hit. The 1-Patchers could see the enemy a whole lot better than the enemy could see them. While the ragheads were groping around in the dark, trying to grab the elephant's balls and squeeze, the Marines could direct their response at their adversary with pinpoint accuracy, flattening it with precise swipes of its trunk.

With Jeckyll having pinpointed a nearby Nexus mortar emplacement, Saxon climbed up behind the M-2's main turret-mounted M242 twenty-five millimeter chain gun, set select-fire for one hundred rounds per minute, and opened up on the enemy position in the nearby hills. The white tracers from the cannon streamed out to the accompaniment of the rapid stutter of the automatic weapon coughing out its rivet load.

Red-black fire poppies sprouted in the distance as ammunition boxes in the emplacement were hit and blew up. Saxon grinned sardonically, maxed select-fire to five hundred RPM, and poured more bullets into the enemy position. Soon there was another and much bigger flash, and this time it was accompanied by a loud concussion and a rising column of incandescent flame that spread into an orange-black mushroom over the target. Scratch one more problem, thought Saxon as he safed the big gun and ducked back down into the APC.

Other elements of the Marine mobile force had by now locked onto individual targets, and were beginning to take a toll on the Al Qadr ambush formations. Jeckyll was using the UCAV to remotely fire missiles at two camouflaged pompom gun pits that the unmanned aerial combat vehicle had identified, as these targets were now probably the most dangerous to the formation. The pits contained what was probably the best field guns in the enemy's inventory, twin Oberlikon twenty-five-millimeter DIANA or thirty-five-millimeter Type GDF-005 AD cannons with computer-controlled laser sight systems. These babies were capable of both high-azimuth and flat-trajectory fire, and they had to go.

The Marines on the ground encircled the remnants of the hostile force, and further decimated those diehard units that chose to put up resistance. Afterward, prisoners were taken back to MF-1 field HQ for interrogation. Papers and other materials of intelligence interest were collected and brought back as well. The captives, Saxon believed, might provide useful supplementary information to complement that already collected by technical resources in the search for the U.S. captives and the Mahdi.

He whose will was law in Iraq, he who was revered as the Rais by his underlings, was personally shown how the elements of this great undertaking would all fit together. In the deep underground facility, secret from all except the Rais, this thing of Allah's holy wrath and divine retribution was shown forth in all its terrible greatness.

The supreme Iraqi potentate saw how that which came first—the Gift—had been augmented, its form subtly and cunningly changed by the able hands of his brother's technicians. Nor had his own appointed *ingineeahs* failed to carry out the difficult tasks with which they had been charged, rivaling, even excelling, those of his brother in the greatness of their own accomplishments.

By the efforts of these skilled ones, that vessel that was first had been altered in such a way as to dovetail with the second vessel, adding greatly to the power and might of the second vessel.

And the Rais saw too how the other modifications that had been made by those who worked even now upon the gleaming steel, who stood upon the encircling rectangle of catwalks, or strode upon its outstretched flanks, had also increased, sometimes subtly, other times more obviously, the power and deadly efficiency of both of these noble and terrible vessels, gifts from heaven to the faithful of Islam.

As one vessel turned within the other, they would together join into a totality that would bring upon the heads of the *kufr* the horrific judgment of the Supreme Lawgiver's unrelenting fire. The combined weapon was a holy weapon, and would be duly blessed by the *sayyidi* to ordain it for use against the hated transgressors of purity.

Now the Rais met with those who would add their flesh and blood to the gleaming steel within the gleaming steel, to the vessel of power within the vessel of power, and by their deaths create a wholeness and a sanctification of all of the Mighty One's wrath and the swiftness of his terrible vengeance upon the heads of the infidel masses, the *kufr* swine of the godless Western realms.

Now those brave *fidayeen* who had been chosen to wield the mighty weapon were brought out to greet the ruler of their nation. Weeping joyous tears, each of the *fidayeen* kissed the hand of the Rais, who embraced them and in turn bestowed upon them the many kisses of his boundless gratitude.

These fortunate ones, whose fate was to die for Allah as *shaheed,* and whose souls would rise up to heaven in everlasting glory, continued to weep at the honor bestowed upon them. The meeting was necessarily brief, for these chosen ones had much yet to prepare for the ordained day's arrival.

For his part the Rais too had much to occupy himself with. But he would not forget these mighty vessels that he had seen, nor the terrible wonders they promised to bring forth in glorious fulfillment of sacred covenant.

Captain Michaels had been left alone for what seemed like several days. His ears, by now attuned and grown sensitive to even the subtlest sounds of the subterranean prison, no longer detected the same level of activity coming from adjoining areas of the base outside his cell.

The tours of the guards patrolling the corridor that the cells fronted had also become less frequent. From time to time there were new sounds: the noises of heavy objects pushed and dragged, and the curses of men who labored to move them around.

Also, the interrogations had stopped completely. Apparently this was not just the case for Michaels alone, but also for the rest of his crew. Their regular communication by tap code made it plain that the others had observed the same set of circumstances.

These new observations, combined with what was already known about a U.S. invasion of the Arabian littoral and Socotra, added up to only one thing. Under the threat of hostile military pressure, the ragheads had commenced the process of abandoning the base.

That was good news on the face of things, but at the same time it could also mean that Michaels and his men were at greater risk than before. The ragheads might be panicked into executing them all, or might even abandon them to die without even the minimal food and water they already got. Michaels tried not to take counsel of his fears, but it was not easy under the circumstances.

It was in the middle of the night when Michaels received an answer to his unvoiced questions. There had been virtually no sound from outside the cell for the better part of the last twenty-four hours. Now there came the heavy footfalls of combat boots tramping on the stone floor of the corridor beyond. A key turned in the lock of the door. Harsh electric light streamed in, forcing Michaels to shade his hurt eyes.

An order was barked and two ragheads stormed in and grasped the malnourished man under the arms. They stood him on his feet and marched him down the corridor. At its end was a large room in which his three crewmen were waiting. Michaels had only caught glimpses of them as they were being led past his cell, and this was the first he'd seen of them since the shoot-down and capture.

"No talk," warned one of the guards.

The captives were thrown some stale crusts of bread and the door clanged shut again.

They immediately began to whisper among themselves.

The jackass dog of a corporal had finally succeeded in doing his superior's bidding. The hydraulic malfunction had been traced, after considerable effort, to a pressure leak in a coupler junction. The four stabilizers, the huge steel struts that anchored the mobile missile launcher, were successfully lowered and locked into position on the rocky ground.

With the crisis now over, the launch crew could now occupy itself with the final phases of setting up the TEL and getting the missile ready to fire. As the captain knew, a launch command could come at any moment, and he wanted to be ready to follow through on it without a moment's delay.

The captain drank some home brew called *siddiqi* from a pocket flask as he settled into his command chair. He took the handset off the secure, signal-hopping radio into his hand, and received a message from headquarters. His commander ordered him to fire the missile, providing the captain with the proper launch-authorization codes.

The captain barked orders at his crew and they sprang into action, going through the motions of the missile-firing drill that had been drummed into them in several dress rehearsals for just such a moment. Soon the coordinates had been programmed into the missile's launch computer and the bird was ready to fire.

The captain issued the launch command. Within minutes the armored vehicle housing the crew shook and rumbled with the man-made thunder of the missile lifting off the TEL's launch rails into the cloudless sky. The captain consulted the chronometer whose digital readout was counting off the minutes remaining until target impact. His lips twisted into a bad imitation of a smile. The American forces would soon feel the sting of the desert scorpion.

chapter *twelve*

Minutes ahead of the incoming missile attack, defense support project (DSP) satellites in geosynchronous orbit detected the heat signature of a Scud launch. The thermal flare produced by the ignition of the Scud's chemical rocket booster stage triggered a signature analysis by the supercomputers of Strategic Command at STRATCOM's Cheyenne Mountain headquarters in Colorado.

Processed at high speed, the identification of the Scud's launch signature was made in seconds. At this point the next step in the automation process was the generation of a series of flash reports over the SPINTCOM, CRITICOM, and other strategic information networks. These served the governments and military forces of the U.S. and its allies as early-warning channels for global events of major consequence.

As the Scud attack's trajectory plot revealed its probable target as CENTCOM headquarters on Darsa Island, troops stationed there were ordered to engage in MOPP-6 NBC weapons-protection routines. The troops suited up in CBW-resistant prophylactic gear including gas masks, gloves, and boots. They bunkered down as PAC-IV Patriot missile batteries tracked the incoming warhead and prepared to interdict the Scud attack.

The CINC was catching an hour of fitful sleep on the couch of his bunker office as the missile-attack warning arrived. The general went to the bathroom sink, turned on the cold water faucet, and dunked his head under the frigid stream, then grabbed the towel his aide handed him. As Patriot batteries acquired the contacts, he had already reached the underground bunker complex's command, control, and communications center.

The Seabees and Army Corps of Engineers who had quickly built the CINC's HQ had in essence dug a large series of pits, lined the pits with poured concrete, embedded enormous spring-loaded shock absorbers into the concrete, and then lowered prefabricated steel bunkers onto the shock absorbers. The excavated earth was then piled back into the excavations, completely burying the structure.

The result, after the life-support air-filtration systems, fiberoptic and mobile comm links, and access conduits were installed, was a buried military nerve center highly impervious to enemy offensives, including direct low-yield or theater nuclear strikes and NBC attacks. While troops up top were in MOPP-6 mode, the battle staff within the CINC's HQ could afford to forgo this cumbersome precautionary measure.

Both topsiders and bunkered-in jib rats watched the rest of the attack unfold; the former via a battery of flat-panel displays, the latter from the dubious protection of sandbagged foxholes and revetmented areas designated for cover during missile attacks. All saw and/or heard the Patriot batteries launching outbound strikes on the incoming Scud. The PAC-IVs tracking the warhead through the skies were not as easy for the eye to follow, but the flare of the explosion as the Scud was successfully hit and destroyed was impossible to ignore.

In a few minutes a blazing bolide of incandescent fragments was all that remained of the missile. Several minutes later, after no further launch contrails were detected by the DSP orbital array and an assessment made by NORAD, the all-clear sirens sounded on Darsa. It was to take several hours more until the scattered Scud debris was collected and analyzed, but the verdict that was to come in was ominous.

The debris would reveal traces of VX nerve agent in sufficient concentration to indicate that the warhead of the Scud had been carrying enough of the dioxin-based chemical-weapon agent to kill a regiment-sized force and destroy the fighting capacity of a division. It meant, in short, that Al Qadr bases on the southern Arabian littoral posed a greater threat than was previously believed.

*   *   *

"**R**ob, where the hell did that damn Scud come from?"
The CINC was royally pissed off. There had been
no indication from Hallsey's own intelligence staff that the
Al Qadr Nexus was fielding Scuds or MRBMs of any kind.
On the contrary, the CIA had issued a warning regarding the
possible existence of mobile launchers in Yemen and Oman
fielded by the Nexus, but this had been downplayed by the
CINC's staff.

"Randy, we don't know yet," replied Hallsey's XO.

"Well, find out, Rob. We can't afford the chance of another strike by a chemical warhead."

"Yes, sir. I'll get right on it."

"You do that."

The CINC turned to the other business that was the subject
of the regularly scheduled morning staff meeting. There were
questions concerning possible Cuban and Libyan involve-
ment in the form of military "advisors" to Al Qadr, and reports of a North Korean mechanized battalion that might be
operating in the high country of the Omani Jiddat al-Harasis.

As to the general's order concerning the Scuds, Hallsey's
XO, Major General Rob Goldman, already had a fairly good
idea of what he'd suggest. There was a Marine snake-eater
brigade basically sitting on its collective rear end conducting
search-and-rescue ops in the boonies. It already had proven
itself highly capable of anti-WMD operations in the Balkans
the previous year. The general didn't like special forces taking the place of regulars, and he'd repeatedly quashed initiatives to use those specwar assets he had available.

This time, the general's horse-handler thought, it might
just be different. Goldman decided to propose that the Marine specialist formation, Force One, be tasked with the
Scud-interdiction role and the related hunt for hidden Al
Qadr bases, launch centers, and Nexus strong points. At least
it couldn't hurt to try.

*   *   *

And the try had flown. The CINC had okayed the op using Marine Force One as CENTCOM's theater Scud-hunters. Once the CINC's orders came down to Saxon at his field HQ, he assembled a suitably configured light mobile force from the manpower and mechanized resources of the brigade. And so it was that Force Tiger, reconstituted as a 1-Patcher mobile recon battalion, had by now reached the final way-point before its main objective, known by the code name Pine Barrens. This was the perimeter of a sector marked by ravines, mountainous areas, steep gorges, and caves; one approximately eighty to one hundred kilometers in circumference.

The satellite imagery of the area, and even SR-71 over-flights, had provided mission planners with high-grade intel, but there was a world of difference between this and the ground truth. In short, conducting a force recon of the sector was a job for specialist infantry forces; a job tailor-made for the elite straight-leg mud soldiers of Marine Force One.

As the mission CINC on the ground, Saxon conducted a map recon before assigning the tasks to squadrons hived off from Tiger's new battalion-strength main force. He had set up his beefed-up mobile field HQ within a squared circle of Bradleys. Above the ring of armored vehicles, a tent canopy had been erected. Comms and electrical lines had been strung, and radio, cellular, and Internet links to the outside world established via CENTCOM's global-mobile network.

Saxon's staff had then set up trestle tables, upon which an array of battlefield computer systems and secure communications rack modules had been placed and wired into the local network. Saxon now hunched over a paper map while One's technicals got the system fully configured. Once up and running, Saxon's techs began to fine-tune the OPPLAN using a tactical map display and mission-preparation software.

Saxon's recon force would in the end consist of four air-mobile squadrons. The four squadrons, each roughly of company strength, and designated by the call signs Raven, Cobra, Rhino, and Ocelot, would be highly agile units that could be dropped into LZs throughout the force recon area at any hour of the day or night and in all weather conditions, conduct their searches, and be helo'd out of the ops zone within minutes of signaling HQ. Or, should circumstances warrant it, the squadrons could call in air strikes, or order up reinforcements in the event of the need for a ground assault on a major target.

The large flat-panel displays were now set up showing the map of the operations zone and the primary force recon objectives that Saxon had marked on it. MF-1's CINC now called in his XO and unit commanders in order to brief them on what was expected to happen.

In the customary informal manner in which he commanded his troops, Saxon went over mission parameters and asked the unit honchos for their feedback. Saxon got some useful suggestions from them, and incorporated the input into the overall game plan. Then he unhitched the leash and let his war dogs run.

Whatever uptick of morale the American captives had experienced on finding themselves reunited was short-lived. Their brief optimism was dampened by the events that immediately followed.

The captives were given some stale maggoty bread and some cold, greasy instant coffee, then were blindfolded and, with hands tied behind their backs, marched off into the darkness and bundled into several late-model Toyota Land Cruisers. The all-terrain vehicles were part of a convoy that soon wound its way slowly and painstakingly along the dusty mountain tracks that spiraled and switchbacked through the arid, craggy landscape of the highland region.

The captives from the downed B-1 bomber crew had no idea of where they were going. Their guards had warned them in English that speaking among themselves was forbidden and was punishable by death. The captives doubted this—were they to have been killed, they would almost certainly have been dead already—but didn't press their luck and sat in sullen silence.

The trucks ground on for long stretches of time, stopping

every now and then, sometimes in small villages clustered in wadis and on the arid mountainsides, at other times on desolate stretches of road. During these halts the Al Qadr, who had been in contact by radio, got out and gathered into groups. There would then be the sound of shouted Arabic as they argued among themselves about the direction to take on the next leg of their journey.

Then, some hours later, the American captives were ordered from the trucks. Their blindfolds were removed, although their wrists still remained tightly bound behind them. While they were still in a region of rocky desert that marked it as part of the Hadramaut plateau, a few miles in the distance stretched a tawny sea of sand considerably different in color and flatness from the surrounding terrain. They were now in the ill-defined borderlands between Yemen and the Arabian Rub' al Khali, or Empty Quarter. By now the sun had risen, and was beginning to radiate an ovenlike heat down upon the sand ocean lying directly ahead.

In time the Nexus pajama men broke their noisy clinch and a group approached the American prisoners. Speaking in Arabic and almost incomprehensible pidgin English, they gestured into the distance, toward the Empty Quarter. In the end, the Al Qadr did manage to communicate the most important aspect of their message with a single, barked command.

"March!" the prisoners were ordered, and rifle barrels prodded their backs by way of emphasis. They began trudging toward the horizon.

Many miles to the northeast, in southern Iraq, a trio of MH-53L Pave Low helicopters, flown by pilots of the USAF's Night Hawks, was reaching the covert mission's final way-point on its inbound track. The Pave Lows were equipped with backstopped GPS and inertial-guidance systems that made them ideally suited to long-range covert missions.

The heavyweight supertransports were escorted by two far more nimble—and far more heavily gunned—Comanche

RAH-1 helos flown by Army pilots who were seconded to the blue-suiters and who had thus earned the honor of no longer being referred to as pogues.

Using their navigational aids, and with additional fuel storage capacity in the upgraded MH-53 airframes that were flying tonight's mission, the Pave Lows had the range and accuracy to insert specialist commando troops into the most unlikely of places.

But that's just what the Night Hawks did for a living. The elite squadron earned its daily bread as a limousine service for clandestine specwar troops. When the snake-eaters got into trouble, the Night Hawks were also first in line to pull them out of a hot LZ.

The moonless night was cold and the mission sortie was hundreds of miles from its starting point at Al-Dhafra Air Base at the northernmost portion of the United Arab Emirates. During the early phases of the antiterrorist war that had come to be known as the War Against the Nexus, the Saudis had kicked the Americans out of their bases in the kingdom. It had become evident that the House of Saud was secretly conspiring with Al Qaeda and the allied Islamic Front to destroy the West. The UAE proved more hospitable, especially when cash incentives were offered, and remained a major U.S. base even after the Saudis later came back into the Western fold.

The Comanches, being well suited to the aerial recon role, surged ahead to scout out trouble and to reconnoiter the mission's target objective. The nimble, compact, and well-armed helos were equipped with a full-featured avionics suite. Comanche pilots could access most avionics, including flight-control and battle-management functions, by means of a head-mounted display (HMD) that took the place of a conventional HUD. The RAH-1 was also equipped with console-mounted MFDs (multifunction displays) for backup or supplemental output.

The Comanches soon overflew the sortie's target zone, their specially muffled rotor system making little sound to warn of their presence. Through thermal-imagining sensors, their pilots saw the complex of buildings that had been previously identified by orbital and SR-71 imaging as a Nexus training facility, false color replacing the gray-scale palate of earlier HMD versions. The installation now appeared to be abandoned. Heat signatures registered by the helo's sensors were not consistent with human habitation in either buildings or vehicles scattered across the desert nearby. There were no warm bodies down there.

The Comanches reported their findings to the mission commander of the troops on board the Pave Lows. These specwar operatives were a mixed group deployed under the command umbrella of the Army's Intelligence Support Activity or ISA. They formed a fusion cell comprised of Army Rangers, Navy SEALs, Delta Force, and even the odd jarhead who deigned to consort with lesser clay for cause and country.

After the RAH-1s completed their reconnoiter, and reported that the base appeared deserted, the ISA commander ordered his troops in for a closer look. The Pave Lows, which had been holding half a klick behind the Comanches, now moved from a hover to a fast transit toward LZs in the base compound marked out by luma-lights dropped from the lead RAH-1.

Once the birds were down at their respective LZs, the ISA honcho ordered his specwar squads to probe their objectives. Silently, prepared for killing, the NVG-equipped shadow troops fanned out toward their objectives. Apart from the possibility of snipers left behind to harass recon teams and raiding parties, the squads were on the lookout for concealed booby traps of various kinds including land mines, tripwire-actuated antipersonnel munitions, pit traps, and other unconventional-warfare devices.

These they discovered in abundance: The former occupants of the base had placed them everywhere their febrile imagination suggested. When found, the booby traps were bypassed rather than destroyed, which would cause unwanted commotion during the recon mission. Of human habitation, the teams found no further evidence at any of the three compounds within the base perimeter. The base was very certainly a dry hole.

When the last of the squads had safely returned to the MH-53Ls and the chopper sortie was again airborne, the cells' commander issued his final orders to the Comanche flight leader. They were concise and simple.

"Frag it," he said.

Moments later rocket salvos had set the desert ablaze in the night. The chopper sortie then turned south, toward its base, and was gone.

Several hundred miles to the southwest and several hours later, two Blackhawk helos swept across a stretch of craggy, almost lunar landscape, their pilots navigating by FLIR. The covert-missions helo dropped to a low hover above the LZ. The copilot signaled that it was time for the squadron to un-ass.

Duly apprised of un-assment time with hand signals from the copilot, One's mission leader, Sergeant Death, passed it on down to his horse-handler, and he in turn to the men. Minutes later the Marine Force One covert operations detachment silently exited the low-hovering chopper, a security team of four Marines immediately taking up covering positions while the rest worked to get out the gear and the FAVs that had been webbed down within the choppers.

Once all gear and all personnel were down on the ground, the choppers elevated, translated, and vanished into the night. They'd be back at the designated LZ for pickup several hours later, or at one of the fallback LZs that had been designated in case of problems. As the last of the rotor noise faded into the wind, the Marines found themselves completely on their own in the enemy's heartland. At Sergeant Death's command they got to work, the land-mobile crews setting up the FAVs for combat duty, charging their weapons, and getting themselves and their gear aboard, the crunchies checking their weapons, lacing their boots, and firing up their NVGs for the first night's recon op.

With the FAVs providing mobile coverage and the other half of the squadron working the terrain on foot, Team Rhino began its night mission, both groups equipped with thermal and infrared imaging gear. Before long the ground element of the squadron came upon a camouflaged installation situated in the cover of a long rift wadi running east-west for at least a mile.

The team leader signaled for the others behind him to work their way forward for a look-see. They had certainly reached the designated Al Qadr training camp area in the heights of the Bar es Safi massif. Ahead of them, between the shoulders formed by two intersecting escarpments, were a cluster of buildings, vehicles, an open area that appeared to be a firing range, and other indications of a terrorist training center. The heat signatures of some of the vehicles showed they had only been recently used. Here was no dry hole such as the ISA teams had found at Salman Pak, hundreds of miles to the north. This base was active.

Sergeant Death deployed his mobile and crunchie units at points surrounding the compound. When all the troops were in position, perimeter countermeasures teams probed for passive intruder-warning systems, hunting for geophone-based sensor chain arrays, differential-force and multi-beam fences, and concealed IR cameras, whether fixed or movable. When the countermeasures technicals reported all countermeasures—including land mines—neutralized and the perimeter sterile, Sergeant Death issued orders for the guard tower sentries to go down.

Blue Man snipers already had the black-pajama men posted in the watchtowers in the sights of their PSG-1 heavy-caliber rifles. These were custom versions of the standard Heckler & Koch Prezisionsschutzengewehr-1 sniper rifle, with a very accurate digital scope developed by DARPA to replace the standard Hensoldt 6×42 LED-enhanced scope and manual reticle.

As a bonus, these watchtowers were prefab types, German-Israeli-made S300 models. Unlike the S100 and S200 series, which are armored models designed for use in areas under constant fire, the S300 series is a low-security model better suited to industrial installations than terrorist training grounds—obviously the pajama men who used the base weren't expecting company.

Aiming at their targets through either the non-armored windows or the large, open rectangular tower entrances just above the top of the steel access ladders, the Blue Man teams loosed their rounds. The guns bucked once apiece as 7.62 × 51-millimeter bullets exited their polygon-bored heavy barrels at a muzzle velocity many times higher than conventional rifles produced, while their low-noise bolt-closing feature reduced the sounds of the shots to low-decibel, subsonic cracks. Each killed their distant targets with perfectly placed head shots. As the taken-down sentries vanished from view or crumpled over the railings, Sergeant Death instructed the next wave of Marines to enter the base.

These, skilled at silent killing with knives and sound-suppressed repeating arms, were already stationed with bolt cutters outside the perimeter fence. At Death's signal they cut openings in the fence, entered the compound perimeter, took out ground sentry patrols, and dragged them from open view.

Now Sergeant Death issued final instructions. His snatch teams were to silently invade the base and abduct prisoners for interrogation. Fire-support squadrons on the perimeter would be ready to intervene if a shit fight broke out, but the purpose of the mission was a snatch-and-grab raid, not an assault in force.

One's snatch teams now snuck inside and stole into the wooden barracks longhouses that were used as troop bivouacs by Al Qadr. The three-man elements grabbed sleeping terrorists off cold dirt floors, slapping duct tape across their mouths and sock masks over their heads before they could even wake up. By the time the Al Qadr pajama men fell from the arms of Morpheus and into the soup, they'd been Chinese-handcuffed and bundled into the FAVs for a ride to the squad's Blackhawk LZ a few hours later.

It was important to interrogate the prisoners before taking more severe measures against the enemy base. Marine Force One's primary mission from the theater CINC was to search out and destroy fixed and mobile missile TELs and terrorist bases. However, its secondary mission was still to try and determine the whereabouts of the missing U.S. hostages.

Later on, TLAMs or aircraft could come in and blow the base to smithereens. The only way Saxon, as mission CINC, could reconcile the two objectives was to take and question prisoners whenever Al Qadr bases were located.

While the team's Arabic speakers were debriefing the POWs, more Marine Force One squadrons were engaged in similar activities in the other sectors of the highlands. When the Blackhawks returned to the clandestine LZs to pick up the teams, they also took possession of the prisoners that the teams had bundled off with them.

The Blackhawks, now returning to clandestine mountain LZs, brought the captives back to Saxon's field HQ for a thorough interrogation by a squad from MF-1's intel platoon. In the case of one of the prisoners, Saxon would be especially interested. This Al Qadr was an American. After questioning, this meant life in the federal pen for him.

chapter *thirteen*

Cruise missile strikes prepared the target for the Marine Force recon teams that stood awaiting the order to go in. The cave complex had been first identified by captured Al Qadr foot soldiers who'd described it as a network of interconnected caverns fortified with concrete and buttressed with steel I-beams.

Some of the military prisoners captured in the recent raids had also claimed to have sighted members of the captured B-1 bomber crew. Their eyewitness testimony was judged credible by the CIA and Marine Force One's intelligence section. For that reason alone the underground base had been spared wholesale destruction by the more exotic fuel-air explosive warheads available to friendly forces, and hit with relatively milder conventional ordnance.

What this added up to was the possibility of armed resistance from Al Qadr soldiers who had been shaken up but not put out of commission. This assessment proved correct. The unfriendlies were holed up in their mountain bunkers, mean as junkyard dogs and spoiling for a fight.

As One's fire-recon teams entered the cavern complex, friendly forces were met with automatic fire and hand and rocket grenades from Al Qadr gunners emplaced in concealed positions. As the 1-Patchers found out to their displeasure, many of these fire positions had been extremely well prepared. Some were protected with sandbag revetments; other positions used the natural convolutions of the cave network to good tactical advantage.

The Marine special recon teams found themselves faced with a pitched battle offered by a determined and well-armed foe whose philosophy was to fight to the death. This posed some tactical problems, but none that were deemed insurmountable.

The USMC had faced a similarly determined and capable enemy under very similar tactical conditions in the Pacific theater of World War II. Then it had been fanatical soldiery that had bunkered itself into caves on the outer archipelagos of the adversary's home islands. They too had pledged never to surrender, preferring death instead.

And then, as now, the Marines had been perfectly glad to oblige their adversaries in their death wish. The same applied today, using the two principal weapons of the Pacific theater, and one modern one.

The two former weapons were the flamethrower and the bangalore torpedo, an extendable pipe charge that could be fitted into small openings and crevices to make these considerably wider in a considerable hurry. The modern weapon was robots that could creep or roll across the cavern floor and deliver a message from the Reaper by remote control.

Before turning from small arms to these more lethal weapons, the Marines gave their Nexus opponents ten minutes to lay down their guns and put up their hands. The Marines didn't really expect an answer, and were not surprised that they didn't get one. Having anticipated this response, the Marines decided that they had every right and obligation to kick some ass.

And so they did.

Midway along the cavern complex were two fortified machine-gun emplacements, essentially large pits in the rock floor surrounded by piles of sandbags several feet in height. Two Chinese Type 80 7.62-millimeter GPMGs had been set up on pintle mounts inside these scorpions' nests, which blocked further passage into the main tunnel of the complex.

While teams of Marine squad gunners threw bursts of cover fire at the enemy installations, Master Sergeant Death's flamethrower team geared up for action. In the old days, in places like Saipan, Kwajalein, Guam, or Makin Island, a Marine would strap a liquid propane tank to his back and charge in behind a stream of fire. Either that, or a Sherman tank would be outfitted with a flamethrower. Today, the Marines had a little robo-helper they'd nicknamed Torchy.

Torchy was a remote-controlled mini-tank equipped with enough napalm to broil every steak in Cleveland on the Fourth of July. Torchy also had a remote-controlled box-fed Minimi MG mounted on it so it could pour hot lead into the enemy's ranks along with flaming napalm. Occupying a secure position, Doc Jeckyll, One's chief technical, sent Torchy on his first errand using a tele-operation rig made up of a head-mounted display and force-feedback gloves that enabled Jeckyll to control and direct Torchy's actions and movements.

When the soon-to-be-charbroiled Al Qadr warriors saw the pocket tank rolling toward them, they subjected it to a volley of bullets and a barrage of hand grenades. It did them no good. Torchy was bullet- and bomb-proof.

Stopping the robot a few yards shy of the Al Qadr position, Jeckyll sent Torchy on his errand of destruction. Manipulating his virtual controls, the Doc triggered the first of several helpings of burning napalm into the first gun emplacement.

The Al Qadr warriors were quickly bathed in a shower of flaming jellied high-test. Their flesh began to char and burn. Their robes and turbans instantly burst into flame. Their eyeballs melted in their sockets and popped from their skulls like blazing jujubes.

The burning hair and scalp beneath their burning turbans soon split from their skulls, which too burned, and the fanatical brains inside them began to cook like chickens in pots of boiling blood. To make sure the barbecued Al Qadr shooters got the message, Jeckyll used Torchy's MG to hose them down with a couple of hundred full-metal-jacket rounds, free of charge from Uncle Sam.

With the first MG emplacement now put out of commission, Jeckyll swung Torchy's weapon-bearing turret around for a second pass at the neighboring gun emplacement. The Al Qadr there were now suddenly less anxious to prefer martyrdom to capture than they'd been mere minutes before. In fact, two of the former lovers-of-death were now trying to escape their comrades with their hands held high.

The difference of opinion among the Al Qadr was quickly settled when the comrades of the would-be surrenderers shot them in the back without a second thought. The two turbaned warriors who'd tried to do the Monkey never made it past the ring of sandbags. Instead they did the Twist, falling over the revetments in bloodied heaps, their arms and heads lolling and swinging while their blood drenched the stone floor of the cavern.

As those left in the emplacement opened up with a fresh barrage of autofire, Jeckyll triggered Torchy's flamethrower again, and a cascade of burning napalm sluiced into the remaining Al Qadr in the revetmented gun position. They quickly achieved martyrdom in exactly the same manner as the charred corpses of their neighbors, first getting a dirt-removing bath of fire, followed by a rinse cycle of 7.62-millimeter autobursts from Torchy's chattering machine gun.

With the path into the inner reaches of the tunnel complex now cleared, the Marine Force One fire-recon teams charged past the smoldering remains of the enemy emplacements and probed deeper into the labyrinth.

They found more Al Qadr willing to be martyred by fire and steel, but in the end, when the entire cavern network had been declared secure and free from unfriendlies, the Marines had still failed to detect a single sign of the presence of the American hostages they had come here to rescue. In this regard the base too had proven to be a dry hole.

Elsewhere in the combat theater, however, the trail was about to get hot again. At roughly the same time as the Force Tiger fire-recon detachment was finalizing control of the de-Nexused underground base, the pilot of an AHW-1 Whiskey Cobra attack helicopter on airborne patrol spotted the dust cloud raised by a convoy of all-terrain vehicles rolling through a high mountain pass.

The airborne patrol consisted of three of these heavily armed yet highly agile Marine choppers, and the patrol had instructions to open fire at will upon any ground forces that were confirmed as unfriendlies.

Since late-model four-wheel-drive trucks of the type favored by the Al Qadr elite made up the convoy, it was a good bet that the chopper crews had in fact encountered fleeing members of the terrorist leadership hierarchy.

Adding to the likelihood that this assessment was correct was the fact that the vehicles were headed at high speed toward the desolate sea of sand that made up the Rub Al Khali, or the Empty Quarter, that lay between Oman and the principle cities of Saudi Arabia.

Although the new and expensive trucks all had their windows rolled up and were undoubtedly air-conditioned, the only human habitations that were found in the Empty Quarter were the fortresses and hidden encampments of outlaws, terrorists, smugglers, and nomadic tribal chieftains. And since the principal sideline of all the above-named was kidnapping and murder, it was a sure bet that the convoy was not occupied by a group of Baptist Sunday school teachers on a tour of natural desert wonders.

The appearance of Kalashnikov muzzles from several of the now-rolled-down windows and sun roofs of those vehicles further confirmed the pilots' judgment. Now the Marine pilot of the lead Whiskey Cobra had positive confirmation of unfriendlies below. The Al Qadr had just punched their own tickets, and validated the attack helo sortie's license to kill.

The pilot issued rapid instructions to the two other choppers flying the mission. They were to stage a lateral attack on the convoy. One by one, the three helos flew in a line to one side of the convoy, getting into a leading position just ahead of the first Land Cruiser.

As soon as the initial vehicle got into optimum range of automatic cannons and rocket and missile strikes, the mission commander would issue instructions to his whizzo to open up on the targets. The rest of the sortie would follow suit.

He didn't realize that giving that order was to also sanction American deaths by friendly fire.

*   *   *

Captain Michaels knew it was do-or-die time. The fat lady was singing a fucking aria. He and the remaining members of his crew had survived weeks of Al Qadr captivity. Now they were about to buy the farm. The ragheads had originally blindfolded them on leaving the place where they'd last been held—Michaels assumed that this was yet another underground base blasted into the guts of a mountain—but had removed their blindfolds when it no longer mattered what they saw. At least they weren't walking anymore. When their bargaining chips—for such his men surely were—had begun to drop, the Al Qadr had relented and put them back inside the air-conditioned trucks. As a bonus, Michaels had persuaded the terrorists to unbind their wrists.

Michaels had picked up enough from his captors to have a fairly good idea that they were heading across the Empty Quarter toward one of the fortresses that had been established there by the several tribal and criminal bands that ranged over the Rub Al Khali.

Michaels knew enough about the lash-up on the Arabian Peninsula to suspect this would represent going from the frying pan into the fire. Al Qadr was basically just a bunch of thugs masquerading as religious reformers, but they at least considered themselves warriors; they all swore *baryat,* an oath of fealty to their immediate superiors and to their Mahdi, which included a sham Arthurian code of chivalry. The Americans' captivity hadn't exactly been a model of Geneva Convention rules, but at least Michaels and his crew were still in one piece.

On the other hand, the nomadic bands inhabiting the Empty Quarter were outlaws to a man, with no scruples whatever and no pretensions toward chivalry, messianic revelations, or anything else. They were pirates, pure and simple, the only difference being that they operated on a sea of sand instead of an ocean of water. Their like would just as gladly kill or mutilate Michaels and his crew as look at them.

The plan of the fleeing Al Qadr honchos was fairly easy to glean. They sought refuge among the chieftains of the Empty Quarter who were unaffiliated with Al Qadr and thus less likely to suffer attack from CENTCOM. The chieftains, obeying the ancient tribal codes of hospitality, would be honor-bound to offer the Al Qadr sanctuary.

But among their breed a favor done always demanded repayment in kind. The spanking-new Toyota Land Cruisers Michaels's captors were driving would surely be part of that payment. Michaels and his men would make up the rest of the fee.

Eventually the fleeing Al Qadr would melt away, toward new sanctuaries in Saudi Arabia probably, leaving Michaels and his crewmen to the tender mercies of their new hosts. He knew that even if negotiations were carried out between the U.S. and his captors, there could be months, maybe years of captivity lying ahead. Michaels was no fool. He had no doubt that if he and his men were not dead in the end, they would be as good as dead.

More to the point, events had overtaken the captives, and the moment of truth had arrived, like it or not. As one of the Al Qadr tried futilely to knock a Cobra helo from the sky with an AK-47 through the window of a juddering truck, Michaels saw the choppers break formation and begin to reform to the left of the convoy. Since Michaels was a pilot himself, he knew exactly what was about to happen.

At the moment it did, Michaels planned to go for broke. Michaels was well aware he had no choice in the matter. He doubted that the helo crews knew Americans were in the convoy, and they would simply frag them all, friendlies and unfriendlies alike.

In seconds the first TOW missile slammed into the roadbed a few hundred feet ahead of the lead vehicle. Michaels, in the third Land Cruiser, was badly jolted as the drivers reflexively slammed on their brakes, but a missile strike was exactly what he'd expected.

Michaels didn't know precisely what had occurred, but he didn't think the Cobra had fired directly into the convoy. If that had happened, all the helos would probably have followed suit in one big salvo and he'd be at the Pearly Gates right now. Since he hadn't sprouted wings, this meant the

AHW-1s had probably just tried to halt the convoy rather than kill it.

It was now or never. The fat lady was singing her ass off and Michaels was in motion. He'd already picked his target, a scrawny raghead wielding a man-sized Kalash seated to his right, and opposite the reforming line of helos. To make his choice of target more appealing, the red stripe above the door handle indicated the lock was not engaged.

Balling the fist of his right hand and propping it against the cupped fingers of his left, Michaels used the bulbous joint of his right elbow as an edged weapon, slamming the sharp knob of his ulnar bone into the temple exposed between the black turban and the scruffy tuft of beard tracing the Al Qadr's upper jawline.

Michaels felt and heard something crack as he reached for the Kalash. When a second hand blow had loosened the terrorist's grip, Michaels wrapped his fingers around the bullpup rifle's receiver. Out the corner of his eye Michaels saw the ragheads seated up front raise their weapons, stretch hands toward him, shout threats and warnings, lower their guns, and get ready to blow him away.

But by this time his index finger was on the Kalash's trigger and he was blindly putting bursts into the forward seat, watching the heavy-caliber bullets trace a line of rips along the upholstery, watching the Al Qadr in the Land Cruiser's forward compartment jump and shudder like electrocuted convicts as the bullets hammered into them.

And then Michaels was clawing for the ATV's door latch, spilling ass-over-teakettle onto the hard-packed earth of the mountain road, struggling to right himself, flailing his arms, and firing long automatic bursts at the sky, praying the hovering gunships wouldn't take him for the enemy as he drained the weapon's magazine dry.

Then, in the kaleidoscope tunnel of his mind, through the blood and sweat that filmed his eyes, he saw one of the Cobras maneuver around, pivoting on an invisible fulcrum in the sky. Its nose pointed toward him and a rocket came off one of the wing pylons, flashing fire and trailing smoke.

A heartbeat later there was an explosion. Everything went dark after that.

As Michaels lay unconscious, he did not see the doors of those Land Cruisers left intact after the rocket strike come open, nor the pajama men in turbans exiting with their hands raised in the air, yet another group of Al Qadr who had learned to do the Monkey.

Unlike the rank and file, the leaders of Al Qadr preferred surrender to death. And they were prepared to trade. The American airmen who were to have been bargaining chips with the scum of the Empty Quarter were now brought out and offered to new providers of sanctuary. What had begun as a battle had ended as a bazaar.

In the mountainous high country of Yemen and Oman, fusion cells—so named because they are made up of mixed commando forces seconded from U.S. and British specwar units—continued reconnaissance and patrol operations in the wake of the success of Saxon's airmobile squadrons elsewhere in the theater.

Like One's special detachments, the squad-sized teams were airmobile. Choppers—in this case the same Blackhawks flown by Delta Force's aviation detachment used by One—would ferry them to positions close to their patrol sectors, and the teams would take it from there on out in complete self-containment.

Their objectives were fixed and mobile missile launchers, including Scuds, SAMs, and whatever else unfriendlies might have out there sitting on TELs, waiting to cause CENTCOM trouble.

Operating mostly by night, the fusion cells rode mountain bikes and fast-attack vehicles to get around the arid, craggy landscape. Sheltering in wadis, caves, and other natural formations, or in spider holes dug by the teams themselves, the fusion cells hid until after sunset, then saddled up and went to work.

The duration of a normal mission might be anywhere from three to five days. The patrols had the final say on how to deal with any targets they discovered. Their standard kit included blocks of plastic explosive for general-purpose demolition, and cutting charges for taking down bridges, overpass spans, and anything supported or buttressed by steel beams. The cells had the tools necessary to blow up missile launchers and supporting infrastructure, such as ground radar installations, when it was judged necessary.

Most often the cells chose to act as observers and spotters for coalition air strikes. There was less risk involved in calling in the fast-movers to put missiles or gravity-delivered ordnance on the target, and the job got done cleaner and better that way. The teams could get in close to their objectives and see things that satellites or surveillance aircraft could not detect in any detail. *Maskirovka* techniques might spoof the cameras of an SR-71 or an orbital imaging bird, but down on the ground the human eye could accurately discern what the electronic eye could not.

For this reason the fusion cells carried lightweight laser target designators on their missions. The LTDs projected invisible death dots onto the targets that had been selected to be hit by an air strike. With the hidden commandos painting, or illuminating, the target in this way, air strikes called in by the cells knew precisely where to place their ordnance.

The fusion cells would illuminate the targets, the fast-movers would come barreling in, strike hard on their overflies, then turn and burn while the target went up in a fireball. Minutes after the sortie's departure, the fusion cells would have melted back into the landscape and another TEL would be history. When day again dawned, manned and unmanned surveillance aircraft would be dispatched by CENTCOM to pass overhead, collecting data for battle-damage assessments at theater CINC HQ on Darsa.

In this way the TELs, mobile radars, training centers, road infrastructure, and tactical command and control nodes of the enemy were gradually but steadily whittled down to the butt-end, and the ability of Al Qadr entrenched in the lower Arabian Peninsula to launch standoff attacks on coalition strongpoints on the Brothers and Darsa was reduced to virtual nonexistence as the war proceeded toward its closing days.

Elsewhere in the area of operations, other units, including Marine forces, did not always fare as well as the fusion cells fighting the Scud war or Marine Force One in its fire recon of Al Qadr sanctuaries, tactical command centers, and weapons of mass destruction.

In the capital city of Rais Khawlaf on Socotra, a mechanized Marine company found itself caught in a lethal quagmire. Met by determined guerrilla resistance, and with the advantage of superior firepower and brilliant weaponry diluted in the urban-warfare environment by the presence of nearby buildings and noncombatants, the Marines were forced to wage an ugly, bloody, door-kicking, house-byhouse fight to secure their objectives.

In doing so they not only had to contend with enemy snipers positioned on rooftops and windows, but also with booby traps of various types and levels of sophistication. Many friendly casualties were turned in during the course of this military action in a built-up area. While the Marines succeeded in capturing Rais Khawlaf, the name of the city would stand in the annals of American war history as a synonym for a hard-fought, barely won, and overly costly battle. It would launch a thousand strategic studies to determine how another Rais Khawlef might be avoided in future combat. And in the end it, like a thousand other battles, would find itself repeated in future wars, study it as they might.

In the long, deep wadi that runs through the center of the arid Hadramaut plateau, which itself stretches from the rockribbed Asir mountain range to the west of the Arabian Peninsula, across most of Yemen and into neighboring Oman, mechanized Marine and U.S. and British Army units sometimes found themselves facing a determined enemy armed with man-portable antiarmor weapons and a will to fight to the death.

These Al Qadr units had been trained by the so-called Afghan Arabs—the remnants of the first Afghan war against the Soviets of the 1980s, from whose ranks the original Al Qaeda elite had been drawn. In the battles of the Wadi Hadramaut, these desert warriors used tactics against American and British mechanized forces similar to those that had worked effectively against Soviet tanks and armored personnel carriers in the Hindu Kush. The enemy attacked the supposed weak points of CENTCOM's armor; they positioned themselves to use natural terrain features to tactical advantage, and they employed a variety of crude but effective booby traps designed to trap, crush, and topple armored vehicles, immobilizing mechanized forces so they could be picked off at leisure.

But their attacks proved ineffective in the end—the Al Qadr had not reckoned with the superior MBTs, APCs, and other armor fielded by the fifth-generation military forces they faced, nor the tactical air that, in the form of Comanche and Whiskey Cobra helos or multi-role combat fighter planes, could be brought swiftly and accurately against their forces, nor the fluid tactics of their adversaries—though the determined assaults by the mobile and well-armed strike units of Al Qadr did slow the advance of friendly armor and impede its effectiveness in taking control of the many hill towns that dotted the Wadi Hadramaut and clustered against its craggy, dusty hillsides.

In these and other sectors of the battle space friendly forces experienced numerous delays, setbacks, and snafus. The enemy had hoped by its strategy of small-unit and guerrilla spoiling tactics to erode homeland support for the war by turning in high body counts, to play on the perceived aversion of Americans and their Western allies to combat fatalities on the part of their troops.

In this too, the tacticians of Al Qadr had made an incorrect assessment. The United States and its allies in the war had determined to clean out a nest of vermin, no matter what the cost in blood, chattel, and sacrifice. The nation had steeled itself for battle, if necessary for a fight to the death. In the end the transnational terrorist state created by Al Qadr, the virtual-reality republic of hatred that it had forged, was doomed to the trash heap of history, do what it might to forestall its fate.

Town by town, the terrorist bastions of the Hadramaut began to fall like dominoes. One by one, the cancerous cells that had taken root on the Arabian Peninsula were strangled, killed, cut off. Day by day, the war against terror ground its forces to finer and finer particles of powder. Moment by moment, the forces of civilization prevailed against those of primordial chaos, until there finally came a day when the theater CINC could inform the chairman of the joint chiefs of staff, who was his immediate superior, that all military objectives had been met, victory could be declared, and the troops could finally be sent home.

But the war was not over, and in some respects the declaration of victory would prove premature.

On the day that President Travis Claymore announced in a State of the Union message that U.S. troops were being pulled out of the area of operations and would be returning home soon, a maintenance worker at the Amoco oil refinery at Houston, Texas, reported for her job as she had regularly and faithfully done for the last two years.

Like everyone else entering the refinery, she had needed to pass through computer-augmented X-ray scanners in order to gain access to the plant, but the scanners did not show any indication that she was carrying a pound of plastic explosive molded to the interior of her vagina and invisible beneath her clothing, or that she was, in fact, a kind of highly lethal human M&M.

At the top of Catalytic Cracking Tower C, located on the north sector of the refinery, the maintenance worker triggered the miniaturized electronic detonator that she'd inserted into the plastic before leaving her home in suburban Houston. The fierce explosion caused the tower to explode into a fireball. The worker, and much of the refinery's north sector, was incinerated in the blazing inferno.

There was little relief in the President's repeated warnings that the Nexus had not been defeated, only greatly harmed, by the recent multinational military action. There was little point in the media's conjecturing about what had led the terrorist bomber to lead a quiet life in a middle-class neighborhood with a husband and three children and then finally do what she had done.

There was no point at all in the probe into the mass murderer's past, which ultimately revealed a carefully prepared cover, clandestine money drops, and a previous identity under which she had spent time in terrorist camps in Syria, Egypt, Yemen, and the Philippines.

The Al Qadr sleeper agent had followed a pattern that others before her had also followed. She had sacrificed her life so that many others would die with her, leaving a by-now-familiar void of pain and hatred in the wake of her actions.

She had been one among many. Part of a twilight army of twisted fanatics who would replace order with chaos, life with death, freedom with bondage, hope with fear. The bombing proved that this satanic force was still powerful, still at large, still a credible threat. Other battles would lie ahead until it was finally stopped, and stopped cold.

One, soon to come, would stun a world that believed it could be shocked by nothing any longer.

chapter *fourteen*

Hassan Ramad Ali, the Mahdi, awaited the day of his apotheosis and ascendency, for it was surely he and no other man who was ordained by Allah to bring the justice of the Koranic sword to this house of iniquity ruled by an apostate king.

As the saying went, "sacred land, profane people."

Allah made no mistakes. He might permit his creatures to err because he had given them the spark of free will. Allah himself could not err. Ever. That the kingdom of the faithless House of Saud, a house that treated with the infidel, a house that brought shame upon the Arab nations, that this kingdom was the selfsame one that housed the sacred Black Stone in Mecca, was to be avenged. The wicked ones who had profaned Allah would soon pay the hard wages of sin. The apostates would do penance for their dealings with the infidel.

In these final days and hours, the Mahdi had slowly removed the velvet cover from the exquisite treasure that he had scattered among the sands of the kingdom.

The Mahdi's golden seeds made up this treasure. These were seeds of destruction and rebirth. From Mecca to Dhahran, they had taken root and were ready to send forth blossoms of fire at the Mahdi's command. Soon, very soon, the golden seeds of change would be caused to bloom like lurid orchids at a mass funeral.

When they bloomed, the heads of the foul apostate princes who ruled the nation would fall and an Islamic republic far greater than Iran's would rise from its ashes. The obscene Crusader forces would be thrown out and destroyed. The infidel would be scourged with fire and cast out of all the holy places. All Islam would then unite under the Mahdi's standard. From there, the *mujahideen* would sojourn west and east, to conquer and avenge fourteen centuries of measureless shame. It was now only a matter of time. The Christians could not prevail much longer. They would be punished. They would fall.

The Mahdi's forces throughout the Arabian Peninsula knew that their emir was nearby and that he would appear among them at the preordained hour. The king suspected as much too, and secretly trembled. But he had no choice in the matter.

Those pilgrims making the *hajj* to Mecca had been converging on the holy city. From Iran, Iraq, Syria, Jordan, Egypt—from the four corners of the Arab world they had come. The Black Stone at the Great Mosque would be unveiled. The king would be in attendance. To hide at this moment would be to invite a cataclysm as great as or greater than that which the Mahdi threatened.

The Omrikanee crusaders had been posted outside the gates of the apostate's holy sites. They were stationed at their bases on Saudi land. They sailed the waters of the Persian Gulf and the Arabian Sea in their mighty ships. But they would soon be as chaff before the wind. On the day of judgment they too would be swept away as dry, crumpled leaves before the hot breath of a blazing inferno.

The Mahdi waited. Confidently he waited. Soon, he knew, that great day would arrive.

Hammon shivered, but not from the cold. The cold and the dark, lowering skies, from which snow, powdery and white as confectioner's sugar, sifted down onto the wooded stretch, were gifts.

Hammon shivered for what he had done.

Snow had already begun to rime the little girl's lifeless body. She lay in front of him like a large doll that had been mistreated by a willful child. The arms splayed one way, the head another, the legs a third. There had been no point in attempting to bury the broken thing. It would have taken a jackhammer to break and turn the frozen earth. Hammon had snapped her neck with a clean, sharp twist, then thrown her down from the high ground into the depression he had selected. All things considered, the chances of the girl's death being ruled accidental were good.

Hammon's mind flashed through the steps that had led to the cold-blooded murder. There wasn't any point in his lying to himself about it being a sudden impulse. It wasn't. He'd been considering the folly of his actions for some time after receiving final instructions from Arthur, his handler, at the safe house. What if the girl showed the money he'd given her? What if she talked? What if . . . any number of things happened?

It had been one matter to have his fun while the child watched when he was just passing routine intelligence. But now, with the magnitude of the operation that was scheduled, and its serious aftermath, he, like many others, would certainly fall under suspicion.

His actions, like those of his colleagues, would be subject to intense investigative scrutiny. Eventually the girl or her mother would be questioned. A link would then be established between them and himself. Hammon's Libyan handlers could not be trusted. Even if they could, where would that leave him? Hammon did not relish the prospect of spending the rest of his days in Tripoli or Benghazi. Besides, he would eventually be sold out, like Carlos Illich Ramirez, called the Jackal, had been sold out by his erstwhile benefactor the Brother Colonel.

All this was happening on an unconscious level, a deep level divorced from his everyday activities. Hammon lived on these two levels, and also on sublevels in between. It was the only way to stay sane—or function with a semblance of normalcy under the weight of his insanity, he had never decided which. The dead drops at the housing project led him to the building's south laundry room, and often the little girl made an appearance. Hammon suspected that she hung around that particular laundry room hoping he'd drop by, eager to earn the money he gave her.

Did she understand what he had been doing? he wondered. Could she possibly have been turned on by it? It was indeed possible, he supposed. Ghetto kids grew up early, far earlier than the spoiled progeny of the suburban rich a few miles away in rural Virginia. Anyway, it didn't matter. All he'd been into was her watching him take his own pleasure, and that had been all. Hammon had no desire to get in any deeper, no urge for physical contact. He liked them to watch while he did it, and he liked them to be very young. That was it.

Hammon had made the last dead drop, and was almost glad when the girl showed no inclination of appearing that afternoon. He'd been about to leave the laundry room when she suddenly came in.

"Hello."

She stood there staring up at him, her large brown eyes shining in anticipation. Hammon at that moment was certain that the girl knew all about what was going on. Maybe not in great detail, but enough. The thought sent a surge of heat through his entire body.

"Hello yourself," he said pleasantly. "How've you been?"

"Okay," she answered. She seemed to be holding something back. Hammon had suddenly felt a twinge of free-floating panic.

"Is everything all right?" he asked her guardedly. "You didn't tell your mommy about ever meeting me here, did you?"

She didn't answer right away, but then shook her head. Hammon no longer felt the heat. Instead, an icy cold now gripped his entrails. And with it came a grim resolution to do what he knew he now must. He forced a smile.

"Are you sure? You didn't show your mommy even a little bit of the money? You didn't tell her anything?"

She shook her head, then corrected herself and nodded, as precocious children will do. Hammon was suddenly angered. The child had talked, and that meant she was a liability. He went over to her and gently stroked her hair.

"Listen," he told her. He had suddenly made his decision.

A new heat had now replaced the old one. "I have a surprise for you. First, let me give you this." He handed her a ten-dollar bill. "You'll get twenty dollars more if you meet me in the woods behind the playground."

As he spoke Hammon realized that it had been settled weeks ago. It was almost like the final act of a play that someone else had written and in which he was but an actor.

Hammon's subconscious had already analyzed the problem, saw what had been necessary, and resolved to carry it out. All that had been missing was the catalyst, and this the little girl had just provided him with it.

"I'll leave first. Then you wait ten minutes and go meet me there. Can you do it? Do you know where I want you to meet me?"

The girl said she would, that she did. And she had. Five minutes after her appearance she was dead, her neck vertebra snapped, her pockets emptied. Hammon made absolutely sure that the area was sanitized of his presence, including footprints—the hard ground was a help here, at least—and left the scene amid the worsening snowstorm.

The circuitous route to his car that skirted the highway side of the housing project, in order to avoid potential witnesses, took him an additional fifteen minutes. Then he was inside the car's leather-upholstered warmth, listening to classical music, on his way home to his wife and a full snifter of Napoleon brandy. And soon it was as if none of it had ever happened. Just like his recurrent dreams of a Huey going down over a stretch of jungle in Vietnam a long time ago.

Hammon had just moved from one level to another.

That was all.

"Coroner's report."
       Jackson nodded at the pretty woman cop, and only turned his attention to the ten stapled pages lying atop his coffee-stained metal desk after her watchable ass was no longer in view. She had a very nice ass, this lady cop, a lot

nicer than his wife's, for example, and it was worth staring at it whenever possible. Her bootie was the one reason that Jackson never made an issue of the medical examiner's policy of faxing over reports rather than e-mailing them.

Sterling Jackson, a detective lieutenant working homicide at the Washington Metro Police headquarters on F Street, then leaned back in his chair and read the first of the ten pages. The reading went fast, mostly because, though ten pages long, the report was actually a series of forms, only some of which needed fairly lengthy elaboration. The multiuser interdepartmental envelope also contained a selection of glossy crime-scene photographs, printed from digital-film originals.

Jackson flipped to the third page and went to the first and only item, the autopsy results. After fifteen years working homicide Jackson knew the medical jargon backwards, and could spontaneously translate the coroner's verdict into plain English. The ME ruled the death accidental. The victim had died of a crushed trachea and shattered upper vertebra caused by a severe fall.

Jackson flipped the report back on the desk and put up his feet. He thought back to that afternoon two days before, when he had stood on the bleak, wooded knoll behind the housing project playground and checked the body over. The pathologist on the scene had also preliminarily ruled the death accidental.

Jackson was a cop and hadn't been convinced. You got a gut feel for what was kosher and what wasn't after a while, and Jackson knew that this one wasn't. Besides, the little girl reminded him of his own kid. Probably, had it not been for this fact, he would have gone through the usual routine, which meant doing practically nothing. The poor did not frequently get justice. The caseload in homicide was too big and the manpower to follow through on all but a few cases far too limited.

In this instance, Jackson asked some questions, made the rounds, done some legwork. An old codger named Mose Kincaid remembered seeing a suspicious-looking man. In particular Mose remembered him because he'd driven a fancy car.

"He was a white man," Mose told Jackson. "Tall, blond hair. Dressed in one of them black wool coats. Drove a real nice car, I think it was a Beamer, maybe a Benz. I noticed him here a couple times. Them social workers dress the same, but they don't drive brand-spankin'-new Beamers."

"You remember anything else?" Jackson had asked. "You didn't get the tag number by any chance?"

"What's that?"

"License plate number."

"Nope. That's all I seen, mister. How 'bout a little somethin' for my trouble?"

Jackson gave Mose a twenty.

"There's a twin brother if you remember anything else," he said, adding, "and I mean anything else I can use. So if you call me, don't try to bullshit me, okay, old-timer?" Jackson handed the dude his card and left thinking that, yeah, that could in fact be something. It might even be a lead.

Jackson knew that with cameras all over the place, including the highways and byways of his fair city, he might possibly catch a break here. But with the large numbers of Beamers in the D.C. Metro area it was still a long shot, unless he did wind up getting lucky. He would have to get lucky in a hurry too, because by next Monday he'd have to declare the case history.

As it turned out, Jackson did get lucky. Because of the snow. The snow that Hammon had considered a gift back there on the frozen knoll.

Traffic was somewhat lighter that afternoon. And just before rush hour, an automatic camera mounted atop a traffic signal pole was automatically triggered when a vehicle skidded to a short stop as the light changed just west of the Capital Beltway at the intersection of Broad Street and Arlington Boulevard.

The automatic camera recorded a series of frames of a black, late-model BMW that had skidded to a stop in the frost-slick intersection box, then backed up behind the crosswalk. Because the driver had backed the car instead of remaining in the intersection, the traffic department did not issue him a summons, nor would the data have been retained in an active file. But a computer alert had instructed all traffic inspectors to send copies of photos showing a Benz or BMW photographed at around the time of the murder to Metro Homicide.

Because of the alert, Jackson had wound up with three sets of traffic-surveillance photos. It was the second set that triggered off the mental alarm bells and gave him the mental confirmation of his gut feel that the kid had been murdered.

Jackson had run the tag numbers of that Beamer through the DMV database. The car was registered to a VIP in the Washington establishment. Jackson next turned to the Internet to see if there were any photos of this guy, and found a fairly good one on a government Website, in which the man was shown in the company of Administration insiders. The photo of the suspect, once enlarged with a few clicks of the mouse, closely matched the description given Jackson by his snitch at the projects.

It was this break that was to ultimately bring the matter to the attention of the DIA's secret Task Force Bravo, though not for a while yet.

Within a sixty-mile radius of the copse of trees in which Hammon's young victim's body had been discovered, Hammon's new case officer, Abel, the man who had suddenly, unexpectedly, and without explanation replaced Arthur, emptied the clip of a Glock semiautomatic pistol into a paper target that hissed toward him along two overhead steel tracks. He smiled grimly as he ejected the spent clip, palmed in a fresh one extracted from his jacket pocket, and holstered the now-warm weapon.

Wolfram Krieger was pleased by his shooting. The shot groups were tight and accurately placed. He, like the rest of the cadre, needed to be drilled and ready for when the day of the mission arrived. All their skills would need to be honed to a razor-sharp edge. Mentally, physically, and spiritually, they would need to be pure. Pure and deadly as king cobras.

This was the one drawback of the operational plan, the one thing that had nagged at him and would continue nagging at him in the coming days prior to the op's launch. Since vacating the training camp at Salman Pak for their European jump-off sites, and then their American final destinations, Krieger's paramilitary action cells required going into sleeper mode.

Any large-scale training efforts would have been certain to draw the attention of national and local police organizations. The entire operation might be jeopardized by this lamentable necessity, and it grated on Krieger's nerves. Even open gatherings of the cells were forbidden, for the same reason. The cells were to remain in hiding until they received Krieger's command to activate.

Each of the cell leaders knew the procedures after this happened. They had been drilled in these over and over again and knew them backwards. Everything from that point would unfold automatically; the unit chiefs were instructed to ignore any command, even from Krieger, to halt the op.

Krieger knew that once he issued the go-order the cells would turn themselves on, arm themselves from the prepositioned secret weapons caches near each cell's location, converge on the target, and carry out the phased martyrdom attacks.

He had perfect confidence in this happening like clockwork. He had personally trained and drilled the squadron leaders and many of the individual shock troops. The virus he was about to unleash would seek to overwhelm, cut off, and kill. What concerned Krieger was the dulling of the sharp edge to which he had whetstoned his fighting forces.

Weeks had already passed, and almost another week was to go by before Strike Day's arrival. In the interim the *fidayeen* would have time to think, time to doubt, time to fear. Even time to turn traitor. It was conceivable that some might at this moment be considering defection to the opposition side, might even already be informing on the operation to the FBI. The fact that the cells were highly compartmentalized—none knew the others' specific whereabouts and none the overall nature of the OPPLAN—such a development could still spell trouble. It would not stop Strike Day, but it might temper the sword that cleaved the head from the American rattlesnake.

Krieger fixed himself a bourbon and soda and tried to cast aside all negative thoughts. The booze would help—it was all he had, having sworn off sex until the mission was complete. Bringing women into the safe house was obviously impossible, but so was even consorting with prostitutes at one of the many fine bordellos to be found just across the Fourteenth Street Bridge, which spanned the lower Potomac west of Metro D.C. Krieger couldn't even risk getting a quick, casual blow job in a rented car. Operational sterility was a must and his cock would just have to suffer a while longer.

The booze at least helped Krieger relax. He flipped on the large flat-panel TV on the wall and watched CNN. It was just a case of nerves, he now assured himself. Krieger had come a long way since Dubai. He was now close to an apocalyptic moment that others might only dream about but that he would live to make reality. It was only normal to feel jittery before the culmination of an op such as that that he had planned.

Everything would change after Strike Day. Krieger had not only been given supreme command of the paramilitary assaults, but of the Libyan sleeper agent, Hammon. It was a signal from his paymasters that they had complete faith in him, or at least judged that no other alternative to his total control existed.

In fact, none did exist. There needed to be a single guiding intelligence behind the American end of the global operations. In the end this feature would prove decisive. Krieger's demand for total control had been questioned early on, but the results of the mission would ultimately prove him right.

The successful strikes would bring about the end of the American empire, the so-called Pax Americana, and the beginning of a true new world order, one where natural law was no longer stood on its head. Soon the weak would no longer rule over the strong. Soon there would be nothing left except the strong.

All that was weak would die.

chapter *fifteen*

Colonel David Saxon cradled his assault rifle—in this case a bullpup Valmet M76, a battle-tested Finnish AK-varient—as he led his men through the labyrinth of subterranean tunnels. The fuel-air explosives had worked efficiently and well. The TLAMs with special ground-penetrating warheads had exploded within the cavern interior.

The enormous incendiary detonations that followed depleted the air of oxygen. The effect of the strikes was much the same as the aftermath of poison gas, only far more severe. Those in the immediate vicinity of the blast front would be torn limb from limb by the severe concussion. Closer, they would be incinerated by heat. Those who merely choked to death, gasping for air in a burning vacuum, were the comparatively fortunate ones.

The name of the underground redoubt was al-Alayah. The complex of caverns was a multistory excavation that had taken years of construction work. Its presence had been completely unknown to military strategists until special forces patrols on the ground had located it.

The cavern complex was buried deep in the Asir mountain range, part of a rocky scarp running along the west and part of the southwest coasts of the Arabian Peninsula. It was here that the U.S. had entertained final hopes of locating the stronghold of the elusive terrorist chieftain who called himself the Mahdi.

Saxon stepped carefully over a charred and blast-maimed enemy corpse, watching out for booby traps. The Marine cadre under his command continued deeper into the cavern complex.

Suddenly Saxon received a communications message via the lightweight E200 Ear Mike that he, like the rest of the MF-1 squad members, wore.

"We have somebody here, Boss. Looks like it could be him."

Saxon reached the section of the underground base a short time later. He was confronted by a strangely appointed area that in appearance was a cross between an Ottoman pasha's throne room and an Istanbul opium den.

Saxon recalled the back-brief materials on the original Mahdi, the one who had terrorized the British Empire in the late nineteenth century. Hassan Ramad Ali, the current, self-proclaimed Mahdi, had convinced his followers that the previous Mahdi had been his incarnation in another life.

Cosmetically, if not physically, this was true. Ali had modeled his own appearance, war strategy, and personal deportment on that of the first Mahdi. He was said to have been in receipt of the original Mahdist Prophecies said to have been hidden before the first Mahdi's death in the Sudan in 1898 at the hands of British troops led by Chinese Gordon at the Battle of Omdurman.

Like the original Mahdi, Hassan Ali ringed his eyes with kohl, wore resplendent costumes, and was seen in video footage to disport himself against sumptuous backgrounds, a far cry from the bleak cavern backdrops of his immediate predecessor Osama bin Laden. Far from squatting on a carpet laid on a cold stone floor, Ali was always seen seated upon a gorgeous throne of rich brocade, his servants in attendance.

It was precisely this throne, one seen in so many video-discs broadcast to the world, that Saxon now confronted. A corpse was seated upon the high-backed regal chair. The cadaver was stiff though not yet decomposed, nor did it even smell much as yet. Saxon approached cautiously, mindful of booby traps.

"Boss, you think this is the guy?"

Saxon studied his face a while.

"Maybe," he said.

*   *   *

Twelve days later, Saxon was back at CENTCOM head-quarters on Darsa Island. He was reporting to the deputy theater CINC on what he had found in the al-Alayah caverns.

In the midst of the brief, the CINC himself came over to personally commend Saxon on the discovery made by his troops. He had some good news for him beyond this.

"Colonel, I just volunteered you."

The general was all smiles.

"For what, sir?"

"You, Colonel, are gonna go to Washington and meet with the commander in chief in the Oval Office. The president has expressed his wish to personally congratulate the Marine who found the Mahdi."

"Is this really necessary, sir?"

"Colonel, the president requested that the leader of the men who found this sonofabitch be presented to him for a ceremony at the White House. He's gonna pin a medal on you personally, goddammit!"

"Yes, sir," Saxon replied.

"Get yourself ready. You leave at 0620 hours. Your orders from HQMC are already cut. They include, for your infor-mation, that some of the men with you on the mission come along for the ride. That's all, Colonel. Dismissed."

"Yes, sir," Saxon said, and left the CINC's office. As he closed the door, Hallsey was already busy chewing his XO out, a regular part of his daily routine.

At 0940 hours Lima, the world learned that while the Mahdi himself might have been killed at al-Alayah, his terrorist organization Al Qadr, was still in business. At 0940 hours, as many of its personnel were just settling into the routine of the morning, Rotterdam's sprawling petroleum sea terminal, the oil jetty, was hit by one of the most devastating attacks in the entire cycle of Al Qadr violence.

Rotterdam's oil jetty projects out into the North Sea from the vast tank farm and underground storage facility at Hoek van Holland. The man-made harbor is deep enough to serve very large and ultra-large crude carriers. A pipeline runs from the oil jetty to the onshore pumping stations.

Even the largest oil tankers are easily able to maneuver in close to the jetty and take on loads of crude. The wide and deeply dredged harbor also makes for effective and convenient offloading of crude oil and other petro-products from oceangoing vessels ranging from supertankers to smaller ships of all types. For this reason the Rotterdam storage and pumping facility is one of the busiest in the entire world.

All this was about to change.

In a coordinated attack a fleet of six light planes converged at low level on the facility and the tankers currently docked in the harbor and taking on loads. Those personnel on the ground, seeing the wave of light aircraft wing in overhead, could not help making an immediate comparison to Pearl Harbor. In the aftermath of the strike, the Rotterdam disaster was to be known as the Pearl Harbor of the Oil War.

After months of investigation following the attacks, Interpol and local police and intelligence agencies in Europe, the U.S., the Middle East, and Russia would piece together the root causes of the devastating surprise attack. The names and faces of those who had piloted the suicide mission's planes would be known within reasonable limits. The scheme for forcing licensed pilots with unimpeachable records to substitute terrorist trainees in the cockpits of the aircraft using kidnapping and blackmail would be uncovered. Many other facts about the operation besides these would also become known.

For the moment, however, only the ominous buzzing of the engines of the planes that converged on the sprawling tank farm and oil jetty were heard, and only the winged shapes materializing out of the morning haze were seen. Personnel on land and on the two supertankers in the harbor sensed, more than perceived consciously, that something was very badly amiss. It all happened far too fast to be processed by the conscious mind. It was just a quickly progressing chain of events that carried its victims along, like kites before the wind.

Some on the jetty began to run. Others stood frozen in their tracks. No action taken did any good. Those who survived the onslaught survived through pure chance alone. Many lived to see the first of the attack aircraft, a single-engine Beechcraft, lose altitude and come barreling across the surface of the harbor toward the flank of the Japanese-flagged supertanker *Yamashita Maru,* which was taking on light sweet crude at the center of the oil jetty.

The Beechcraft plowed straight into the flank of the *Yamashita Maru*'s hull, instantly exploding into a fireball. The explosion was enormous. The Beechcraft had been packed full of high explosive.

The force of the explosion tore a huge gash into the plate-steel skin of the tanker. The enormous heat and molten fragments of shattered hull immediately became shrapnel that ignited the containerized crude stored within. The primary explosion was followed by an even larger fireball that broke the hull in the center, sending two halves of the supertanker to the bottom of the harbor.

At the same time, the other planes in the suicide squadron were nearing or striking their intended targets. Two aircraft struck the central tank farm in the storage complex. The impact easily ruptured the tanks that the planes crashed into, igniting millions of gallons of crude oil, gasoline, and other fractions of the petroleum refinery process stored in the tanks.

An enormous explosion was heard as far away as Belgium. Its shock waves traveled along the bedrock for miles around. In the nearby city of Rotterdam, the blast front was fierce enough to shatter windows. The dense pall of sooty, jet-black smoke from the burning installation darkened the skies of northern Europe for weeks on end. The burning lake of oil spread hazardous toxins across the European landscape. The destruction of the major fuel entrepot paralyzed Western Europe, which was dependent on the oil that flowed from this facility via the supertankers that docked there and trucks that debarked from it to overland destinations.

The catastrophe was also to have major repercussions

many thousands of miles away, especially in the United States and Japan.

The first Oil Riots took place less than a month following the discovery of the Mahdi and the disaster at Rotterdam. The riots began spontaneously, first in Los Angeles, then in New York, and quickly spread to other large cities across the country. Within a week the nation tottered on the brink of civil insurrection.

Gulf War veteran Timothy Lomax had been to the VA clinic in Pittsburgh's Point to get his semiannual medical exam. As a victim of Gulf War syndrome, Lomax needed twice-yearly testing in order to claim benefits under new federal legislation. Since the walk-in exams could be done at any VA hospital in the country, and Lomax was a short-haul trucker, he'd formed the habit of dropping in for his exam anywhere in the tri-state area his run happened to take him to at the time. Today he took a run down by car from his home in Youngstown, Ohio. Lomax planned to kill two birds with one stone. He'd have his exam and his son Timmy would get to see the Fort Pitt museum near the tip of the Point.

It was in the maze of streets in the Point, as he was on his way back toward the Ohio-Pennsylvania border, that Lomax realized he and Timmy were surrounded. The crowd had materialized without warning. In hindsight it had to have gathered fairly quickly, yet in a totally unplanned way. Whatever had sparked it, Lomax was soon surrounded by a mob of shouting hooligans and crazed looters, smashing shop windows, overturning parked vehicles, and trying to set whatever would burn on fire. Lomax knew he'd find one of the bridges that crossed the Allegheny River due west. He began driving a twisting course through the confusing labyrinth of streets in the Point, avoiding the larger avenues where the mob ran rampant even if it meant driving the wrong way down one-way streets, always bearing steadily westward, toward the river.

It was near the corner of one of the mobbed-up avenues that he saw the Korean shop owner being hauled out of his convenience store by a bunch of skinheads, one of whom was brandishing a length of clothesline tied into a crude but efficient-looking noose. To Lomax's right the side street was clear, and he could see one of the bridges in the distance. Lomax hesitated as the skinheads tried to fit the noose around the head of their struggling victim.

A moment later he'd told Timmy to get down on the floor beneath the dash and had drawn his .38. Leaning on the horn, Lomax barreled up the street, praying the goons up ahead would have enough smarts to get out of his way. The gunshots fired into the air through the open driver-side window helped persuade them to beat it. In seconds Lomax had pulled to a screeching stop between the skinheads and their victim with the passenger side window powered down and the rear door unlocked.

"Get in the back!" he shouted at the shopkeeper, who wasted no time doing precisely that, the makeshift clothesline noose still draped around his neck. The Korean was dropped off near his home on one of the adjoining side streets free of the mob, and Lomax soon was across the river and into neighboring Ohio, none the worse for wear aside from a shattered rear windshield and part of a swastika that one of the skinheads had tried to spray-paint on the car's trunk. By this time the Pittsburgh police had its riot squad out in force and was in the process of quelling the disturbances that had broken out in the Point.

What Lomax did not know was that a news cameraman in a Channel Seven chopper had captured most of the incident. Several frames from the video feed produced good images of Lomax's face. Within twenty-four hours of the aftermath of the national epidemic of riots, that face was broadcast on nightly news programs across the country.

When Lomax's neighbors phoned the media, he became a national hero and his name a household word. A nation besieged by photos of bearded men bearing apocalyptic messages of doom and ultimatums of destruction longed for a hero. Timothy Lomax suddenly found that he himself was that hero, albeit a reluctant one.

Lomax had no desire for publicity. All he wanted was to get on with his life. He had no desire to be in the public eye or at the center of events. The last thing on earth he'd ever wanted to be was a word, household or otherwise. The media camping out on his doorstep changed all that for Lomax. His paperboy became a celebrity. His mail carrier became a frequent guest on talk shows. His barber, the last man standing on a survival program set on a desert isle.

And though Timothy Lomax tried like hell to hide out and hope it would all go away, the summons from President Travis Claymore to attend an award ceremony at the White House finally made Lomax into a celebrity too. The president himself had phoned Lomax to ask him to attend. Lomax felt he had no other choice except to agree.

When he replaced the phone in its cradle, he looked at his son Timmy Junior.

"Well, Dad," Timmy had asked. "What you going to do?"

"I guess we're both going to Washington, Timmy," Lomax replied.

Ta'lab emerged from the simulator and massaged the cramps from his tired arms and legs. The technicians had made several improvements to the delivery end of the mission since Ta'lab and his comrade, Quzah, had began their training, but the Lords of the Skies were still extremely cramped. Of course, their time spent inside the Baal Samin capsules would be limited, and so they could bear the burden of discomfort for the duration of the mission.

Nevertheless, stress effected performance and the importance of the mission demanded no tolerance for failure. For this reason they had done all humanly possible to make the capsule more bearable.

Unfortunately there was little they could practically do. The design on which the delivery system was based had been taken directly from the only known prototypes in existence, those used by Nazi Germany and Tojo's Japan, and although modified from contemporary sources, could not be greatly changed.

Fuel stores, guidance, the modifications necessary to retrofit the system for human interaction, and the extensive weaponization itself, all prevented more than token improvements. Still, it would have to do, and both Ta'lab and Quzah were prepared to make successful use of what they had been provided with to carry out the mission.

Here was the sun before its rising of the morning. Here was death, winged destruction, directable by the forces of stainless holiness. Those who would speed death on its mission were now fully prepared. They had practiced and drilled, over and over again, until they were no longer human but robotic in programmed thought and action.

In their dreams they saw themselves commit these wonderful, terrible acts, bringing forth the blossoming flames of annihilation, and in their waking moments their prayers to Allah contained and encapsulated these very same dreams. The profiles, outlines, colors, shapes, even the slant of the sun upon their targets, were like afterimages burned into the retinas of the eyes of those who stare too long at the heavenly orb. The images of these future targets were present at all times. They were now at the core or nucleus of their lives.

These two, Ta'lab and Quzah, would fulfill the dream that had been entrusted to their care. They would not falter. Both were top performers. Each sought to outdo the other. They would rest and continue the simulations, again and again.

Soon their targets would be obliterated.

The so-called "terrorists" had turned out to be punks. Wannabees. Since the war against Al Qaeda had begun following the attacks of September 11, 2001, the copycats and wannabees had crawled out of the woodwork. Here was yet another bunch of maggots.

Clinton, whose Task Force Bravo had been alerted by the FBI when the bust had gone down, had been along for the collar and questioning that followed. He had to admit that these were the best pseudo-terrorists he'd seen yet, and he'd seen a few.

They claimed they were from a secret fighting cell that had trained to attack airports across the country. This admission, and the fact that they had been found lurking on the boundaries of Washington National Airport (DCA), four miles from the central District on the lower Potomac, was what had brought Clinton in.

The DIA's special task force had reciprocal agreements with police agencies nationwide under the Homeland Security Department umbrella. Any reports about, or information concerning, terrorist acts to be committed at U.S. military bases or airports, including commercial jetports, were to be directed to the task force.

Although the terrorist training encampment at Salman Pak had been abandoned, the terrorist cadre, including the European and American training staff, was still unaccounted for. It was assumed that cells from this encampment were now at large and preparing for a major strike somehow connected with the extensive geometrical grid patterns on which they had trained, and that these patterns conformed in layout to a military base or airport somewhere in the continental U.S.

But the crew that had been nabbed at DCA turned out to be gangbangers playing some demented game. Clinton listened to the feds' questioning, asked a few questions himself, then realized he had reached another dead end. Clinton still didn't attach credence to the explanation that the lines, rectangles, squares, and circles on the Iraqi desert necessarily meant what the consensus believed it meant. However, since Clinton had no better theory, that's what he had to work with for the time being.

As it turned out, his visit wasn't a total loss. There was a D.C. homicide cop present at the interrogation who wanted to talk to him.

Clinton consented to meet with the cop, whose name was Jackson. Jackson ushered Clinton into a vacant conference room and told him about the case of the murdered little girl.

"I've got to drop the case," Jackson admitted, concluding his brief.

"So why try handing it to me?"

"Because you might be able to do something with it. Here's the deal," Jackson went on. "We—I guess I really mean *I*—have one bonafide suspect. This guy's been seen around the projects a lot. Folks who live there took him for a social worker. At first all there was to go on was a description of the suspect and his car.

"But I got lucky. An automatic camera caught a vehicle matching the description only a short time after the murder. I ran the plates through DMV. Then I staked the guy out."

"Did you question him?" Clinton asked.

"No."

"Why not?"

Jackson laid glossy color surveillance photos on the desk. "This is the perp. Recognize him?"

"Yeah. Sort of. The face is familiar. Connected with the White House, right?"

"Right."

Jackson flipped over the photo. There was a data sheet on the perp taped to its back.

"That's who he is."

"Che infamita."

"What's that mean?"

"That's Italian for oh, shit."

"You sure don't look like no Italian, man."

"I'm not."

"Anyway, now you see my point? I don't want to touch this dude. Not without more than I got. Another thing. This homey's history can be traced back only so far. There's something dirty . . . maybe a better word's spooky . . . about him, if you know what I mean."

"Yeah," replied Clinton. "I get your drift."

But Clinton didn't realize just how dirty or spooky the suspect was, or how close Hammon was to carrying out his assignment. Had he any inkling of all this, he would not have returned home to his family, dinner, and cable TV that night, but gone straight to his office instead. Nor would he have permitted the D.C. Metro detective's tip to fade into the background as other leads were pursued in the coming days and weeks. He would regret this later on, when everything reached the meltdown point.

For the moment Clinton had more important things on his mind.

book three

Against the Habitation of the Strong

Behold, he shall come up like a lion from the swelling of Jordan against the habitation of the strong: but I will suddenly make him run away from her: and who is a chosen man, that I may appoint over her? For who is like me? And who will appoint me the time? And who is that shepherd that will stand before me?

—JEREMIAH 49:19

chapter *sixteen*

Saxon was now back at Lejeune. He would remain at One's operational headquarters for the next week while the trip to Washington was finalized. All the while Saxon hoped he could avoid the ceremony. Others might covet the pomp and circumstance, might crave the international media exposure, but not him.

What's more, Saxon had picked up some bad political storm warnings on the wind. Hardly had he been back in his office at Lejeune than rumors had begun filtering in. The president didn't only want to pin a medal on Saxon's chest—the grapevine had it that the commander in chief wanted to recruit Saxon to serve as chief deputy to White House National Security Advisor Ross Conejo.

This news—which Saxon got from more than one source—immediately put Saxon on his guard. It didn't take a Ph.D. in political science to know that this was exactly the same post in which Oliver North—also a light colonel during the Reagan Administration—had served under then National Security Council honcho Robert C. "Bud" McFarland. The news smacked of another effort by the One-haters to remove Saxon from leadership of Marine Force One, replace him with a unit commander of their own choosing, and then disband One entirely before Saxon's White House tour was over.

Saxon was not a politician or a glad-hander or a would-be media personality. He was a straight-leg, mud-eating dog soldier. That's all he ever had been, that's all he ever aspired to be. Either death in battle or retirement with four stars pinned to his shoulders, those were the only options he considered as being in the cards. And again, White House visits by Marine light colonels could prove disastrous to a career, as that other Marine recruited for duty at the Reagan White House ultimately found out.

If the president asked Saxon to do an Ollie North at the NSC, Saxon would flat out refuse. He didn't want to spend any more time in civilian clothes than he had to. He didn't want to get caught up in White House power politics. He didn't want to work for a Bud McFarland. He didn't want to get mixed up in any kind of high-echelon muck.

Besides all that, he wasn't about to give up the command of the best damn outfit in the U.S. military, Marine Force One. The force was as much Saxon's obsession as it had been the brainchild of General Patient K., who had seen MF-1 through a hundred internecine battles that were legendary at the Pentagon. No way was Saxon about to let himself be eight-balled.

Saxon sat in his office and tried to work it all out in his head. What was going on? If this was a sneak attack on Marine Force One, where was the fire coming from? Saxon didn't have to look too far for the usual suspects. The Office of the Navy and its staff had been fiercely opposed to MF-1 from the beginning, proposing an expanded role for its SEALs instead of the creation of an entirely new formation.

It made no difference that there were some very sound operational and philosophical differences between the SEALs and MF-1. The SEALs were commandos in every sense of the word, while MF-1 was super-infantry. Their skill sets might overlap, but MF-1 and the SEALs were operationally suited to entirely different combat roles. Each had their part to play in the big picture. There should never have been any reservations about One's establishment, although there had been.

Having thought it over, and convinced that he wasn't just being paranoid, Saxon decided to phone his godfather, General Patient K. Kullimore, and lay his concerns and reservations on the general's table. With some luck, Patient K. might be able to turn things around. Saxon picked up the phone and dialed the general at HQMC (Pentagon), keeping his fingers crossed.

* * *

The residents of the city of Suez, which straddles the canal of the same name, turned out to watch the spectacle. The passage of an American carrier battle group through the canal was not an altogether rare event, but neither was it something you saw every day.

U.S. CBGs had several options of reaching the waters of the Arabian Sea, the Gulf of Oman, and the Persian Gulf. These included the Pacific route from bases in California, through the South China Sea, and then through the Straits of Molucca, rounding the Nicobars into the Indian Ocean, of which the Arabian Sea was one of its northern reaches.

Since the mission of the U.S. Navy routinely took its vessels to the four corners of the globe, the Pacific route was as feasible as the Atlantic route that reached the Middle East via the Med. In this case the CBG had already sailed into the Med weeks prior to the orders from CINCPAC directing it to proceed into the Persian Gulf. There it was to conduct highly visible exercises within sight of the shores of Iran, Iraq, and Saudi Arabia, to name but a few of its intended spectators.

Throughout the month of Ramadan, the U.S. warships were to create a noticeable presence in the Gulf region. Although the reason for the orders had been implied rather than stated, the clear intent of the mission was to bolster the Saudi regime against attack by neighboring Arab states. In fact, less than forty-eight hours prior to the instructions to steam from the Med into the Persian Gulf, the Royal House of Saud had contacted the White House with a request that had originated those very orders.

"Your highness, a pleasure," the president had said, scribbling a note to the national security advisor, who flanked his desk in one of the brocade-upholstered chairs that awaited White House visitors. The note asked what time it was in Riyadh, from where the king was phoning. Conejo checked his palmtop, then held up twelve fingers.

"Mr. President," the king went on as the president nodded to the NSA. "I hope that my call finds you in good health.

I also hope that I am not disturbing you at any important time."

"Not at all. I'm all ears."

"That is good, sir," the king went on. "I do have a trifling matter to speak with you concerning. It is not terribly important, I hasten to add. But it is something that you might consider, should it please you to assist my country."

"I'm ready to hear and consider any request you might have to make, your excellency," the president returned.

In the beginning Clayton had found it hard to deal with the devious circumlocutions of Middle Eastern leaders. The Arabs and the Israelis both played the same game. It was something deep in the cultures, this beating around the bush and not getting right to the point, something that dated back to the days of the caravans and the Silk Road. But he'd learned to hear them out and be patient. Eventually they always got to the point, as did King Abdullah after a few more minutes of playing the humble supplicant.

With his throne sitting atop the largest proven petroleum reserves in the world and reserves critical to U.S. energy needs, the king really didn't need to mince his words. Sure, the politeness was refreshing, compared with other national leaders—the Brits, for example, who chewed your ear off in their equally polite but always obstinately blunt way. But at least the British prime minister cut the chatter soon after the preliminaries were over and got straight down to business.

"Mr. President, I thank you for graciously consenting to consider this request, which I might add is an official request from my government to the people of the United States."

"Understood, sir."

Now at last he seemed to be getting to the point.

"Mr. President," the king went on, "our intelligence apparatus has furnished me with compelling evidence of the possibility of the repeat of something like the grave troubles that accompanied the religious observances at the Great Mosque in 1979."

"I'm familiar with them, your excellency."

The president might have added that the CIA-prepared National Intelligence Digest, which he received every morning, had for the last week been full of the same reports. The POTUS assumed his opposite numbers at Two Dzerzhinsky Square, 10 Downing Street, and in other global capitals had read pretty much the same reports.

Knowing this, he already had a good idea of what the king wanted, and in fact the king, citing concern for insurrection at the mosque sponsored by Iran, Iraq, or even local Al Qadr forces operating as secret underground cells, did indeed ask for a United States presence in the Persian Gulf for the duration of the extended holiday.

No *kufr* could set foot in the holy cities of Mecca or Medina, this was true, and so no U.S. troops could actively engage in the defense of the Great Mosque or the Kaaba that it housed in any case. But a carrier group in the Gulf might very nicely persuade those bent on disrupting the services during the holy month that a powerful ally was watching with an interest in maintaining the peace.

The president exchanged further pleasantries and courtesies with the Saudi maximum leader, and the conversation ended with the president promising to phone back later that night (it would be morning in Saudi Arabia by then) with his decision. Both leaders knew that this was merely a formality and that a carrier battle group would quickly be dispatched.

The king knew it because there was—for the time being, at least—a vast sea of oil beneath his throne. The president knew it because he'd already made up his mind to order it done days before, just as he'd known that the king would phone him and ask for it. Forty-eight hours after the phone call, orders had been cut and the CBG had begun to steam out of the Med, and through the locks of the Suez Canal to the delight of many of the Canal Zone's inhabitants.

Many, but not all.

Amid the crowd that lined the locks of the canal, and hidden in concealed places farther inland, scanning the passing ships through powerful binoculars, others witnessed the passage of the battle group through the portal to the Red Sea with alarm, contempt, and hatred. They were agents of Al

Qadr, and they were not at their observation posts merely to pass their idle hours.

They were men on a mission, and each of them had their orders. Some video-recorded the procession. Others snapped photographs. Still others scribbled digital notes on palmtops, and yet others did nothing except carefully scrutinize every aspect of the ships, the weapons visible on board and the sailors moving about on their decks, filing the details away in their heads.

While their activities differed, all of these observers had one thing in common. Each of them would report their findings back to Al Qadr, for analysis and possible action against the Crusader infidel hordes.

King Abdullah, leader of the House of Saud, conducted the customary *majlis* prior to the commencement of the ceremonies that would soon take him from Riyadh, the capital, to Mecca, the holy city. Abdullah, aged beyond his years by the many cares that he entertained, showed the strain that he was under. His face was haggard, his eyes were dull, and his movements lacked their former alertness.

While he was relieved by having received the positive news of the U.S. decision to send one of its mighty carrier forces into the Persian Gulf, he was nevertheless far from convinced that anticipated troubles would be forestalled, either by its presence or anything else. The rot had set in far too deeply by this point.

Saudi Arabia's closely monitored press and servile electronic media gave no hint of the insurrection that roiled beneath the surface of the staid theocracy. Yet even these rigorous domestic controls could not keep the lid on everything now happening.

Though managing to remain a medieval theocracy in many ways, Saudi Arabia was, like it or not, part of a networked world. The Internet could not be censored like its national media. Despite the strictest Saudi suppression measures, news could be secretly broadcast over the Web. Slowly, reports concerning the newest assassination attempt on his highness had begun to leak out, as did the news of wholesale arrests.

Such was the concern of the royal family that none of those condemned had been executed in public as was the general custom. Instead, military executions at remote desert outposts had been conducted by emergency tribunals set up by the Saudi armed forces. The bodies of the condemned had been buried in unmarked desert graves.

The king had been warned not to attend the annual unveiling of the Kaaba—the Black Stone sacred to Islam—at the Great Mosque in Mecca. Despite the extra contingents of military troops—including Pakistani soldiery who would not hesitate to open fire upon Saudi nationals, and were often used by the Saudis as border guards for this reason—and despite the conspicuous presence of the American Navy in the Gulf, the king's advisors had not deemed his appearance advisable.

There was an undercurrent of rumor that bespoke serious trouble ahead. Neither the king's inner circle of counselors, nor he himself, had forgotten the 1979 uprising during Ramadan at the Great Mosque.

Then, hordes of Iranians on *hajj* to Mecca had sparked massive riots.

Within a short time the Great Mosque was taken. Armed gangs of rioters entrenched themselves within the precincts of the mosque and within the labyrinth of tunnels that ran beneath its floor. At one point the mosque and the sacred Black Stone were both in jeopardy of being blown to smithereens by the interlopers. Months of fighting had been necessary to clear the holy site of the last vestiges of the mob. The attempted takeover and fierce struggle to dislodge the Iranians had left the entire kingdom shaken to the core and had sent shock waves rippling through the Muslim Middle East.

Still, the king would not heed his counselors this time. He had decided to go to Mecca, for to remain behind in Riyadh would be to admit the truth behind the rumors of turmoil in the kingdom. He had resigned his fate to Allah. Let his will be done. King Abdullah settled into his chair and took the first of the questions from those who had come to the *majlis*.

When the petitioner stood, produced a small nine-millimeter automatic, and began rapidly firing, the king could only sit in frozen panic, as the trigger was squeezed again and again and the weapon jerked and bucked in the assassin's outstretched hands.

Jackson knew he was on a mission. But he couldn't help himself. He knew he should have just dropped the case. That's the way things worked. You dropped them after a while and you filed them and you pretty much forgot all about them.

What was the point of beating a dead horse? If you didn't make a collar within a reasonable time, then pressure would come down for you to drop that sucker and pick up another case that might net a suspect.

Each department had its own unwritten rules concerning how much time you had, but it boiled down to a formula of manpower vs. caseload multiplied or divided by the twenty-four hours in each day. There was no way to get around it. If the case went unsolved within whatever that period happened to be, it had to be filed and forgotten. And if a cop was dumb enough to get himself caught up in an investigation that was headed nowhere, then that cop probably deserved all the grief that was augured in his tea leaves or the lumps on his head.

Jackson pondered this wisdom even as he did just what he knew he shouldn't be doing, staking out and following the high-profile suspect around Metro D.C. and then out into the Virginia suburbs at the end of the day. He considered this especially stupid considering what his investigation had already turned up concerning the suspect.

Maybe if he hadn't gotten lucky with the DMV's automatic camera images he might have dropped it. Probably would have. But the photos had led to a positive make on the car and this to a make on the driver, who turned out to be a member of the White House staff. This development had given Jackson some sleepless nights.

Once Jackson had ID'd the suspect, and knew his name, he had gone back to his snitch at the projects. It wasn't hard to find old Mose. The codger was in his apartment as usual, chewing on tobacco and working on one of those ships he made in old whiskey bottles.

"What can I do for you, Lieutenant?" he asked with a smile. Jackson knew he'd expect another sawbuck, and he was ready to make his own play.

"That guy you told me you saw the day of the murder. You still remember him, old-timer?"

"Yep. Got me a real fine memory. Remember the first piece of ass I ever had, in fact."

"OK."

The old dude was playing with him, as old dudes sometimes did, but Jackson wouldn't go there.

Instead Jackson pulled the photo of the suspect from his coat pocket. It was a full-face surveillance photo he'd snapped himself with a digital camera on one of his stakeouts, but of another guy. He had two more like it, both ringers.

"This the guy?"

"Nope."

It hadn't taken Mose but a moment to shake his head.

"How about this?"

Jackson showed him the other ringer, getting the same response.

"What about this homey here?"

This time it was the suspect.

"That's your boy, Lieutenant," Mose declared. "No question in my mind."

"Would you be willing to testify to that in court?" asked the cop.

"I'd have to think about that one, Lieutenant," Mose replied immediately.

Jackson gave him some more money and left. Mose had ID'd the suspect without pause or hesitation. He'd make a credible witness too, that sharp old coot. But Jackson knew he'd need more, considerably more to go on, before he could bring his case to the captain and get an arrest warrant so he could make a collar on this particular suspect.

Although there was a murder involved, this was not the first case of vice involving a Foggy Bottom big shot and one of the District's poor black residents, nor would it be the last. There had been plenty of other cases, some that had made the news and resulted in local scandal. In most of them Jackson had seen the guilty party go free or get off with a pro-forma slap on the wrist.

So Jackson had started tailing the suspect, working on his off hours when necessary, neglecting his mounting caseload, hoping for a smoking gun, and telling himself he'd give it up by the next day if he hadn't found it. But the days mounted like the files piling up on his desk and in his computer, and even as Jackson got in deeper and deeper, he began seeing things about the perp—he thought of him as that now—that were convincing him there was more to him than met the eye.

The way he moved around, for example. It was effortless, natural and totally guileless; but Jackson, who was good at surveillance and really hard to spot if he didn't want to be seen, could tell he was dealing with a professional at the game. The perp was extremely careful about his movements despite outward appearances. He varied them a lot, and went where he went via circuitous routes that allowed him to double back and check on pursuit. Here was a guy, Jackson was sure, who was trying to spot a tail wherever he went, just as a natural part of his daily routine.

But why? What would make him so nervous? Sure, if he'd just murdered a little girl in cold blood, that might explain it. But not to the extent that his movements indicated. The perp was on his guard everywhere, all the time. This was an ingrained habit, not just a reaction to recent guilt. Jackson was sure of it.

Jackson was a master of the game too, and while the perp had almost shaken him off on several occasions, Jackson had ended up tailing him to a suburban street on a cul de sac on a rainy day. He had seen the perp park his car, walk over to a mailbox, reach under the mailbox, and take away something that he'd found secreted there.

Jackson had not followed the perp after he had driven away.

Instead he had walked back to his own car, parked several blocks away, gotten in, driven the car to the nearest strip mall, bought a stamped postcard at the postal station there, addressed a brief and mildly obscene love letter to Jennifer Lopez, care of Disney Studios, Hollywood, CA, driven back to the cul de sac, mailed the post card at the letter box, and then driven away again.

In the process Jackson had seen what he had anticipated finding on the letter box. It was a white chalk mark, sort of a right-handed squiggle. Hard to spot unless you looked for it. Meaningless to anybody. Unimportant to anybody.

Unless you happened to be a spy.

Brown eyes ringed with kohl, his splendid robes of many colors shining beneath the klieg lights that illuminated the throne room, the Mahdi prepared to issue the latest of his cyber-*fatwas*.

"Behold, you believers and infidels alike! Behold the hand of Allah and the wondrous majesty of his works! Praise Allah, worker of miracles, maker of wonders, righter of wrongs! Let the wicked tremble! Let the righteous rejoice!"

The Mahdi smiled and stroked his long black beard with spidery, bejeweled fingers. Then he pursed his lips and went on.

"Your leaders tell you that I am dead. They proclaim, these deluded ones, from their judgment seats of false righteousness, that their armed might has triumphed over the sanctity of the faithful.

"I ask you, believers and unbelievers alike, do I appear to you now as a ghost? Is he who speaks to you now a corpse rotting in the grave? Or is he a man of blood and flesh, brought back to the world of the living by the power of Allah?"

The Mahdi fell silent. He gestured. From off-camera a *mujaheed* in black turban and flowing *shalwar qameez* appeared bearing a tray laden with fruit, pastries, wild honey in silver serving dishes, and other assorted delicacies. The camera panned back to a wider angle. The Mahdi selected a bunch of dark purple grapes, and plucked a few from the bunch. For the next several minutes he made a show of chewing and swallowing the grapes that he leisurely popped into his mouth.

"See that I eat, thou believers and unbelievers alike. See that I have returned unharmed to walk among the living. To enjoy the savory fruits of Allah's bountiful blessings. To carry out Allah's unchallengeable will. For he who Allah has given a destiny to follow cannot be harmed by the bloody hand of the infidel, not even with all the weapons of the unbelievers' technology at their disposal."

The Mahdi now reached for a shank of lamb, took it from the platter, and lustily tore strips of hot, steaming meat from the bone with his teeth. When he had chewed these at a leisurely pace and downed water poured from a jeweled golden ewer into a chalice of cunningly chased silver, the Mahdi concluded his *fatwah*.

"Be thou warned, oh, believers and unbelievers alike, that the wrath of Allah has waxed full, and will soon strike down those who do not heed him. Number the days, thou wicked, for before long you shall see the wrath of heaven descend upon you, and the fires of hell rise to consume you. Then will you cry out for Allah's mercy, but it will be too late. Repent yourselves now or risk the vengeance that fast approaches."

The Mahdi once more fell silent. Again he reached toward the serving platter resting on the low sideboard by his throne. Now he brought a live dove from the platter, its wings clipped, its beak and legs bound. A small American flag had been draped around the bird's neck. Smiling broadly, the Mahdi stroked the dove's soft, feathered head. Then, in a single motion, he savagely twisted and snapped the harmless creature's neck in two. As the image dissolved, the Mahdi glared into the camera, his burning eyes the last thing viewers would see before the screen went dark.

chapter *seventeen*

The would-be assassin of the Saudi king had failed in his mission. As he shouted "Death to the apostate!" and fired, one of the king's bodyguards launched himself into space, knocking aside the Saudi ruler. The bullets intended for Abdullah slammed into the brocade back of the throne upon which he sat.

Having failed in his bid to eliminate his target, the gunman next tried to martyr himself with a blast to his own temple. Unfortunately for him the weapon misfired, and he was brought down by the crowd attending the *majlis*.

The next task of the king's security staff was to prevent the crowd from tearing the appointed killer limb from limb.

On recovering consciousness in a guarded room on a sealed-off floor of the King Faisal Specialist Hospital in Riyadh, the assassin underwent preliminary questioning. The fact that the intravenous stacks not only bulked up his arteries with glucose solution, but also injected a steady flow of a painkilling barbiturate mixture that had effects similar to truth serum, helped loosen his tongue.

Unfortunately, there wasn't much the shooter was able to tell his questioners. Saudi security and police already knew the shooter's identity: Haseeb Azzam, a Riyadh native who lived in one of the poorer subdivisions west of the downtown section. They knew Azzam's religion too: Shiite, but this also had been suspected.

The ultra-orthodox Wahabi branch of Sunni Islam practiced by the house of al-Saud, and the official religion of the kingdom, looked down upon the large Shiite minority in its midst. In Saudi Arabia, Shiites, who occupied the lowest strata of society, made up a restive underclass opposed to the ruling regime. It was from the ranks of Saudi Shiites that the first cells of the Hamas terrorist organization had been recruited in the early 1980s, followed later on by conscripts to the nascent Al Qaeda.

The investigators didn't find out much more, though. Unfortunately for them, they had suspected as much too. While drugged, the gunman revealed that he had belonged to a Mahdist fighting cell, revealed the location of the safe house used by the cell to meet and to plan its operations, also revealed the names of most if not all of the other members of the cell. Beyond that Azzam revealed nothing, because he had nothing more to reveal.

The investigators had little doubt that when they raided the safe house it would have already been vacated, and that when they rounded up Azzam's fellow conspirators, they too would have little to offer by way of useful intelligence. Only the upper echelons of the Al Qadr power structure knew the big picture, and they were far out of the reach of anyone in the kingdom, or elsewhere.

In the case of Azzam, the investigators' hunch was right on target. The shooter's drug-induced confession got them absolutely nowhere. Even as he lay recovering from his injuries in the hospital room, Azzam was sentenced to death by royal decree.

Less than two weeks later his head would be cut off in the traditional public execution ground on Dira Square between Riyahd's downtown mosque and the tall clock tower at the center of the plaza. Such beheadings generally took place after noon prayers on Fridays and always attracted a sizable crowd of Riyadhis. In the meantime, the Saudi security service would be put to work making more arrests.

At a secret location in the northern Iranian desert, the Dasht-e-Kavir, the two Tu-22 Tupolev Blinder-A jet bomber aircraft were brought out of their hiding places.

The airstrip had been carefully prepared over the last several months. Experts recruited from the cast-off brain trust of the former Soviet Union, skilled in the operational art the

Red Army had called *maskirovka,* had gone to work to create an elaborate deception scheme.

A site selected for a natural cavern system that ran beneath the desert crust had been enlarged into a concealed underground hangar spacious enough to berth and service two medium-range jet bombers.

While the excavation progressed below, construction crews installed a pneumatically controlled access hatch above the sloping entrance to the bunkers. The hatch, made of a sandwich of reinforced concrete and structural steel, was visually, thermally, and magnetically camouflaged from all known overhead imaging and surveillance systems flown or orbited by the U.S.

Since these were the best, they were the only ones that really counted. If the U.S. sensors could be spoofed, then it was a given that those of the Russians, or commercially operated satellites, would also be deceived. Surface crews topped this immense access hatch with thousands of cubic tons of sand, rock, and vegetation that had been carefully removed from the site and just as carefully replaced.

They worked during slack times when no satellite coverage was known to be over the area. Those in the Iranian, Iraqi, and Libyan security services in charge of knowing those things had paid extremely well for the satellite coverage intel and the intel was judged highly reliable. Nor did their agents in place detect any U.S. reaction to the construction project after the fact, bolstering the credibility of the intel.

The months of planning and hard work had paid off. Now, as the Strike Day that had been the object of so much sacrifice, planning, and labor finally arrived, everything was ready. The two retrofitted Tupolev jet bombers were taking on full loads of fuel, more than sufficient reserves necessary to fly the history-making mission.

While fuel was taken on, the bombers' avionics systems were being checked by technicians as the pilots and aircrew went over their respective preflight checklists. Everything seemed to indicate that the mission would be a go.

As the high-octane jet propulsion fuel flowed into the

planes' storage tanks, still other technicians used specially modified bomb-loaders to equip each of the twin aircraft with single missiles. These munitions superficially resembled U.S. long-range cruise missiles, except for a variety of modifications to the hulls and solid-fuel propulsion systems that would turn them into weapons far more lethal than their original builders had ever intended.

The technicians handled their charges carefully. They were irreplaceable, one-of-a-kind munitions. There were no backups and there could be no mishaps. They worked with total focus and complete diligence, knowing that any slipups could spell their deaths.

There were no mistakes. Soon the aging jet bombers, originally of Soviet manufacture, were fully fueled and fully loaded with their munitions cargos. All aircrew of the two Tupolevs had checked off every item on their preflight manifests and had programmed their flight vectors, including way-points and the initial points for ordnance release, into onboard navigational computer systems.

Now, beneath the cover of darkness, the camouflaged access hatch slowly and noiselessly retracted into the desert floor to reveal the yawning black rectangle of empty space below. All lights in the bunker complex had been extinguished and crews worked with the aid of night-vision goggles.

When the hatch was fully retracted, electric tugs slowly pulled the two bombers, one after the other, up the grade of the gently sloping ramp to the surface. Here too, crews working with NVG support were busy at their own appointed tasks. The crews were handpicked military engineers, sworn to secrecy.

Manning graders and bulldozers, some prepared the desert floor as a makeshift runway for the Tupolevs. Trailing behind these, others inserted infrared strobes into the hard-packed desert crust to mark the boundaries of the clandestine runway. After the bombers took off, these would be removed and the desert floor sanitized.

Every facet of the operation proceeded smoothly. Within a short time the bombers were on the surface, their turbine engines powering up. At the signal to take off, the pilots pulled back their throttles, set flaps, and increased thrust. The howl of the maxed turbines now filled the desert night.

Those on the ground watched as the planes sped forward, reached the limits of the runway, then rotated into belly-up ascent postures and rapidly climbed to the first stage of their outbound flights. Within seconds nothing except blue wing lights, faint as distant stars, were visible against the black, moonless sky. Even the last echoes of the thundering turbines had died away by now, and soon even these harbingers of imminent destruction were gone as well.

Other things would also disappear forever. Among these would be the crews that had served so loyally the cause of their nation. The Iraqi *sai'qa*—commandos—had inserted clandestinely by helo as the final preparations were made. None of the engineer crews had noticed their arrival. They had come in secret, like dark angels, death's heads beneath their cowls.

Within minutes of the takeoff, the *sai'qa* began executing every living thing on the ground and below it with bursts from their silenced automatic weapons. When single shots to the head of each victim guaranteed that their work was complete, the hatch above the underground hangar was re-closed and permanently sealed. Nothing but the night wind and the undisturbed sand remained as the *sai'qa*'s helos lifted off again, moving westward, toward Iraq, in the same direction that the bombers had flown.

The Oval Office occupies the West Wing of the White House. It overlooks the Rose Garden. It is where the president meets with his advisors, poses for the press corps, and conducts much of his official business.

But the Oval Office is a small room by comparison to other chambers in the presidential mansion. The Blue Room, like the Oval Office, is also ovoid in shape, but is considerably larger and much more comfortably appointed for the reception of visitors.

The Green Room, adjoining the Oval Office, is also sometimes used for this purpose. But above the Oval Office, on the White House's topmost story, is the Yellow Oval Room. It's larger, better-lit, and has a better view of the presidential mansion's North Lawn. It was here that the sitting president, Travis Claymore, preferred to receive important visitors.

And so it was that Lieutenant Colonel David Saxon, who had not been able to avoid a meeting with the POTUS after all, now stood as the president entered the room and shook hands with those in attendance. Saxon, dressed in his A-uniform bearing the globe and anchor of the USMC and the number 1 on his right shoulder patch, was uncomfortable in these exalted surroundings. He couldn't recall the last time he'd worn a tie—One didn't do much parading. But there he was, tie and all.

Flanking Saxon were a lot of VIPs. Some he recognized. There was the vice president, the secretary of defense, the national security advisor, and the secretary of state from the civilian side.

From the ranks of the military had been drawn the Marine commandant and General Patient K., who, HQMC aside, had personally ordered Saxon to attend. Saxon's refusal wasn't an option. He was attending as a Marine and as a 1-Patcher. To stay away would be to dishonor the Corps and the unit he commanded. Saxon had to keep the appointment. Patient K. had made it clear that there would be no wiggle room here.

There were others in attendance too. Saxon had been introduced to a civilian whose face he'd recognized from the media. Timothy Lomax was the hero of the Pittsburgh Oil Riot. Lomax and Saxon shook hands, and this immediately sparked a flurry of flashbulbs. The *Washington Times* would plan to give the photo-op several column inches in that day's evening edition.

After the ceremony, picture editors selected the shot of the Marine light colonel and the First Gulf War veteran shaking hands, Saxon's regular Wasp features in counterpoint to Lomax's African-American profile. It was the kind of symbolism of unity that the editorial board wanted to promote

against a sea of hostile America-haters and Americans dis-
satisfied with the status quo alike.

Unfortunately that picture would never make the front
page. It was destined to be displaced by breaking global
events that would rivet the nation's attention for a long time
to come. The two heroes who met during that brief photo-
op in the Yellow Oval Room would also make the news, but
in a way that none had ever expected or could have predicted.

At the Pentagon they had a word for it as they did for a
lot of things. In Pentagonese it was a BFO, which stood
for a blinding flash of the obvious.

It was the BFO that hit Bill Clinton like a ton of bricks
that wound up making the crucial difference on Strike Day.
Clinton had received the prospectus for a condominium con-
version of a warehouse in Alexandria he was considering
buying into.

His posting to Washington, D.C., would be semi-
permanent. The property might prove valuable as an invest-
ment even if he were transferred. Clinton was sipping an iced
Coke when he skipped to the architectural drawings of the
floor plan of the individual units.

Something clicked in his mind. In his mind's eye there
was a juxtaposition of the squares, lines, and rectangles that
made up the geometrical patterns of the imagery taken from
the desert floor of Iraq to the architectural drawings now in
front of him.

Could it be that they had been wrong all along? he wondered. Clinton and the task force staff had considered the
possibility of the geometrical patterns applying to an architectural structure, but had rejected this interpretation early
on.

One reason was the inclusion, in the exercises taking
place, of commando preparations for storming commercial
aircraft. Another was the flat two-dimensionality of the dia-
grammatic figures themselves.

It seemed obvious and intuitively correct that the schematic outlines represented an airport and that the planned attacks fit the pattern of a commando-style terrorist strike on a major air terminal, commercial or military. This interpretation was bolstered by the testimony of the convicted terrorist, Nazir Hamadi, who was captured in 2002 before carrying out a strike on Chicago Midway Airport and had revealed plans to destroy still other major airports in the U.S. in coming years.

But what if the mock attacks on jet aircraft practiced at Salman Pak were actually diversions, diversions deliberately intended to confuse orbital surveillance and ensuing intelligence analysis?

What if the aircraft served as training surrogates for something else—something resembling the interior of a passenger cabin of a commercial jetliner. Something with aisles, seats. And in those seats, instead of air travelers, there were . . .

And what if the paradigm that intelligence analysis had developed was entirely wrong? What if the intelligence data that Task Force Bravo had been studying was actually a kind of code or cipher, only a cipher in three dimensions?

What if the series of activities that Bravo had believed to be set up as a sequence of training exercises was not sequential at all? Instead, what if each group conducting commando exercises at Salman Pak were rehearsing separate phases of a coordinated strike, phases that could be linked together during the actual assault; linked like modules, strung together like beads on a chain . . .

What if what they had believed was a jigsaw puzzle was really three-dimensional chess?

What if someone very clever had set them up?

Someone very bold too. Like Wolfram Krieger, the rogue NOC who had deliberately exposed himself to satellite surveillance at Salman Pak while executing two suspected traitors. Krieger had been well aware that he'd shown enough of his face for biometric matching to confirm his identity, but he hadn't cared. That meant he'd wanted to be known as the executioner of the U.S. intelligence assets.

Clinton stopped what-iffing and set down the glass of Coke. His hands had suddenly gotten clammy in the palm.

He felt like someone had just walked over his grave. He had a hunch that he knew what the actual target of the commandos might actually turn out to be. He got into his car and headed back to his office.

On the way he pulled out his cell phone and made a few fast calls. He wanted his staff assembled and ready to work.

The ominous sense that a clock was ticking and the second hand was approaching the zero mark dogged Clinton as he backed out of the garage into a rain-drenched morning. His tires made a sizzling sound as he pulled out of the black-topped driveway of the rented A-frame house. It struck him that it was like the sound that a lit fuse made, burning down to a bundle of dynamite.

chapter *eighteen*

Jackson's shirt was drenched. So were his Jockeys. Part of that was from the pores; the rest from nature calling in its markers after three pots of black coffee drunk to keep him awake. Protocols demanded that the feds be brought in at this point in the investigation, and once the feebs came marching in they tended to take over the show. That's precisely what had happened. Arrests had been made under federal warrants. Jackson now stood on the sidelines as agents from Justice and the FBI interrogated one of the suspects.

But Jackson hadn't given the feds everything in his kit bag. There were leads in this case he still planned to run down by himself for the time being. Having eyeballed the suspect servicing a dead drop, Jackson had called in some markers. Jackson's access privileges on the Metro computer system stopped at data rated classified by the government. The deeper he probed into the suspect's past, the more "Access Denied" messages began cropping up. Jackson knew he needed a way around the system.

In order to get into the databases of federal law enforcement agencies, he would require the joss of higher-ups. This meant a lot of red tape, a lot of paperwork, a lot of questions, and a lot of resistance. Jackson knew that when the time came, he would need to fast-track it. This is just what he did.

Metro's intelligence division occupied office space in a separate building on F Street. It possessed discrete, dedicated computer links to federal databases. Those links connected it directly with the spooks. The listing on the lobby directory gave no indication that the occupant of a suite of fifth-floor offices had any connection to D.C. Metro, no indication that it was anything besides the back office of another business concern in a building full of them.

Jackson had helped one of the division honchos out of a tight spot two years before. Eddie Conklin owed him one. It was time to pay up. Jackson had phoned from his cell on the way over. Conklin was expecting him.

Jackson laid it all out to Conklin in his office. The little girl's murder, how he'd linked the suspect to the crime, the homicide detective's trailing the perp to the dead drop, the whole nine yards. Conklin listened, nodding at times.

"Come on," he finally said. "We'll check it out."

Jackson was ushered into a vaulted room accessible only via a cipher-locked steel door that opened onto a small vestibule monitored by an armored security cam, followed by a second cipher-locked door. On the other side of door two was a large room in which personnel with name tags pinned to their shirts were busy at computer terminals, banks of phones, and printers spitting out streams of telexes, hard copy and faxes.

Conklin logged Jackson in at the security desk near the door and handed him a yellow-coded visitor's pass. His was blue.

"Where you are now has got a history. This used to be the D.C. headquarters of Centac. Ever hear of it?"

"Yeah. They were a counter-drug organization."

"Much more than that. Centac tracked global narco-conspiracy. It used RICO statutes to prosecute global criminal organizations. The FBI inherited this infrastructure. We got it from the feds."

"What happened to Centac?"

"The feds disbanded it. Centac made a lot of people in law enforcement look like assholes. It did too good a job, made a lot of enemies. But the important thing's we inherited its database. Not even the NSA had some of the information Centac had.

"Because of this we were able to do some horse-trading. We told the spooks, 'We show you ours if you show us yours.' The upshot is that Metro intel has a periscope up everybody's rectum. We can look into the bowels of the Jus-

tice Department, CIA, NSA. See all, know all. We're proc-
tologists to the whole fucking world."

Conklin led Jackson over to an unoccupied workstation,
told him to sit, and logged onto the system.

"Let's do a proctological workup on your asshole."

He meant the suspect, Jackson figured. He wasn't wrong.

Conklin began to compile a digital dossier on Jackson's
suspect, working his way backward from his current
whereabouts to the earliest data concerning him. The recent
data, including a set of three-sided Bertillon photos, finger-
prints, IRS income information, and all the rest, were readily
available.

The data showed nothing new, nothing Jackson had not
already been able to find out for himself. The suspect was a
highly regarded professional with a distinguished career history. He lived in a renovated Tudor-style home in Fairfax
County, Virginia. He drove a late-model import. He had no
arrest record. His lifestyle was in perfect keeping with his
annual salary. A Vietnam War veteran, who had been dec-
orated with both the Silver Star and the Purple Heart, he was
now a key member of the White House staff in a position of
extreme respectability.

Nothing there to indicate he was also a child molester,
murderer, and foreign intelligence operative.

"Let's dig deeper," Conklin suggested. "But this could
take me a while. You got any idea how many friggin' databases I can search? Then there's servers that might not be
on-line right now, network slowdowns, all kinds of shit. This
could take days."

"It's early yet."

"Suit yourself."

But it didn't take days, or even many hours. Less than an
hour later the suspect's sterling patina had flaked off like
gold plating on an obscene statue. Under the missing patches
they were beginning to see unpleasant things.

In two hours—it would have been faster if not for a
crashed server at Interpol HQ in Brussels, necessitating an
overseas phone call and fax—the gold plating was almost
completely stripped away. Beneath the golden Apollo there'd

been a phantasm with horns, cloven hoofs, and a forked tail.
    Hammon.
    After trips to the bathroom, Conklin and Jackson grabbed
coffee and sandwiches in the intel division's small cafeteria,
tucked away in a room off the main operations space. Over
the small pastel-veneer table they went over what they'd
found out.
    "So this guy goes down in a chopper crash in Nam. He's
supposedly captured by the NVA. The rest of his crew is
never recovered and are presumed dead. But about a month
later he walks out of the jungle and collapses in front of a
squad of Army Rangers. His story is he's been making like
Rambo for the last week in the bush, after having escaped
from a ville where the VC held him while moving him north,
presumably up the Ho Chi Minh Trail.
    "He's decorated with the Silver Star and Purple Heart for
this. He comes back to the world, okay? Now he's back in
Baltimore with the wife and kid—not incidentally a little girl
about the same age as the victim—what, about a month,
right? And then, lo and behold, his two loved ones perish in
an unfortunate highway accident. Our boy is miles away at
the time, coincidentally.
    "Years go by. We're now in the last year of the Carter
Administration. Our man is now very busy in the Middle
East. He's working for one of the Seven Sisters as a security
specialist. He spends a lot of time in Saudi, a lot of time in
Libya. Then Qaddafi kicks all the Americans out of Libya.
This is early eighties. Our man is one of them. He never
goes back. Not to Libya anyway. But he travels a lot. Germany. Morocco. Paris. Rome. He goes on foreign vacations.
Nothing wrong with that. Doesn't effect his security clear-
ance. In fact, when he moves into his current job, the traveling helps him do it, gives him just the right background
for his work."
    "And he's now doing a lot more traveling than ever be-
fore," Jackson put in.
    "Right. On-the-job travel. A lot of it. But it gets you think-
ing. It's all circumstantial. He might be a sleeper. He might

be the Ghost of Christmas Past. He might be anybody or anything."

"But I saw the drop."

"Exactly. You saw the drop."

"And if we stake the drop out. Who knows?"

"Right. Who knows. Fuckin' Santa could piss down the chimney."

Conklin finished the sandwich. He had enough juice with the police commissioner to go over the head of Jackson's boss, if necessary, but he'd lay it on him anyway to satisfy department protocols. He'd also bring the feds in; he'd have to now that it might be a national security matter. Conklin hit the phones. Bells soon began to ring all over Washington.

A joint FBI-Metro force had staked out the dead drop that Hammon had last used. With any luck, they believed, they might catch the opposition's field agents servicing the drop prior to the next pickup.

It didn't happen right away, but it did ultimately happen. In the end they arrested two Libyan nationals, one who was placing a coded message in a magnetized capsule beneath the mailbox, the other waiting in a nearby car. Both had diplomatic immunity and wouldn't say a word.

But Hammon didn't have diplomatic immunity. And the morning of Strike Day was the morning that Jackson and an FBI field agent, armed with a federal bench warrant, were on their way to the White House to take him in for questioning.

Inside the first Baal Samin, named for the Mesopotamian Lord of the Skies, Ta'lab felt the familiar sense of weightlessness as he fell through the open bomb-bay doors and plummeted into empty space. Behind the Plexiglas cockpit bubble he heard the wind shriek like something wounded and enraged.

Then the solid-fuel engine automatically ignited and a deafening roar filled the cramped cockpit, blotting out the keening of the high-altitude winds with its man-made thunder. A steady shudder now filled the entire airframe, trans-

mitting itself up the bones of Ta'lab's skeleton and almost
making his teeth chatter. He kept his jaw clenched, as he had
learned to do from the many hours of simulator training, and
focused on the controls on the console before him, the joystick to his right, and the mission that lay ahead.

Only seconds had passed since he had fallen from the Tupolev's underbelly, but already Ta'lab had traveled far from
the larger and much slower aircraft. He craned his head to
seek it out there in the night skies, but it was long gone,
swiftly heading back toward a landing site whose location
he had not been privy to due to the security compartmenta-
tion of the operation.

Besides, he did not care. His role was to function as an
instrument of divine vengeance. What others did with him
while using him in that role was of no consequence.

He was content to be their willing tool, as others before
him had been, including those righteous martyrs who had
destroyed the World Trade Center and part of the Pentagon
on September 11th. All he prayed for was the chance to
surpass them in the extent of destruction he would cause the
unclean enemy.

The images that now came unbidden to his mind reminded
him of the thirst for vengeance he would soon slake. Ta'lab
again saw his young brothers, wounded in American air
strikes on Baghdad long ago, again watched them slowly die
of their wounds, septicemia, and lack of medical treatment,
again felt the helplessness and the rage, again recalled the
vow he had then sworn to repay the dogs in their own coin
who had rained down their bombs and forgotten the inno-
cents they had murdered.

It would not be much longer, he knew.

The crude cockpit of the converted air-launched cruise
missile in which he sat using rudimentary aeronautical controls had no radar or FLIR. The technicians that had converted the American standoff-range missile that had been
retrieved from the wreckage of the crashed B-1B Lancer
bomber had only been able to shoehorn so many refinements
into the retrofit.

The Baal Shamin's rudder controls were muscle-power

controls linked to external control surfaces. Cockpit instru-
mentation was limited to an altimeter, compass, and a digital
clock showing elapsed time to target. Finally, there was a
red button on the console. When depressed, it would activate
a five-second timer that would detonate the fuel-air explosive
charge that took up most of the seven feet worth of fuselage
trailing behind him. He did not know it, but the payload of
jellied incendiary would have been near-worthless had not
Iraq received the electronic detonation timers known as Col-
umbine Heads that Wolfram Krieger had transferred to Al
Qadr cutouts on a windy mountain in Dubai.

Ta'lab was about to stage the first kamikaze attack on an
American warship since the Pacific theater of World War
Two. His target was to be the heart of the CBG that was
now steaming down the Red Sea toward the straits of Bab
el-Mandeb between Yemen and Ethiopia, through which the
battle group would traverse into the Arabian Sea en route to
the Persian Gulf.

The nuclear aircraft carrier *Dwight D. Eisenhower,* and
many of the other vessels that made up the carrier task force,
would never pass through the straits. Instead, ships and men
would go down to a watery grave at the mouth of this portal
into the Arabian Sea, and the wrecks would serve as a permanent memorial to America's impotence in the face of the
power of Islamic *jihad.* Osama bin Laden had shown them
how to do it. He had sent a little boat to destroy the frigate
Cole years before. Now a far greater American warship
would come to an ever darker fate: the *Eisenhower* was to
be at the epicenter of the blast.

At the speed it was traveling from the initial point at which
the Tupolev had released it, the Baal Samin soon came
within visual range of its target. Through the night-vision
goggles he wore, Ta'lab now received visual confirmation of
his target. At this point he knew that he was ultimately
doomed no matter what.

Although he had no threat-identification radar, it was certain that he had already been detected by early-warning radars forming a hemispheric electronic detection shield
around the carrier force, including those from the EA-6B

Prowler electronic intelligence aircraft that flew in a figure-eight track around the CBG.

Without a doubt F/A-18 Hornets flying combat air patrols had been alerted to the intrusion and had scrambled to intercept the incoming missile. The Tupolev had been equipped with jamming equipment, but there had never been any question of the bomber aircraft being of great effect against the counter-countermeasures capabilities of a U.S. carrier group.

No. What would enable Ta'lab to reach and annihilate his target was the speed and stealthiness of the Baal Samin. Its solid-fuel rocket engine propelled it forward at supersonic velocity, while its fuselage shape and small size relative to a conventional manned aircraft gave it an extremely small radar cross-section. Computer projections showed that given these factors the mission could work. Ta'lab knew in his heart that he would carry it out successfully.

A dime-sized point of yellow-white light suddenly appeared on his left visual hemisphere. In moments it had expanded to silver-dollar size, then to the size of an automobile hubcap. Ta'lab responded quickly. He knew what the glowing disk signified and heralded. One of the Hornets had launched a missile, probably a Sidewinder. The disk was its exhaust contrail, viewed from a forward angle, growing larger as the missile approached, jinking and turning to mirror his maneuvers. Ta'lab remained calm. The simulations had prepared him for this eventuality. He knew he could meet the challenge, defeat the threat.

Ta'lab jinked the Baal Samin and changed altitude, invoking the evasive maneuvers he had practiced until he practically rehearsed them in his sleep. Moments later the Sidewinder whose exhaust contrail had alerted him to its presence shot past only a few feet above the al-Sharq's fuselage. A heartbeat later it burst into a dazzling explosion somewhere in the indigo western sky.

Ta'lab saw yet another two missile contrails wink into existence, and knew that more weapons had been fired at him. But this had been anticipated as he reached the inner ring of the concentric circles he envisioned as the final lethality envelope surrounding the CBG, and he knew precisely what actions to take. Jinking again, he dropped the manned missile even lower, so low that its underfuselage almost skimmed the surface of the waves.

Flying this low down on the deck, he knew that electronic surface clutter would render even missiles with the most advanced search-and-track systems ineffective. He was not wrong. Twin shock waves, one following a second after the other, soon buffeted the hurtling Baal Samin, but Ta'lab was untouched and still remained on course to target. The compressed airflow beneath the al-Sharq's wings and underfuselage that pilots call surface effect, even helped boost his speed.

Directly ahead of him Ta'lab could now see the amidships portion of the *Eisenhower*'s vast hull. The *fidayeen* was now well inside the carrier's projected lethality envelope. Nothing could prevent him from succeeding now, he knew.

Aware of the Baal Samin and the grave threat it posed, the *Eisenhower* was now attempting to turn and steam out of range. Let it try, thought Ta'lab. It could no longer escape its fate and his long-delayed vengeance.

Phalanx deck guns, their search-track radars tuned to the signatures of missile-sized objects like Baal Samin, were now also firing at the incoming missile. Let them fire, thought Ta'lab. Nothing would stop him from riding the pale horse of death down the throat of the infidel oppressor.

Ta'lab depressed the red console arming button and kept his hand steady on the control joystick, laughing at the glowing lines of white twenty-millimeter tracers that burst toward him across the face of the black waters.

In seconds the martyrdom he had trained for had become accomplished fact. Flame and death engulfed the predawn darkness, and in his final instant of life the new *shaheed* believed he saw fragments of the shattered *Eisenhower* explode like pinwheels into space.

S ecret Service agent John Mulderig watched the Marine delegation leave the Yellow Oval Room. The Marines were on their way to the Capitol, where they were to meet with Senate members of the Armed Services Committee who would present them to the Congress.

Mulderig, chief of White House security, was pleased by their imminent departure. It meant fewer persons to take notice of during the concluding twenty minutes of the ceremony. Mulderig was a veteran of the Secret Service. Presidents and their families during the last two Administrations had been protected on his watch.

Apart from his duties, Mulderig also liked and genuinely admired the current president. The PUTSO—that was how Mulderig liked to think of him, inverting the characters of the acronym POTUS that stood for president of the United States—was a man after his own heart. A regular guy who could appreciate a good joke. Mulderig knew that because the president had shared a couple of real dirty ones on more than one occasion with him. That was the president, thought Mulderig. A great guy, and a respected statesman.

Which was why it would be too bad that the president had to die. Maybe not today. Maybe not tomorrow. But soon. And for the rest of eternity.

Too bad also that Mulderig was the one about to kill him.

Unfortunately Mulderig, who had been a sleeper agent for a succession of paymasters under the code name Hammon for decades, had been given his orders. He had also been assured of a small fortune and, if necessary, a new, and third, identity—since he was not actually John Mulderig, but a turncoat named Birch Medlo who had originally assumed the dead Huey crewman's identity on KGB orders—after the execution had been carried out.

And since he had been given the weapon and the basic scenario, it was a question of when, not how, the deed would be done. He would waste the fucker. That much was a given.

Hammon's new handler had made it clear that the president was to die by some means that could be considered natural. His death was to be trumpeted as a divine punishment for his sins against Allah, the Mahdi's brave freedom fighters, and several other deserving martyrs to the cause; proof of the iniquities of America. Most of all, the PUTSO's death would serve as justification of the terrible vengeance that the Mahdi's forces were to exact on the United States on Strike Day. For this reason Hammon had been provided with a weapon that dispensed untraceable and nearly instantaneous death.

The fountain-pen-shaped weapon could be quickly fitted with a molded plastic pistol grip. Touching its muzzle anywhere to the victim's body and depressing the trigger would quickly and unobtrusively inject the bio-engineered virus into the target's bloodstream. The victim would die within minutes. It would appear to be a sudden heart attack by massive cardiopulmonary congestion. The virus itself would not be traceable. It could even be made to look, if need be, as if the president had choked on a pretzel.

The U.S. president's death could come before, during, or after Strike Day. The choice was up to Hammon. The sleeper agent would bide his time and pick his spot. Now that he had received his instructions, he would find the precise moment to use the weapon.

Within six months he would be able to take early retirement. Hammon would opt for this, and settle down to a comfortable life, a life he had seen led by the wealthy patricians whom he had served while he stood by like a faithful watchdog, ready to bark, spring, and bite at their beck and call.

But in a short while Hammon was to discover that he was wrong about the bright future awaiting him. His plans were in fact about to change, and his options were about to zero out. The president was now shaking hands with Lomax, the hero of the Pittsburgh Oil Riot, and camera strobes were flashing.

At that moment, the phone rang. An aide went to answer it, spoke for a moment, glanced Hammon's way. He then punched a button on the desktop communications console and walked with a briskness that masked an effort to inconspicuously control his agitation toward where the president stood.

The aide then whispered in the president's ear. Both of them now looked at Hammon. In that instant Hammon realized that he had been burned, that his cover had been blown, that the game was suddenly over. Moments later the door opened and two men entered. One was white, the other was black. Both were cops. It was written all over them, in their faces, their movements, and especially on the gold shields on their jackets.

Hammon was about to go down. And he knew he *would* go down, one way or another. Either for killing the little girl or for espionage. He now had no choice in the matter. His options had run completely out. This was crystal clear. But he would not go down without taking his target down with him. That much was also a certainty. That much he could do. Right now.

Hammon drew his service pistol, took aim at the president's face, and began pumping nine-millimeter bullets into the nearby target as fast as he could jerk the weapon's trigger.

chapter *nineteen*

The United States Capitol was constructed to be symbolic of the people of the United States. It is a monument to the concept that the will of the American people is paramount, and that nothing may supersede it.

In recognition of this fact, federal law forbids any structure in the immediate vicinity, save the Washington Monument, to rise above the Capitol, and building heights within a square mile are limited to 130 feet to insure that the Capitol can be seen from as far away as possible.

The Capitol forms the centerpiece of the Federal Triangle, an architectural trinity created by the Capitol, the Washington Monument, and the White House. Constitution and Pennsylvania Avenues form the two long sides of the triangle, the latter leading directly from the White House to the Capitol. The base of the triangle is formed by the west bank of the Potomac River.

Between the Capitol and the Washington Monument stretches the Mall, a grassy expanse lined on either side by the Smithsonian Institution buildings. On Capitol Hill, to either side of the Capitol, stand the House of Representatives and Senate office buildings. Behind the Capitol on either corner are the Library of Congress and the Supreme Court, buildings whose classic facades give them a deliberate resemblance to the temples of ancient Greece and Rome.

It might be argued that this triangular wedge of real estate represents, symbolically and architecturally, the heart of the United States of America. It might be further argued that Washington's Federal Triangle also contains the brain trust of the American government, playing daily host, as it does, to the elite of the elected legislature of the American republic.

Given these facts, it could also be argued that to invade this triangular sanctuary with a hostile force would, in a single stroke, deal a crippling blow to the nation.

That to submit this vital area of the republic to a scourge by fire or, as it is called in military terms, a reconnaissance, or recon by fire, would be to blast a bullet into this heart and so cut off the lifeblood of the nation.

And since the dominating architecture of the District is the Greco-Roman classical style favored by Thomas Jefferson, the destruction of the Federal Triangle would also be the symbolic destruction of two thousand years of Western civilization in a single master stroke.

Such wholesale devastation is precisely what the Mahdi had in mind. And it is what his well-laid plans called for during the American phase of the coordinated attacks on Strike Day.

Directly in front of the Capitol, flanking the Mall to north and south, between the seat of Congress and the Library of Congress and Supreme Court buildings that themselves flank the Mall, are two circular parks. The parks, partially encircled by stands of elm and poplar, lie within easy walking distance of the Capitol, yet far enough away to afford striking views of the Capitol dome and the Statue of Freedom that surmounts it.

Facing east, the nineteen-foot-high bronze statue is of a warrior Amazon, clad in flowing draperies, whose right hand rests on the hilt of a sheathed sword and whose left holds a laurel wreath and a soldier's shield. This lady warrior wears a star-encircled helmet crested by an eagle's head. She stands on a globe of iron with the words *E Pluribus Unum*—One Nation United—incised on a band that encircles it.

The feminine statue *is* America. She is America as much as the Statue of Liberty in New York Harbor is America. Moreover, she is a gift bestowed upon America by Europe, for just as Lady Liberty was brought from Paris, so Freedom came from Rome. She too stands as a bridge connecting the United States with other civilizations that have bequeathed their legacies to the cultural destiny of Western man.

In November of 1862, when the fifth and final section, the head and shoulders, of the statue were to be raised into place, a special ceremony was declared by order of the War Department. At the final moment when this last section of Freedom was lowered into place and Old Glory displayed from the statue, a thirty-five gun salute was fired from a field battery on Capitol Hill.

Moments after the final gun fired its salvo, it was answered by a salute from the twelve forts that at the time constituted a line of fortifications surrounding the city of Washington. At precisely noon on the second day of December of 1863, the last salute of the last answering gun died away and the flag of the United States flew unfurled over the head of the statue. She has stood as a symbol of the national spirit, in peace and war, ever since.

This made Freedom a target for the one who hated this tradition and those who enshrined and protected it; a target now destined to draw fire from entirely different guns. These would be fired not to salute Freedom, but to destroy her and the nation she represented.

Twin circular parks stand before the east front of the Capitol. The parks normally have a high level of foot traffic on any given day. Especially when Congress is in session, as it was on Strike Day, and on a clear, mild, and sunny afternoon, as was also the case, there is usually a large pedestrian turnout. So it was today, as Strike Day was about to commence in the North American sector of operations.

Inside the Capitol, in the chambers of the Senate, the first news of the near-simultaneous Ramadan attacks on both the USS *Eisenhower* and the Great Mosque in the Saudi holy city of Mecca had just begun trickling in. As had been the case during the Al Qaeda strikes of September 11, 2001, the reports were at this initial stage confused and disjointed, as well as overly optimistic, and the extent of damage, as well as the precise nature of the attacks, was still largely un-known.

At the western crook of Pennsylvania Avenue, within the south facade of the White House, the president had also received this information via the CRITICOM and SPINTCOM global tactical communications networks. The president had just arisen from beneath a pile of Secret Service human shields who had jumped in front and on top of him as Hammon fired at close range. He was still in a state of shock and trying to absorb what had happened through badly hammered senses.

The president had not seen Timothy Lomax vault across the Yellow Oval Room and wrestle with Hammon for possession of the intended murder weapon. He had not seen the weapon discharge into Hammon's solar plexus as the men grappled for it on the floor. Nor had the president seen the pandemonium that resulted as the White House medical staff and emergency services were radioed to the scene.

Now, as the president was dragged from the chamber by the same Secret Service agents who had knocked him down minutes before, he saw the emergency services working to resuscitate the fallen assassin. He did not know that they were to fail, and that Hammon was to die within a matter of minutes. At the same time, Lieutenant Colonel David Saxon was in a limo flying the flag of the secretary of defense, just leaving the North Portico gate of the White House for Pennsylvania Avenue.

It was at this moment, when these and other events were taking place in near simultaneity, that two backpackers reached positions between the midpoint of the two circular parks and their boundaries with the eastern front of the Capitol building.

Both backpackers were young male Caucasians, a familiar sight in a vicinity that was a magnet for tourists from all over the world. But the rucks of these two sightseers didn't contain the usual array of assorted gear. Instead they each held a specially downsized missile launcher, whose three-hundred-meter range made it an effective weapon to strike an object on the Capitol dome.

Both shooters had rehearsed their intended strike on Freedom at training bases in Libya, and at Salman Pak in Iraq, and knew they could accomplish it successfully. Both had exceptional marksmanship skills, and both were pledged to die as martyrs after the fact. Having synchronized their actions, both quickly shucked their packs, removed the missile launchers; in one smooth series of movements, they knelt, sighted, and fired.

Both missiles struck their intended target, one a split second following the impact and detonation of the other. The Statue of Freedom was broken in two by the twin explosive bursts, her shattered torso crashing down and rolling over the Capitol dome to plunge into the broad plaza of the east front. As panic swept the crowds below, many members of which had been injured in the attack, both *mujahideen* saw uniformed Metro police rushing toward them.

They next did what they had been trained to do at the mission's conclusion. They flipped micro-toggles sewn into the heavy canvas of their rucks, detonating the fragmentation grenades taped together inside each backpack. The twin explosions were further proof that Al Qadr had struck, and Strike Day had commenced.

As the bloody chunks of the fragmented martyrs splattered the grass and strange strips of meat suddenly and obscenely hung from the leafless branches of trees, other strollers in the parks pulled out combat knives, compact submachine guns and machine pistols, and mini-grenades. These began attacking any targets of opportunity that presented themselves, indiscriminately raking them with bursts of automatic fire, throwing grenades, shooting into the blast front as the grenades exploded. Running, shooting, grenading.

But also using their knives.

While women screamed, they gleefully followed them, plunging the K-bars they'd been issued into their breasts, backs and stomachs. Many of the *fidayeen* were themselves attacked and cut down during the attacks by the service revolvers and shotguns of Metro cops.

It didn't matter to the mission. They had surprise working in their favor and they knew they would die anyway, no matter what. Many *shaheed* who were not mowed down by police guns used their last grenades and bullets on themselves.

Others signaled to their comrades and ran—firing bursts from their weapons into the air—from the two parks toward the shattered plaza fronting the Capitol stairs, where truckloads of other attackers were now being disgorged near the broken remnants of fallen Freedom, to press the attack home.

Some five minutes before the RPG attacks from the twin parks commenced on the Capitol, occupants of the nearby Russell Office Building heard a single loud bang. It originated from somewhere in the depths of the building. A tremor followed that made desks shake all the way up to the top floor.

The first thought of most of the staff in the building, which housed bureaus of the Department of State and other government agencies, was that the building had been bombed. Panic seized hold of many staffers. But after a few minutes, there was no sign of smoke or new concussions. Those who reached the custodian's office by phone were assured that it was probably the furnace acting up again. The super would go down and have a look.

Two stories beneath the lobby level of the building, the cause of all the confusion was clearly apparent. Two small C-4 charges had blown out a large section of subbasement retaining wall. The charges used had been shaped, in this particular case, prismatic charges. The blast waves had been channeled and focused. The charges had not been intended to do major damage to the Russell building. All they'd been intended to do was to open a sizable breech in a two-foot thickness of old concrete.

This they had done, creating a gaping aperture in the wall large enough for the sixty men in the black caftanlike garb that al Qadr's warrior elite call *shalwar qameez* to quickly pass through into the darkness beyond. There was no light in this place, and a musty odor permeated the motionless air. The attack force, its members' faces hidden behind lightweight night-vision goggles, had come prepared for this eventuality. Switching on the NVGs, they were able to navigate through the darkness as they had drilled over and over again.

At the head of this force was Wolfram Krieger. His blood was pumping in his ears. He was keyed up. The operation he had planned and nurtured was now finally taking place; it was finally becoming reality. This knowledge turned him on, gave him an intense high with which no drug, no sexual experience could ever compete.

A thousand images whirled through his brain. This is what it is like to die and have your life flash before your eyes, he thought. He knew what was happening. It was the berserker euphoria of battle that was taking hold of him, body and soul.

This time it was far more intense than he'd ever known it, yet he had in fact experienced it before. Since his first taste of it as a mercenary in the years after Saigon fell and the Americans pulled out, he'd known it, loved it, lived for it.

For two years he'd sojourned among the scattered opposition forces, essentially carrying on the long-defunct Phoenix program under other auspices. The principle was still the same. Assassinate key members of the Vietnamese hierarchy in an attempt to destabilize the new Communist leadership loyal to Ho.

Krieger's force was a ragtag assemblage of Montagnard tribesmen, displaced Saigonese, and a smattering of mercenaries from around the world with ties to the old-boy paramilitary network. Most were not Americans because of the CIA's need for deniability concerning the assassinations, but some were.

Of course the entire operation was foredoomed to failure, and if this was not known on the fourth floor of the CIA's off-Beltway headquarters at Langley, Virginia, from which funding and logistical support for the opposition were dispensed, it was known to all combatants in the field.

Krieger knew it, but he had no complaints. He'd not been a player in the game to salvage the respectability of Cold

Warriors who were fighting a losing battle on the Asian subcontinent.

On the contrary, Krieger's overtures to the CIA and his subsequent recruitment were part of what they called "opposition research" in operational slang. Krieger was sheep-dipping himself. Those early days were to serve as his crucial baptism under fire. In the post-Nam covert war in Southeast Asia, he had learned the tradecraft of organizing and leading indigenous paramilitary formations against entrenched enemy forces.

Again and again, in a succession of shadow battles in clandestine ops zones throughout the Cold War and beyond, the lessons Krieger had learned and the skills that he had honed had served him in good stead. In many ways today's attack was a culmination and an inevitability of those years spent in a dozen-odd twilight wars.

Today a scalpel force of trained commandos would strike a lethal blow to the heart of the American republic. It was the blow that the neo-Nazi underground had theorized about for decades, yet had never even come close to carrying out. Anthrax spores on letters were nice, but they didn't cut it. Today it would become a reality. Once struck, this blow would destabilize the nation, weaken and tear the social fabric in a manner that could not ever be repaired.

The destruction of the twin towers in New York had shown those who plotted the overthrow of the Zionist Occupied Government of the U.S.—the ZOG, they called it—how the deed could be done. This bold new action today would finish the job. With the federal government crippled, with the nation challenged from without and within, the secessionist movement in the Deep South would stand a fighting chance.

It could happen. The dream Krieger cherished might come true.

A white Aryan state could be created. Self-reliant, strong. Populated by free white men and women. Answerable to no power on earth except itself.

Today its foundation would be poured in blood.

*   *   *

Krieger reined in his thoughts. He focused now on the tasks of the immediate present. Only minutes separated his force from the battleground in which many would die, and he had to think clearly, quickly, precisely. Once again, for the hundredth time, he went over the coordinated progression of steps that lay ahead.

He and his force were now inside the old pedestrian tunnel that had connected the Russell with the Capitol between 1908 and 1960. Long ago the tunnel had been permanently sealed and replaced by a short-run subway system connecting the Capitol with both the Russell and Dirkson Office Buildings in January of 1960, and which serves it to the present day.

With the new subway in daily use, the existence of the old tunnel had become forgotten. Nevertheless, architectural plans were on file and available from the Library of Congress. Krieger had researched those plans, which showed the original access points of the old tunnel in the basement of the Russell and revealed where the old tunnel was separated from the new in several places by only a foot thickness of concrete. Krieger had checked the feasibility of breaching the tunnel wall with engineers. When they'd deemed it doable, he'd started on the operational plans.

Now these plans were being made reality. Krieger's force of *mujahideen* negotiated the old tunnel at a brisk lope. Like a wolf pack they moved swiftly along the old concrete walkway that was as free of obstructions as it had been decades before when the tunnel had originally been sealed.

The tunnel was not very long. It had been designed for easy access between the Russell and the Capitol. In only a few minutes the force had reached the hidden junction between the old and new tunnels as indicated on architectural plans.

At a signal from Krieger his sapper team emplaced a second pair of shaped C-4 charges. The prismatic munitions, filled with molded plastic explosive, were rapidly affixed to the wall. The demo team used portable pneumatic hammers to secure the munitions with steel bolts through eyelets in their metal casings. Lengths of det cord were then run to a digital hand-detonator unit and at a second signal from Krieger, the wall-breeching blast was initiated at the throw of a single-pole switch.

With Krieger in the lead, the *mujahideen* force poured through the blown-out breech in a matter of seconds. The pale, dusty light that streamed in through the clouds of cordite was sufficient proof that the NVGs would be no longer necessary and in fact would now pose an encumbrance. Krieger's strike team was hard-charging into the well-lighted interior of the new subway tunnel. Here they also knew they would encounter the first targets of opportunity of the strike, and possibly even some scattered armed resistance from random police personnel or various persons with reason to be carrying pistols.

The operational plan had taken all of this into consideration, however. As the strike force spilled out of the old tunnel, the *mujahideen* hurled antipersonnel grenades and sprayed automatic fire from the bullpup Kalashes they ported at any bystander in their paths. Business-suited men and women on the platform who had been awaiting transport to other sections of the Federal Triangle found themselves gunned down without warning or mercy by the suddenly attacking terrorist force.

Stepping over the bodies of the dead and wounded, the strike force raced toward the twin stairways that were its immediate objectives. These two short flights of concrete stairs led directly to the circular Rotunda beneath the Capitol dome.

Once inside the Rotunda, the force had been trained to split into two main action groups. One action group would speed to the left, and invade the meeting chamber of the House of Representatives on the south wing of the Capitol. The other section would race right to invade the Senate chamber. Both lower and upper houses of the Congress were currently in session.

The OPPLAN crafted by Krieger called for the infliction of total, indiscriminate carnage both to those targets encountered in the Rotunda and those victims found in either chamber of Congress. Anything that lived was to be attacked and killed. United States senators and congressmen were to be mercilessly gunned down. So were visitors, be they tourists, sightseers, or persons connected with the government. Anybody, anything, was to be considered a target. And killed.

The statuary, artwork, and other national icons and symbols inside were to be destroyed as well, for the Moguls had discovered two thousand years before on invading India that to annihilate the fabric of society, it is not merely blood that must be spilled, but national treasure must also be turned into smoldering garbage. History taught that when a society saw its wealth in a trash heap, its spirit was often broken. This lesson would be repeated here, today.

Krieger's black-pajama force continued to pour through the ragged breach in the tunnel wall. They had replayed these culminating minutes of the history-making military assault on America countless times, at Salman Pak and the training camps in Libya provided by the Brother Colonel. Their bodies functioned almost automatically by now. They were no longer flesh-and-blood human beings. They were homicidal robots bent on total destruction.

Many were additionally high on the amphetamines that had been provided them before the battle, but even those who were not wired on speed were floating on an adrenaline-fueled berserker euphoria as they hived off into two groups, raced along the subway platform, and double-timed it up the two flights of stairs to the mezzanine level of the Rotunda, hollering shouts and battle cries as they ascended to martyrdom and slaughter.

Moments later the first wave of strike commandos had successfully negotiated the stairs and reached the Rotunda floor. They came up firing bursts from their automatic weapons and tossing grenades to left and right. Who they hit and what they shot did not matter at this point. Only the smoke and the concussion, the sour stench of cordite in their nostrils, the blood that coursed hot and singing in their veins, and the cries of panic from their frenziedly running victims as they joyously went about their butchery mattered.

Later, when each of the two teams reached their final destinations—the two halls of America's bicameral legislature—they could, with more sober deliberation, pick out targets of opportunity for special treatment and individual punishment.

As part of their extensive training, Krieger's cadres had spent dozens of hours studying the faces, mannerisms, and favored positions on the House and Senate floors where the elite of the American legislature were to be found. Key senators and congressmen had been targeted for death in this way. Each member of the strike force would be paying close attention to who they encountered when they reached these final objectives.

For the moment, their training and zeal called for them to unleash as much automatic firepower and grenade fragment clouds as possible as they boiled up from the depths of the subway tunnel and hard-charged across the mosaic-tiled floor of the Capitol Rotunda. Krieger, leading the elite group of fighters that was to spread death amid the Senate chamber, like the rest of his force, had only limited situational awareness at this point of what was happening around him.

With the smoke, confusion, and noise of the killing ground, his perception of the battle was largely limited to a circle of approximately a dozen feet in any direction within the confined space of the Rotunda. But this too had been expected and had figured into the calculations of the OP-PLAN.

Like the rest of his men, Krieger fixed his mind on moving steadily and swiftly toward the Senate chamber, mowing down anything in his path, remaining intently focused on his final objective. His consciousness fragmented his perceptual stage into a series of swiftly moving images, changing, shifting sounds and smells. His reality was like something seen between the pulsing flashes of a revolving strobe.

As he ran across the Rotunda floor, firing and tossing grenades, he glimpsed citizens being shot, blown up by fragmentation bursts, and in some cases being run through by thrusts of razor-sharp combat knives and rifle bayonets. Reveling in this orgy of destruction, Krieger continued to move, fire his Kalash, and hurl his grenades. Because of this tunnel vision, he did not immediately realize that not all of those who were incarnadining the colored mosaic floor of the Rotunda with their blood were among his intended victims.

chapter twenty

Near the First Street turnoff that would bring them around to East Capitol Street and the Capitol entrance, Saxon heard the distant thud of explosions and the staccato chatter of automatic-weapons bursts from directly ahead on Constitution Avenue. He had no doubt what they meant, and it was more than the simple and obvious fact that all hell was breaking loose. The worst-case scenario that had been planned for by One had indeed come a cropper. A major new terrorist strike on America was under way.

Thanks to the BFO that the blue-suiter captain on the DIA intelligence planning staff at the Pentagon had been hit with, security preparations had shifted from expected attacks on military and commercial airfields to attacks on the District itself. Using this new paradigm, computer matching of the geometrical patterns that were photographed during surveillance overflies of the Salman Pak training area had narrowed the field of potential targets to D.C.'s Federal Triangle with a high level of probability.

Though the timing and nature of the attacks were still unknown, plans to counter them, should they materialize, had hastily been drafted. Security forces had been pre-positioned to meet a large-scale terrorist offensive, whatever form it took.

Some of these friendly forces were openly in evidence. Others, like a platoon of Marine Force One hard-chargers, were much less visible, though just as ready to repay fire with fire and death with death should an all-out al Qadr offensive take place.

To meet the threat Saxon's men had been deployed in and around the Capitol. Some were in plain clothes, others in

AG-344 Class-A uniforms, including service caps. Some circulated around the Rotunda as sightseers. Others were discreetly positioned in adjoining areas, such as the chambers used as art galleries and museum displays, while still others occupied visitors' seats in the House and Senate galleries.

Each of the Marines shared one thing in common: they all carried shoulder bags of various sizes, shapes, and colors. Perceptive visitors to the Capitol might have noticed that while most arrivals went through the usual metal detector archways, other visitors passed through a special, separately located, section. These VIP visitors presented an ID card that was swiped through a card reader, and placed the fingertips of their right hands on a biometric scanner. After these checks—and without a search of their carryalls by the normally attentive Capitol guards—the VIPs were waved through into the Rotunda lobby.

The VIPs—a security element of Marine Force One personnel—was on scene to bolster the ranks of the normal security staff at the Capitol. Nestled inside their carryalls were automatic weapons and webbing heavy with mini-grenades and extra ammo clips for the SITES Spectre M-4 SMGs the team had packed along.

Beneath their civvies and A-uniforms the Marines wore lightweight body armor. The grenades were mini-Stingballs, which mixed the standard flash-bang with a twenty-meter fragmentation cloud of hard rubber ball bearings designed to incapacitate rather than kill. Their ammunition, for the same reason, was restricted to Glaser safety bullets that mixed low-ricochet potential with high stopping power in direct frontal hits. This was the same type of ammo favored by Delta Force for airline hijack takedowns because of its low toxicity to innocent bystanders.

The decision to pack the short-barrel and extremely compact SITES Spectre M-4 was motivated by the need to further reduce risk to friendlies as much as possible. The Spectre M-4 was a portable "room broom" reliable under sustained fire conditions, and like most true SMGs, was chambered for the nine-millimeter long or parabellum round, the bullet of choice for close-quarter and hostage-interdiction missions. Finally, the Spectres used by the team were equipped with sound suppressers, the intention being to deny the opposition the ability to sight on muzzle flash and return accurate fire. The lashup wasn't perfect, but it was the best that could be done on short notice. It would fly.

When the first explosions of the RPG attacks on the Capitol dome and the statue of Freedom were heard, the Marines inside the Capitol quickly reacted as they had trained to do, unshipping their weapons and seeking out terrorist targets. As the first wave of black-pajama men attacked from the Capitol's east front, the 1-Patchers engaged the attackers with speed, agility, and surprise.

Nevertheless, the Marines were not prepared for the emergence of a second wave of al Qadr shock troops from the two mezzanine stairways leading up from the subway level directly below. Caught off guard, the Marines reacted only as the main force of the second wave of attackers had reached the Rotunda floor.

It was at this point that Saxon's limo, flying the SecDef's and American flags, sped down East Capitol Street to a screeching, strut-crunching halt in front of the Capitol. About to exit the vehicle, Saxon and his Secret Service driver were met by a scene of utter pandemonium. But Saxon had come equipped with a suitable fire extinguisher, which he'd stashed in the limo's trunk.

The driver popped the trunk using the dashboard unlocking switch and threw open the driver's-side door. Hardly had the door opened when a jagged line of indentations pockmarked its metal skin. The steel-jacketed rounds did not penetrate the door, which was well-armored, nor did another volley from an AK-47 do more than flake off shards of the front windshield, which was made of a bullet-proof polylaminate material. Though the tires were not hit, they would not have deflated under fire or shrapnel bursts either, being reinforced with a strong yet lightweight steel mesh.

While the driver threw bursts of fire from a MAC-10 submachinegun at the easily recognizable enemy in their black *shalwar qameez,* Saxon was already pulling out the box-fed M60A3 7.62-millimeter light machine gun he'd stashed in the limo's trunk. Slinging bandoliers strung with mini-Stingballs around both shoulders, he hefted the Maremont Pig in his hands and charged the weapon, chambering the first of the two hundred rounds in the high-capacity box mag mounted beneath the MG's receiver. As an afterthought, Saxon one-handed the American flag clipped to the car antenna and managed to shove the pole under his webbing where the bandoliers crossed behind his back. Old Glory waved in the wind as Saxon set off across the East Front plaza toward the Capitol stairs.

While the driver kept up phased salvos of .45-caliber covering fire from the MAC-10, bystanders were treated to the unique sight of a Marine light colonel in dress uniform, flying the flag and charging up the flights of steps leading to the Capitol entrance while cutting loose with machine-gun bursts to left and right.

The M-60 wasn't just for show either. The colonel was scoring his share of hits with the Maremont too, sighting on the black-clad ducks in his shooting gallery, confident that muzzle flash meant enemy, not friend. The black-pajama men who fired at him from semi-concealment were forced to tuck in their heads or have them chopped off by white tracer streams of steel-jacketed bullets. Those terrorists in Saxon's path who were stupid enough to remain there, were cut down by concentrated bursts of heavy-caliber autofire as the Pig spoke the only language their breed understood.

It was an object lesson for their pajama-clad kinsmen to stay clear of the dragon that had suddenly appeared to spout a fiery breath of death into their broken ranks. Continuing to fire his Pig from the hip, Saxon negotiated the final flights of broad, majestic stairs and disappeared inside the east front entrance. He was now inside the Rotunda, in the midst of the utter chaos that whirled around him.

A vast mural occupies the interior of the Capitol dome, or canopy, as it is otherwise known. This mural is called

The Apotheosis of George Washington. It was painted, over the course of many years, by the naturalized American artist Constantino Brumedi, who also conceived of and carved most of the series of bas-reliefs in stucco on the Rotunda frieze, until his death shortly after completing the frieze mural depicting William Penn's treaty with the Indians.

The Apotheosis remains Brumedi's masterpiece. The enormous mural depicts George Washington, draped in pale violet, rising to infinity over a gorgeously resplendent rainbow. Female figures, including two representing the personifications of Liberty and Victory, and thirteen maidens, each crowned by a single star, symbolizing the original states, flank him, raising a banner emblazoned with the motto *E Pluribus Unum*.

Six groups on the perimeter of the fresco, each depicting ancient gods such as Ceres and Minerva and figures from American history, including Benjamin Franklin and Robert Fulton, depict scenes symbolic of national events. Brumedi had created the figures to give the illusion of three-dimensional depth to the striking composition.

Today, beneath the glory of the canopy fresco, death stalked the Rotunda. Only a few circuits of the clock had elapsed since Krieger, at the head of his *fidayeen* assault force, had bounded out of the depths of the new subway tunnel, but to his telescoped sense of time, these fleeting minutes seemed like hours. Though his situational awareness was now more coherent, he still witnessed the scenes of battle as fragmented glimpses, frozen between the strobe flashes of combat-challenged awareness.

Nevertheless, Krieger now knew that the attack had met serious resistance and that the benefits gained by surprise had been compromised. All around him, in the smoke-filled Rotunda, he witnessed his men being met by opposing forces and being killed or badly wounded in sporadic firefights. In many cases the slaughter of his men took place against the unlikely background of the Rotunda frieze itself.

In one glimpse of the battle Krieger saw a black-pajama man being killed before a frieze mural depicting the surrender of Lord Cornwallis at Yorktown. His attacker was a soldier in a Marine Corps dress uniform who plunged a combat knife into the top of the *mujaheed*'s head. The black-pajama man's brains spurted out through the aperture, adding to Cornwallis's problems by spattering the Redcoat general with gore.

Elsewhere another black-pajama man was raked across the midsection by a sustained burst of automatic-weapons fire from the silenced muzzle of a 1-Patcher's Spectre SMG. Nearly cut in half by the zigzagging bullets that had punched through his abdominal region in a three-second burst, the man in black pajamas performed a sort of ballet dancer's pirouette that ended in a dying swan act against Pocahontas rescuing John Smith. Both the Indian maiden and her boyfriend were given a bloodbath by the perforated al Qadr fanatic before he crumpled to the tile floor of the Rotunda.

Not even George Washington reading the Declaration of Independence, flanked by Benjamin Franklin and Thomas Jefferson, escaped a drenching in terrorist blood. Under a hailstorm of hot studs from another 1-Patcher's subgun, yet another luckless terrorists's terminal Aztec two-step sent him crashing into the part of the frieze at Jefferson's gartered feet, where he collapsed in a blood-leaking mess. As the deflated terrorist went down to his final doom, his bloodied hand clawed at the frieze, painting an I-Ching pentagram of dripping blood across the two Founding Fathers. Above them, a small boy depicted seated in a nearby tree playfully waved a handkerchief, as if to bid farewell to another bad actor who'd gotten his just deserts.

More prosaic endings overtook other members of the black-pajama assault force trapped by Marine Force One opposition fire inside the Rotunda. Across the Rotunda's mosaic-tiled floor, bodies in black pajamas were sprawled in a variety of tortured death positions, limbs and heads splayed in an assortment of highly unnatural angles.

Still, many of Strike Day's attackers had not died without taking their enemy along with them. The tiles of the Rotunda floor had now become slippery with the mingled blood of terrorist forces, their civilian victims, and those mysterious defenders who had appeared to challenge Krieger's terrorist army.

While some elements of Krieger's shock troops had certainly reached their ultimate targets in the chambers of the Congress, he knew that the full goals of the operation could now no longer be effectively met, and that the operation was terminally compromised. How severely would become plain within the next few minutes, but full success of the operation had been dependent on complete tactical surprise, surgical precision, and maintaining a sustained operational tempo.

Before the senators and congressmen were executed they were to have been paraded before the newsmedia's cameras. Their deaths—for some, throats slit in the manner of pigs, for others a bullet in the back of the head while kneeling bound and on all fours—were also to be recorded and instantaneously beamed across the world.

Still, Krieger took heart. Maybe enough of the operation's goals could be salvaged to make it all come out right in the end. Above all he hoped that his own escape route was not compromised. Krieger had no intention of dying for the cause, still less of dying for someone else's cause. His was to lead the Nexus to glory and let them deal with the consequences. The old subway tunnel from the Russell was not the only subterranean passageway that led from the Capitol to safer shores. There were others, including one below the Senate chamber that could be reached from the basement. A small C-4 charge and he'd soon be inside the vast storm-drainage tunnels that honeycombed the District. While Krieger knew of many escape exits from that warren, it was a. labyrinth in which no pursuer could find him once he'd reached it.

Krieger pressed forward, sprinting for the Senate chamber. Those luckless or foolish enough to get in his way were cut down by well-aimed bursts of automatic Kalash fire. He was soon through the senate chamber doors and charging into the chamber itself. He was relieved to discover that many of his black-pajama men had survived the ordeal by fire in the Rotunda and were now in the final act of gaining possession of the chamber. Like sockeye salmon, they had reached their spawning ground.

Krieger permitted himself a graveyard grin as he stormed into the hall, his combat-booted footfalls echoing on the chamber's terrazzo floor. The operation could still prove a success. He knew this in his guts.

S axon chanced a forty-millimeter grenade strike, hoping that no friendlies were in range of the strike's splinter envelope when it hit the heavy wooden doors.

He had handed the Pig and webbing to the Force One master sergeant called Chicken Wire in the midst of the fight for the Rotunda, being hailed by the 1-Patcher squad automatic-weapon meister from out of the chaos of blood, death, and smoke. CW had clutched at the weapon like a puppy handed a soup bone, and disappeared amidst the smoke and chaos of battle with a *hoo-yah* on his lips and the Pig chattering like a long-lost lover in his arms.

Divested of the Maremont, Saxon now ported the bullpup Kalash with its undermounted M203 grenade launcher he'd taken off CW together with a spare clip and M79 rounds. Saxon would chew the 1-Patcher's head off later for disobeying orders and bringing along the weapon, but for now he was glad of the heavier firepower the weapon gave him as compared to the Spectres.

As Saxon braced the weapon in a double-handed grip, a high-explosive M79 can was already chambered and ready to roll. Ahead, the heavy doors of the Senate chamber were being hastily swung closed by furtive figures draped in sweat-stained black. Saxon wanted to get inside that room in a hurry. They'd discussed the inclusion of shotguns to fire door-breecher shells in One's kit, but logistical considerations had ruled this out. The HE can would have to do.

A burst of automatic fire from the Kalash stopped the pajama men in their tracks, and a second burst persuaded the Al Qadr to duck for cover rather than return fire. Before they could reposition themselves or get him in their sights, Saxon launched two HE canisters in rapid succession. The grenade rounds struck the door with loud concussive reports, throwing up clouds of smoke and debris as the bursts chewed up the wood.

Before the dust could settle Saxon was loping into the chamber on a low crouch, fast-tucking sideways as he entered to reduce his target profile. This was fortunate, because a black-pajama man had drawn a bead and was ready to cut him down with a long burst of 5.45-millimeter steel as he barreled on through. With the jagged line of Kalash tracers passing harmlessly through empty space, Saxon snapped an answering burst off at the attacker that stitched a line of spurting red pocks across his upper torso and sent him dropping to his doom.

The scene inside the Senate chamber was one of utter carnage. Several senators and their aides lay dead, the victims of the Al Qadr suicide attack. Others, more fortunate, faster on their feet, or less brave than their colleagues, had taken refuge beneath chairs, desks, and behind statuary, and were momentarily safe.

For others the situation was far more precarious. These senators had been taken hostage by the black-pajama men who had stormed the Senate chamber. The captives pressed Al Qadr gun muzzles to their heads, and in some cases had their hands duct-taped behind their backs. The captors of the U.S. legislators saw them as mere bargaining chips, nor did the hostages' gender matter. Male and female senators alike were both under the gun.

As Saxon charged into the Senate chamber he didn't face the lions' den alone. Behind him were the angry survivors of the Rotunda shock assault with Marine Force One troops in the vanguard, backed by a few uniformed Capitol guards who'd made it through the firestorm alive. The *mujaheeds* in control of the Senate chamber—as their comrades in the chamber of the adjacent House of Representatives—were outnumbered and outgunned. They remained alive only because they held a hole card: the hostages.

Otherwise Krieger's operation had gone bad in the can. Still, while the attackers could not prevail as successfully as originally planned, they could still rack up a significant vic-

tory. The *fidayeen* continued to hold hostages as human bargaining chips. Among these were the senators from major
constituencies, including California, New York, and Texas.

These were powerful and well-known figures on the
American and global political landscape. The death of any
one of them would still serve to strike terror into the enemy's
collective heart, as the guidebooks to *jihad* had taught, and
the deaths of all would be viewed as a crushing blow to
American power, wealth, and prestige.

"Who's in charge?"

Krieger carefully removed his balaclava, taking care to
keep his Sig semiautomatic pistol firmly pressed into the
temple of the lady senator from New York State whom he
held hostage. It was hot behind the mask, and events had
reached the point where concealing his face was no longer
necessary.

Saxon stepped forward.

"I am," he said.

"We have met before, have we not?"

"At a peep show on the Ku'Damm," Saxon replied in
German.

Krieger laughed.

"Our old acquaintances in GSG-9 would not take kindly
to being described in such terms, my friend. It is Saxon, is
it not?"

"That's right, Krieger," Saxon replied. "So why don't we
can the bullshit? You played a fast game but you didn't
score. Release the hostages and tell your men to lay down
their arms."

"Not an unattractive offer, my friend, under the circumstances. Except that at this stage I doubt these fanatics would
obey my orders anyway. They are not soldiers like you and
I. A soldier knows there is a time to fall back and regroup,
even a time to surrender. Fanatics know only to kill and to
die.

"Therefore I am afraid I must decline your kind and generous offer to surrender. Instead I propose that it is you and
your personnel who drop their weapons and permit the safe
passage of myself and my troops to Dulles Airport. A fairly

spacious helicraft is to be dispatched to ferry us from the Capitol to Dulles. Once on board a 747, for which I also ask, we will release the hostages unharmed."

Saxon said nothing, thinking of a response. But he had been checkmated and he knew it. Krieger tightened the pressure of the Sig's muzzle on his hostage's skull and again told Saxon to drop the Kalash. Saxon saw no other choice. He put the gun on the floor.

"Do we negotiate a deal?" Krieger asked after a brief pause. "Or do I kill this famous lady and give my men the order to take the lives of their hostages too? That's one order they'll obey, I assure you."

Saxon did not answer. Death's messenger had just whispered in his ear.

Blue Man One was the code name of the master gunnery sergeant who led Marine Force One's sniper detachment. Blue Man One was not only deadly accurate with a variety of sniper weapons, but like any good sniper, was also adept at concealment and *maskirovka*. The operational art of the sniper called for functioning as a forward observer almost as frequently as it called for a well-placed round at long range. A sniper worth his salt was adept at both combat disciplines.

Blue Man had been given his orders. He was one of the two MF-1 snipers secretly posted in the chambers of each house. Unlike the rest of the Marine security force, their instructions were to deploy to positions of concealment where they could bring their deadly skills into play should hostage scenarios develop.

The weapons they carried were short-barreled Commando autorifles specially modified by MF-1's master armorer. These modifications included a sinusoidal re-rifling of the barrel to impart a faster rate of spin to the round fired by the weapon, modifications to the charge of each custom-loaded round to further enhance the kinetic energy value of each round, and modifications to the standard silencer accepted by the Commando in order to more efficiently silence the custom loads and suppress muzzle flash.

During the storming of the House and Senate chambers, the Blue Man sniper teams had been responsible for whittling down the opposition numbers while more visible members of the Marine security details at the Capitol dealt openly with the invaders. The sniper teams now remained in hiding, ready to drop those black-pajama men who believed they held the whip hand in the final confrontation.

"Blue Man One to Saxon."

The words came in over the wireless earbud Saxon had worn into combat. The team members were all equipped with American Avionics EM-500 series Ear Mikes, which enabled both reception and transmission via the inner ear. The specially tuned microphone that was part of the one-piece earbud picked up vibrations directly from the auditory canal. No separate microphone was needed for transmission; the single unit functioned as both receiver and transmitter.

"Blue Man team has picked its targets. Nod when you're ready."

Saxon was about to do just that when the lady senator from New York decided the issue for all concerned. Summoning her wits and unarmed combat training learned during her years as First Lady, she chose that instant to lash out with a stomp to the metatarsus of the man who held her hostage. It was a dangerously foolish move to attempt. But this once it worked like magic.

As the kick connected, Krieger's grip relaxed just enough to allow her to break free and pivot out of the way. Hollering for her to get down, Saxon yelled for Blue Man One to fire and launched a flying tackle, landing hard on top of the senator and shielding her body with his own. Krieger tried to draw a bead on his former hostage, but was unable to accurately fire as Saxon lay atop the former president's wife—a near miss from Blue Man One had spoiled Krieger's aim.

Hit by chips of wood and plaster off to his right, Krieger knew instantly he was being fired on by a concealed sniper, and that his sudden flurry of movement in trying to draw a bead on the target had probably saved his life. While Krieger dived for cover behind the Senate podium, the sniper team used the confusion to open up on the targets each Marine had selected.

On the heads of those targets infrared laser-designator beams had painted death dots visible only to the Blue Man shooters. Silenced high-velocity bullets instantly drilled holes in those heads, clean on one side, ragged with gore on the other, dropping the terrorists before nerve spasms could jerk triggers and send bullets auguring into their captives.

Now Krieger was up again, his drawn Sig side arm tracking for fresh targets. Nearby he saw Saxon bundle off the lady senator into the protection of one of the anterooms adjoining the chamber. Lining up the sights so two white dots marked the spinal vertebra between Saxon's shoulders, the Sig braced in a two-handed match grip, Krieger smiled and squeezed the trigger.

Nothing happened. The hammer dropped and blowback tripped the slide, but no brass was ejected. It was a hangfire, a damn cook-off. Krieger's smile changed into a frown. Saxon had turned and was now trying to rush him. Before Krieger could unjam the Sig for further use the American would be on him. Flinging the now-useless pistol aside, Krieger pulled his combat knife from its belt sheath and held it blade-out in the knife fighter's attack-defend position.

It was a good knife, a seven-inch K-bar reground with a serrated cutting edge. It would work as well as a gun.

Maybe better.

Especially since Saxon was unarmed.

"Catch, Boss."

As Krieger advanced, brandishing his cutlery, a 1-Patcher broke from the circle and tossed Saxon his general-issue Marine combat knife; one equally long and sharp. Krieger's charge stalled and he grew wary as Saxon also took up a knife fighter's stance and gestured for him to come at him.

Krieger's gallows grin returned with a vengeance as he and his opponent began warily circling one another, feinting with their drawn edged weapons. The Marines now formed a circle around the combatants, a *cordon sanitaire* through which nobody would pass. They would not fire on friendlies, but they would try to hold anyone off who might attempt to come between the two antagonists. This one contest would be settled in the ancient manner of gladiators in the Roman amphitheater, of heroes in single combat.

Their knives flashing, Saxon and Krieger continued to circle and feint, parry and dodge. Both were skilled knife fighters, each evenly matched against the other. Suddenly they closed and one, then the other, drew blood. Backing away, they circled again, more cautiously this time, their glinting blades inscribing deadly arcs through empty space. The stress of this mortal combat was grueling. In a matter of minutes the moves and countermoves of each combatant began to grow less precise and controlled as both opponents were cut again and again.

Blood now streamed down Saxon's face from a wound on his scalp. Krieger's left hand was useless; one of Saxon's strikes had severed the long flexor tendons in his arm. The contest had now degenerated into a battle between two injured, angry primitives. They were men in a cave, fighting against a backdrop of shouts and flickering torchlight. They were blood-crazed savages squaring off on the sands of a pagan arena.

The contest ended when Saxon's blade thrust home into Krieger's heart. Saxon could not honestly claim credit for the death strike. Later, he could not even remember having delivered the coup de grace, only recall how one moment the two were locked in mortal combat, and the next Krieger's eyes were wide in pain and horror, and his limp body had begun its slow descent to the floor.

And then a smile had crossed Krieger's features, and he nodded as Saxon's knife emerged from his rib cage, dripping with arterial blood. He tried to say something, tried hard, but no words emerged from the mouth that struggled with such difficulty to form them.

What Krieger had wanted to say was, "See you in hell." But his words had turned to blood and now only this crimson fluid escaped his mouth. As his life ebbed, and Krieger sank to the carpeted floor of the Senate chamber, his last earthly sight was of balance scales of good and evil painted on one of its walls. The last sounds he heard were the echoes of gunfire tapering off as the defenders of the Capitol over-whelmed the mauled and decimated terrorist assault force.

Across the city the guns and explosions were falling silent, their martial clamor replaced by the keening wails of ambulance sirens, emergency services vehicles, and onrushing fire trucks.

Soon the nation would begin to mourn its dead and rebuild its monuments.

And soon after that it would be time to pay the bastards back.

Again.

epilogue

The well-dressed foreign gentleman in the first-class hotel suite in the heart of Paris switched off the cable TV in his sitting room. He had been watching the American president give his address to the nation, talking of courage, renewal, and the strength to soberly face the new trials that lay ahead.

The foreign gentleman in the suite sipped his bourbon. It was liberally diluted with water because he had not had the opportunity to do much drinking during the last several years and was no longer as used to straight alcohol as he'd once been. Earlier, as a young man, he had flaunted his native Saudi drinking prohibitions as many others had: by frequently flying from Riyadh to the glamor capitals of Europe, where every vice could be satisfied to the fullest.

Then, Western clothes had been donned and pricey French cologne had been slapped on smooth-shaven cheeks minutes after the jetliner's no-smoking sign had winked off. For the rest of the flight the complimentary-drinks cart had gotten heavy custom. Once in Europe, debauches of sex, drinking, and drugging had rewarded the numbing abstinence of days spent in the kingdom.

The gentleman's taste for these pleasures had not left him during the last few years spent on the run and in hiding. Because he again had leisure to enjoy them, in some ways the debacle of the attacks on Mecca and the United States had proven a blessing, possibly from Allah, possibly from nobody.

But he was not one for philosophical or theological hair-splitting, and besides, he did not really care. The Mahdi sought power, that and nothing else.

Religion was a path to that power. Religion—despite the mind-conditioning to which he'd subjected his loyal but clueless underlings—*was* that power. The power of masses so drunk on heaven that they would murder and maim every living thing on God's earth in heaven's name at the Mahdi's command.

Still more importantly, the West continued to be as vulnerable today as it was when his late forerunner Osama had begun the great fight. Patience had always been the Mahdi's greatest virtue and weapon; it still was today, as it would surely prove to be in the years that stretched ahead.

This and the fact that he still had plenty of money would insure that he could lay his plans carefully and well. His relative bin Laden was not the only one in the family with a fortune at his disposal. The Mahdi would wait and bide his time. His new identity was bullet-proof; he'd prepared it for years prior to his escape from the Middle East and it could not be compromised. New chances would come. In the meantime there was Paris, Rome, and many other glittering capitals of Europe in which to lie low.

The foreign gentleman left the suite and clicked the door secure behind him. Time enough for a leisurely stroll beneath the linden trees along the well-heeled Boulevard Ney, and perhaps a bite at a nearby restaurant.

The evening, as it fell, was beautiful, and Paris, even to the Mahdi, was always a paradise on earth.

DAVID ALEXANDER

Marine Force One.
A special detachment of the Marine Corps whose
prowess in combat and specialized training sets
them apart from the average grunt. They charge where
others retreat, and succeed where others fail.
They are the best America's got...

MARINE FORCE ONE
0-425-18152-9
As tensions continue to build between North and South
Korea, Marine Force One is sent on a recon mission
that reveals North Korea's plans to use chemical
weapons against the south. But before they can report
to H.Q., they are ambushed and overwhelmed by a
relentless pursuit force.

MARINE FORCE ONE: STRIKE VECTOR
0-425-18307-6
In the deserts of Iraq, there's trouble under the blister-
ing sun. Using an overland black-market route that
stretches from Germany to Iraq, extremist forces have
gathered materials to create a new weapon of devastation. It's a hybrid nuclear warhead that needs no
missile—it can be fired from artillery. And it could cast
a radioactive cloud over the entire Middle East.

Available wherever books are sold or
to order, please call 1-800-788-6262

B532